Don't miss the other books in
The Bridesmaid Chronicles . . .

*First Kiss* (July 2005)
*First Dance* (August 2005)
*First Love* (September 2005)

## Praise for the novels of Karen Kendall

"Sassy and sexy . . . a writer to watch."
—Susan Andersen

"Effervescent . . . witty . . . fresh . . . fun."
—Christina Skye

"If you find a Karen Kendall book up on the shelves, don't hesitate to grab it. You'll enjoy it, guaranteed."
—A Romance Review

"The incomparable Karen Kendall is back with yet another rollicking comical romance, which will have the readers laughing their hearts out. . . . [She] is indeed a masterly writer." —Road to Romance

"Will leave you howling with laughter."
—*Affaire de Coeur*

"A terrific love story . . . filled with laugh-out-loud humor." —Reader to Reader Reviews

"Smart, sassy, and sensational, this is the contemporary romantic comedy of the year."
—Romance Reviews Today

"A fast-paced, amusing, and heartwarming romp."
—Romance Reader's Connection

"Fans of amusing yet serious relationship dramas will delight in Karen Kendall's *I've Got You, Babe*."
—The Best Reviews

## ACKNOWLEDGMENTS

This book would not have been possible without the support of Kara Cesare, Rose Hilliard, Anne Bohner, Claire Zion, Kara Welch, and so many others behind the scenes at NAL. I'd also like to thank Kimberly Whalen and Celeste Fine for their endless patience, hard work and straight-faced answers to innumerable stupid questions.

Thanks to the towns of Fredericksburg and Gruene—you'll always have a place in my heart! And especially to Debbie Schumann and Troy Rose of Grape Creek Vineyards, who couldn't have been kinder and took me on an impromptu tour.

Dennis Fallon, what can I say? You've come a long way, baby, from your days playing garage guitar with my husband! I love to hear you any chance I get, even living vicariously through my characters. Listening to Two Tons of Steel is always a pleasure.

Finally, thanks to Kylie Adams and Julie Kenner for being a lot of fun to work with; Wendy Wax for just being there, my Dad for supplying those Italian words and Don for putting up with my madness, scary deadline hair and gross consumption of chocolate. Love you guys!

# First Date

## The Bridesmaid Chronicles

## KAREN KENDALL

A SIGNET BOOK

SIGNET
Published by New American Library, a division of
Penguin Group (USA) Inc., 375 Hudson Street,
New York, New York 10014, USA
Penguin Group (Canada), 10 Alcorn Avenue, Toronto,
Ontario M4V 3B2, Canada (a division of Pearson Penguin Canada Inc.)
Penguin Books Ltd., 80 Strand, London WC2R 0RL, England
Penguin Ireland, 25 St. Stephen's Green, Dublin 2,
Ireland (a division of Penguin Books Ltd.)
Penguin Group (Australia), 250 Camberwell Road, Camberwell, Victoria 3124,
Australia (a division of Pearson Australia Group Pty. Ltd.)
Penguin Books India Pvt. Ltd., 11 Community Centre, Panchsheel Park,
New Delhi - 110 017, India
Penguin Group (NZ), cnr Airborne and Rosedale Roads, Albany,
Auckland 1310, New Zealand (a division of Pearson New Zealand Ltd.)
Penguin Books (South Africa) (Pty.) Ltd., 24 Sturdee Avenue,
Rosebank, Johannesburg 2196, South Africa

Penguin Books Ltd., Registered Offices:
80 Strand, London WC2R 0RL, England

First published by Signet, an imprint of New American Library,
a division of Penguin Group (USA) Inc.

First Printing, June 2005
10  9  8  7  6  5  4  3  2  1

Though it's a lighthearted romantic comedy, this book is dedicated to the victims of Alzheimer's disease and their caretakers. My heart goes out to them, especially those who are affected by early-onset Alzheimer's, which runs its course so breathtakingly fast.

# Chapter One

*If home is where the heart is, I need to work on being more heartless.* Sydney Spinelli stared at the accounting mess in front of her, and reflected that there were some things you'd only do for family.

Just like Sydney's mother, South River, New Jersey, had received a face-lift in the last few years. In spite of this, she didn't want to be here.

A town of about fifteen thousand, South River was known for some apparel manufacturing and not much else. Sydney's father Marv loved the place, probably more out of habit than anything else. He'd become a big fish in this small pond. Marv shared with it an inferiority complex: He'd resent Howard Johnson, king of the road motel, until dirt got shoveled over his short, round body. South River felt much the same about nearby New Brunswick.

Bobby, Marv's postman, ambled through the door. He brightened when he saw Sydney muttering at the computer screen. She looked up with a tolerant smile and waited for his inevitable question.

"Hey, Syd. Good to see you. What's new?"

"Not a lot, Bobby." She accepted the stack of mail from him, nodded her thanks and paused expectantly while he worked up to his next inevitable question. "How's your sister?" Every male in town asked the same thing.

"Julia's just fine. You want me to tell her you said hello?"

"Yeah." Bobby gave her a bashful smile. "Well, see you around."

"Okay, Bobby. Take care." She turned back to the computer. *What's new? Absolutely nothing. Not in ten years, maybe twenty.*

Oh, if anyone were to get technical about things, the carpet was new. Her father Marv had ordered replacement shag six months ago, resulting in another vast, depressing brown lawn under all the vintage 1974 furniture.

Nineteen seventy-four had marked the utterly ungrand opening of Marv's Motor Inns, the year that Sydney had her fifth birthday. A photograph, slightly askew, hung on the faux wood–paneled wall in front of her desk. Marv beamed with pride, resembling a pudgy, plaid-clad Bonaparte. Myrna, Sydney's mother, had a bad blond beehive and didn't quite carry off the part of Josephine. Sydney winced at her own five-year-old image: She sported a snaggletooth, a dress in green polyester plaid and one of Myrna's horrifying home haircuts.

The photo had been snapped just as she yanked little Julia away from the radiator. Myrna didn't appear to have noticed—her smoggy blue gaze focused on the camera lens—but judging from Julia's expression, the normally sunny child had resented her big sister's interference. Her petal pink lips formed a midhowl "O." Her Gerber-perfect eyes sparkled with angry tears. Her sculpted, dimpled chin jutted at a resentful right angle from the rest of her pampered little body.

Julia had grown from an adorable baby into the blond teenaged goddess craved by every boy in school.

Sydney . . . hadn't. She looked wryly away from the photograph and sighed. Well, hell. At least she'd lost the snaggletooth and the green plaid dress. And the once-orange hair was now auburn.

She squinted at the computer screen again. The family had come a long way, financially speaking, since 1974. Marv could hire a platoon of accountants to do this miserable job. He could burn the office to the ground and build a compound with an indoor swimming pool. But no.

*Fuhgeddaboudit.* Here she sat, in the same old dump, tracking the gradual embezzlement of Betty Lou Fitch, Marv's bookkeeper, over a thirty-year period. Betty Lou had disappeared with the funds about three weeks ago, and Marv had threatened, pleaded and blackmailed Sydney until she'd agreed to leave her own business, hightail it to South River from Princeton and figure it all out—no pun intended.

Her eyes were crossing from glaring at the computer screen. Still, matters could be worse: Marv had only transferred his records onto the machine as of 1992. Syd shuddered at the thought of going through thirty fat, handwritten ledgers.

She stood up, yawned and stepped accidentally on Humphrey, Marv and Myrna's long-suffering basset hound. "Sorry, boy! I'm so sorry . . ."

Humphrey gazed up at her piteously and didn't even grunt. Since he was ignored by everyone else in the household, he seemed to consider being squashed by her size nine foot a sign of affection.

Sydney bent down, kissed him and gifted him with a nacho cheese–flavored Dorito, her chosen poison during stressful times. He licked at it but left it on the floor and followed her to the watercooler, his droopy bloodshot eyes full of adoration. She drank some water from a pointed paper cup—so annoying, what genius had designed a cup you couldn't set down?—and then allowed him to slurp the rest of it.

The front door burst open. "Da hell is dat dohg doin' heah?" Marv said, taking three pugnacious steps forward. His ducktail quivered against the fat folds at the back of his neck, which swallowed the heavy gold chain he wore until it tunneled out at the side.

"He's lonely. Ma's out all day."

Marv snorted. "Dohg's too lazy to get lonely. Besides, Marcella's there."

"Marcella vacuums him."

"You find my money yet? *Un*believable, that Betty Lou! You can't trust *no*body."

Sydney restrained the urge to point out that Betty Lou had stolen less than the amount she'd deserved in back vacation pay, Christmas bonuses and 401k contributions over the last twenty years. It still didn't make the theft right, and Marv would blow a gasket.

"You heah from dat useless sistah o' yours? I can't get holda her, an' I want her receivables."

Sydney sighed. "She's not useless. And it's high tourism season right now, so I'm sure they're run off their feet."

Marv grunted.

"She's going to do great there, Pop."

Marv grunted again. "You find that money, Syddie. Okay?"

"I'll find it, Marv. Don't worry."

At the end of the day, Sydney turned with a wince into the circular drive of Marv's latest acquisition: a house that could only be described as a palace dipped in gingerbread batter. Syd sat staring at the monstrosity from the driveway, reluctant as always to enter the place. It shrieked pretension, from the ornate motifs frosted onto the brown stucco exterior to the tasteless fountain erupting like a volcano of new money from the landscaping. She averted her eyes from the swan paddleboat tied to a Grecian arcade at the edge of the man-made pond. Several fake ducks were anchored in the water at intervals, too, among faux lily pads with painted resin frogs perched on them.

Sydney closed her eyes briefly, took a deep breath and then inched her Acura forward into the "arbor" which hid the automobiles not parked in the garage. She opened the car door and knocked off yet another bunch of the rubber grapes clustered at artistic intervals on the trellis that made up the walls of the arbor. "Come on, Humph." The basset hound slunk out of the car. He, too, viewed the house with a jaundiced eye.

Sydney wanted passionately to hunt down Marv and Myrna's interior desecrator and burn her at the stake. If the woman had only stopped with the inside of the house. But no! She had massacred the outside, too.

Her parents were the laughingstocks of the entire town, and they didn't even realize it. Syd slammed the driver's side door, hitching her purse over her shoulder. She bent down, retrieved the cluster of grapes, and jammed them back into a bare spot on the trellis. Every time she pulled in here, she managed to accidentally harvest another bunch of grapes, whether it was with her shoulder, her briefcase, or the car's door. Marv's spare Mercedes was parked too close to her spot, giving her very little leeway.

Humphrey dragged after Sydney, stopped to sniff the air and looked even more depressed when he caught Eau de Marcella.

Syd was veering for the side door, what Marv called the service entrance, but Marcella had already spotted her. The wide double doors of the Gingerbread Palace opened noiselessly and the creepy housekeeper stood waiting for her at the top of the stone steps.

Sydney pasted a smile on her face and changed direction. Marcella's smooth olive face betrayed no emotion whatsoever and she stood sentrylike in her black dress with the white lace collar and starched white half apron. Syd had decided that the housekeeper was an android, and that she had an extra eye in the back of her head.

Without fail she opened the front door for family members and guests, but only the side door for any maintenance people or salespersons. Marcella was an expert in matters of condescension. A recent addition to the family, she had come with the house—undoubtedly part of the décor.

Myrna had confessed to Sydney that she was actively afraid of the woman, but Marv liked the prestige of having her.

"Doll-baby," Myrna whined, "she swipes my dirty laundry off the bathroom floor while I'm in the shower! She returns it clean two hours later. I know I shouldn't complain, but it's just *weird*. I don't like her sneaking in there while I'm naked, and I don't like another woman handling my personal washing."

"So why don't you tell her that?" Sydney asked.

"I'm afraid she'll put a curse on me."

"Because you won't let her wash your panties?" Myrna nodded.

"That's crazy, Ma. If you can't tell her yourself, then have Pop tell her."

"He says most women would beg for worries like mine."

Syd supposed that he had a point, but still, her mother shouldn't be terrorized by a uniformed panty thief in her own home.

"Hello, Marcella," she said now to the housekeeper. "How are you?"

Marcella nodded without expression and reached for Sydney's computer bag. She had the habit of mugging family members of their belongings right when they came in the door: coats, purses, bags. Syd hung on and a minor tug-of-war ensued. "I'm going to check e-mail again right now, so I'll take it up," she said firmly.

The housekeeper finally let go. She didn't like anyone disturbing the carefully orchestrated surfaces of the house. God forbid that a gas station receipt or movie ticket stub should mar the hall table or kitchen counter. Marcella even alphabetized the family mail on a silver tray.

Sydney felt Marcella's evil eye square in the middle of her back as she went upstairs, and resisted the urge to straighten her top or brush lint off her backside.

She entered the guest room she currently occupied, wrinkling her nose at the rococo reproduction antiques. Marie Antoinette would have felt comfortable in the room, but she did not. Such an abundance of gold and carved curlicues made her itch. She kicked off her shoes and unzipped her computer bag, placing the laptop square in the middle of a writing desk with elaborate, S-shaped legs. The thing could have galloped here from the court of Louis XVI. Sydney shook her head and hit the computer's ON button.

The information she needed from Marv's tax attorney was not there, but there was a new e-mail from her younger sister, Julia. "BIG NEWS!!!" was the heading.

Sydney clicked it open.

"Syd!!!!!! Oh my God, call me as soon as you get this!!!!! I am over the moon!!!!!"

*Huh?* Had Julia stumbled into a buy-one-get-one-free shoe sale at Neiman's? Added another pair of

Christian Louboutins to her collection of torturous footwear?

Even as Sydney wondered, another e-mail from "CrownJule" popped up on her screen. This one said "No time to call, but . . ."

She clicked on the heading to open it, and almost fell out of her chair.

Subject: No time to call, but . . .
Date: XXXXXXX
From: CrownJule
To: numbersgeek, vshelton@kleinschmidtbelker

GETTING MARRIED!!! To the most amazing guy, Roman Sonntag. Gotta fly, xoxoxo Julia. PS not sure how to break it to pop and ma? Don't say anything! Promise!

Sydney reeled. *What?* Her little sister had some "splainin" to do. *Oh, no, she is NOT flying off, not before talking to me first . . .* Sydney lunged at the phone and dialed the Marv's Motor Inn of Fredericksburg, Texas.

After being fired from her job as a buyer for Nordstrom, Julia had accepted Marv's decree that the only thing she was good for was running the smallest motor inn in his domain. "And she'll probably screw that up, too," Marv had said uncharitably. "She's not the responsible child."

Sydney knew it was useless to point out that Julia hadn't "screwed up" at Nordie's. She'd ordered exquisite clothes. She just didn't have a very good head for figures.

Julia had more of a figure for good head—or so the joke had gone in high school. Sydney still remembered the only fistfight she'd ever gotten into—because Chucky Malone had made that very comment.

She'd punched him in the eye. Never mind that Chucky, after recovering from his shock, had then spanned her face with his ham hand and pushed her head into the lockers. She'd just kneed him in the balls, too. And then she, Sydney Spinelli, straight-A student, had gotten suspended from school for three days.

At least Julia had snuck her a family-sized bag of nacho cheese–Doritos to keep her company. And she'd been able to watch all the soaps.

Today Syd was an accountant and had curbed most of her tendencies toward violence. Chucky Malone, however, was now in the Middlesex County jail, serving a sentence for grand theft auto. He'd never quite lived down getting sucker punched by a girl—and Sydney was okay with that.

The Marv's Motor Inn phone rang and rang before it was answered by some kid with a hick accent. *Naw, Miss Julia warn't thar, ma'am. Could'ee take a message?*

Sydney tried Miss Julia's cell phone, but she wasn't picking up. She threw the phone in frustration. What the hell did Julia mean, she was getting married? She'd only been in Fredericksburg for a *month*.

Sydney herself couldn't even *meet* a man in a month, much less marry one. And Marv was going to have a coronary. Roman Sonntag? What kind of name was that? Was he Italian or German? Oh, God, probably both. A man with the morals of a Sicilian alley cat and the anal-retentiveness of a German general. Roman Sonntag?

Julia had always had packs of men barking at her heels, but this was the first time she'd gotten engaged to one. Most of the poor guys had been unmemorable; only a couple stayed in Sydney's mind. There'd been Santiago, the Argentinian boy who'd sobbed uncontrollably while warbling Latin love songs under her window . . . before passing out cold in the hydrangeas. And then there'd been Somers, who'd sued Marv for eighteen thousand dollars after Julia lost the family heirloom necklace he'd given her.

The rest of them sort of ran together in Sydney's mind. She told herself that this engagement was no different than the boyfriends. It would be done, over with, in a few weeks. Except . . . Marv had given Julia such a hard time over the Somers situation that she'd sworn the next boyfriend was the last. In fact, Sydney clearly remembered her sister swearing on every Jimmy Choo in her closet that her serial relationships were over.

Was it possible that she'd marry this Roman person just to make a point?

Sydney turned the college class ring on her finger, tugging at the blue topaz in the center of it. Then she drummed her fingers on the ridiculously ornate desk. She drummed them until they hurt and her nails vibrated. And then she logged on to an airline Web site, keyed in her password and arranged a flight to Texas.

# *Chapter Two*

Alex Kimball was known in boardrooms across Texas for his piercing, eagle-eyed stare. He leveled it now, growled from deep within his chest and waved his arms for good measure.

The emu due north of him—a giant goddamn chicken—just bobbed her head and tilted her crazy beak. That she did so to the bass beat of the Stevie Ray Vaughn pulsing from the open door of Alex's Suburban probably made the bird talented.

He didn't care. "Get back on the other side of that fence, you friggin' feather-face, or I will tie a knot in that silly long neck of yours. I will sprinkle your ass with Tabasco and eat you raw for breakfast." He surged toward her. "Yah!"

The ostrichlike emu executed a step-ball-change and flapped her wings. Then, ignoring Alex completely, she twisted her neck backward and buried a long beak into her tail feathers. Apparently he was far less important to her than an itch. Alex would have gladly used the Suburban to nudge her back into her pen, but there were about seventeen of the birds—not to mention their chicks—to contend with.

Sighing, Alex plucked his cell phone from his pocket and dialed his Uncle Ted's number. "Ted, it's me. Chickens've flown the coop again. I have over a dozen of them here and they're not cooperating. What d'you say I just shoot 'em all and we scramble any remaining eggs? . . .

"No? C'mon, Ted, this is the great state of Texas we live in, remember? Whatever happened to *cows*? Nice, normal, four-legged critters. Easy to feed, herd and eat. Easy to market . . .

"No, Ted. I'm not dissin' you. Not doubtin' you, either. Big guy, I am still a venture capitalist. Just never been involved in a venture quite like this one, okay? Yeah, I'll wait 'til you get here. I'll do my best to keep 'em somewhat contained. Just hurry."

Alex hit the OFF button and stared at Bad Mutha Emu. "Women usually fall at my feet, darlin'."

The emu bobbed her head again and opened her beak to display a black tongue and wide gullet. Then she made a weird grunting noise.

"Charming." Alex wiped sweat from his brow with the back of his hand.

Edward Kimball, his father's brother, had operated a thriving San Antonio law practice at this time last year. Alex would never understand what had made him trade that in for a cussed emu ranch, of all things. And Ted couldn't start small, either. No— he'd invested over a million dollars in these bizarre birds.

"It's the new beef, Alex!" he'd said. "Mark my words. Emu will hit menus all over the world. Low fat, high protein, no danger of mad cow disease . . . great with beer, wine or tequila. The oil is restorative and excellent in cosmetics. And the boots you can make out of emu hide! Move over, ostrich, elephant and alligator. Emu is the new 'It' skin."

Uh-huh. So here Alex was, chicking—uh, checking—on the investment for which he'd mistakenly helped round up the cash. *Christ Almighty.*

Problem was, emu meat had aroused only mild interest across the country and now even that was fading. And Aunt Susie had gone all earth mother and freaked at the concept of processing the birds for distribution.

"Nothing will be killed on my land!" she'd declared. "It's just not right."

The result was just what Susie ordered: No processing was done on Kimball land; the birds were purchased and shipped elsewhere. At least that was the plan. The actual purchasing was going slow. Alex hoped that emus weren't highly sexed birds; otherwise the Kimball flock was going to overrun all of the Texas Hill Country.

Ted and Susie were still developing a new cookbook: *Recipes from the Cordon Emu*. Somehow Alex didn't think the French would be too impressed, though he himself made a mean emu chili and was perfecting a spicy, chipotle-based emu barbecue sauce.

The sadistic Texas sun started to steam him in his own juices, and he climbed back into the Suburban, hunkering down in front of the AC. No matter how many years you lived in the Lone Star State, you never got used to a Texas August. He was sure his toes had melted and become grafted to the lining of his Lucchese ostrich boots.

"Ostrich," he said aloud, and made a gun out of his finger. He aimed it at Bad Mutha Emu. "Pow."

She bobbled her head and pretty much ignored him until Uncle Ted showed up with a couple of field hands, Bud and Smudge.

Ted was an unusual figure of a man: a string bean with a potbelly. Truth to tell, he resembled an emu himself. He swung down from behind the wheel of a Jeep, mock-saluted Alex and strode right over to Bad Mutha.

"Hello, Beautiful," he said to her. Then he grabbed her chick under the chest, holding the wings down under his arms. The chick didn't like it much, but couldn't do a damned thing about the situation besides wriggle his little three-toed legs. Uncle Ted de-

17

posited him on the other side of the downed wire fence and said "Shoo." Bad Mutha followed and joined him.

*So simple. Why the hell didn't I think of that?*

Bud and Smudge did the same and soon all seventeen birds were two-legged-trotting back north. The field hands produced a coil of wire and set to repairing the gap in the fence—probably made on purpose by a teenager, just for fun.

Alex felt like a fool.

Uncle Ted grinned and snapped his gum. "All there is to it. Chick gives you problems, just grab 'er by the breast."

"Yeah," said Alex in wry tones. "Next time I'm in a bar, I'll remember that."

By the time they'd exchanged some more easy banter, Alex had devised a whole new recipe for Szechuan Shredded Emu. He couldn't wait to make it at home.

He drove slowly, drinking in the landscape and letting the idea of home curl into his belly. The gray tarmac sliced through fields unusually green for this time of year. The cedar and mesquite trees, normally scrappy and rugged, sported luxurious foliage and seemed almost drunk with complacence. The heavy rainfall made for an explosion of vegetation, and the grapes and peaches reveled.

Unfortunately the rain had also bred an explosion of young mosquitoes and flies that feasted on miserable steers and quarter horses; fleas were as thick as fur on outdoor dogs and cats.

Why had it taken tragedy to bring him back here? He'd taken so much for granted—family, home, women and money.

He'd had everything and known everything until the phone call from his father two months ago.

He'd known the sky was blue. He'd known catastrophe, a snake, struck quickly—but he'd always sidestepped it. He had not known his own limitations.

"I need you to come home," his father had said.

Alex cited twenty different business obligations.

"I need you to come home," his father repeated.

"Why?"

"Just come, damn it."

So Alex cancelled meetings and conference calls, put off correspondence and hitched a ride with his best friend, Roman, who'd been in San Antonio on business. Roman—though he must have known, like the rest of the town—pretended not to, thinking it was a family matter. Alex, oblivious, enjoyed a Shiner Bock, wondered what his wily old dad was up to, and heard the unbelievable news that Roman was engaged.

Say what? To whom? A Yankee from New Jersey? He had to be kidding. He was not.

Before he'd fully digested the news, Roman dropped him off at the gorgeous old limestone Kimball casa. The first thing Alex noticed was the peculiar state of the flower beds. They were well-tended as usual—his mother was meticulous—but the color scheme, if you could call it that, was bizarre and there were several clumps of . . . dead branches? Not plants that had died, but cut limbs, "planted" in a careful mix of potting soil and mulch.

Alex gave them a curious stare as he strode up the flagstone path to the front door of his childhood home. He felt a little guilty that he hadn't made it home to visit his parents in over three months. Well, he was here now. He'd find out what his father wanted soon enough. He opened the screen, pressed the latch and walked in—to the heresy of crumpled laundry on the formal living room couch. He blinked. Not in thirty-five years had he ever seen such a thing.

The house was spotless, its soft yellow walls and beautiful dark wood trim the same. An oil portrait of his grandfather hung over the stone fireplace; comfortable chairs in hideously expensive fabrics still retained the shapes of the last derrieres to be seated in them. That was goose down for you.

Crystal sparkled from the old mahogany breakfront; touches of highly polished silver gleamed from various corners. Not enough to be oppressive or pretentious—just enough to look casually elegant.

"Mama?" he called. He set down his overnight bag and walked into the kitchen. It was redolent as always with delicious cooking smells: sautéed garlic and onion, olive oil, rosemary and a waft of pinot grigio. Two loaves of fresh-baked bread were cooling on a wire rack. Mama had always been a helluva cook. Hundreds of recipe books from all over the world lined the shelves of the large, airy kitchen.

"I see you." His mother's voice was sharp and bright with . . . *fear*?

Somewhere in the back of the house, no doubt from his father's office, came the rumble of a male voice on the telephone.

"I saw you walk into this house like it's your own," said Mama. Her eyes reflected sheer terror— and not a trace of recognition.

*What? It* is *my own.*

"You'd better stop right there, mister, because I've called the sheriff." Always high and girlish, the timbre of her voice had risen an entire octave. A misplaced lock of her salon-rinsed blond hair trembled on her forehead. Her mascara had smudged under her hazel eyes, and into the laugh lines that only made her more beautiful.

*Sheriff?*

"Don't you come one step farther!" His mother, the woman who'd given birth to him, brandished a knife in her right hand and the cordless phone in her left.

"Mama?" He held out his arms.

"Not one step! I'll stick you like a pig!"

*Jesus.* What in the hell was going on? Alex swallowed. "Mama, it's me. Alex. What are you doing?"

"Thought you'd help yourself to the Francis I silver, did you?"

*Huh? No! Who is this crazy woman, and where is my mother?* "Mama!" He unconsciously stepped toward her, but she gave a frightened squeak, the noise of a field mouse, and retreated behind the central butcher block.

Horrified at the pathos and helplessness of the sound, Alex froze. He closed his eyes, praying that when he opened them his world would make sense.

In the back of the house, Alex heard his father's boots; he was emerging from his office. "Dad? Get in here!"

"He's dark and dangerous-looking," his mother quavered into the phone. "About six foot two, and he's *in my kitchen!*" Her voice rose yet another octave. "Please send someone right away!"

# Chapter Three

DON'T MESS WITH TEXAS, the sign read. Sydney raised a brow. "Wouldn't dream of it," she muttered. "All I want is my sister back."

She stepped on the gas and her rented Ford compact strained to reach seventy miles per hour. Though the Austin airport had yielded nothing more surprising than Texas wine and loud chili-pepper neckties, she was beginning to realize that she'd arrived in a foreign country. No doubt about it: Jersey didn't feature pickup trucks with gun racks and bumper stickers that read I BRAKE FOR ARMADILLOS.

And the farther she got from Austin, the scarier it became. She passed big spreads of wire-fenced land dotted with brush, scrub trees and water storage tanks, a business called Big Rack Taxidermist and another called McCoy's Building Supply Center. McCoy's, for real?

She expected to then roll by Hatfield's Demolition,

but instead the next business of interest proved to be something called the Wild Ride Saloon. Hmmm. She had a feeling they weren't referring to horses.

After the Nutty Brown Café came big signs for a new Polo Club. Weirder and weirder: She could have sworn they rode Western in Texas. Polo? Oh—it was a housing development, perhaps represented by Ranch Real Estate nearby.

Syd passed the American Red Brangus Association—what the hell was a brangus?—and tried to imagine her sister Julia living out here. She failed miserably. Julia's Manolo Blahniks would catch in every gopher hole from here to San Antonio. She'd bounce all her checks from the Cattleman's National Bank. And Syd couldn't possibly picture her employing anyone from Ole Yeller Landscaping.

Julia, purchasing hay for thirty dollars a bale? Hanging out in the 101-degree heat astride a longhorn? Or perhaps—Sydney snorted—chomping down on a piece of Whittington's Beef Jerky. Yeah, right.

She ignored the rumbling of her stomach, not wishing to risk stopping at a barbecue place called the Pit, even though it smelled more promising than its name. She saw signs for Johnson City, birthplace of Lyndon B., and her stomach asked if she wanted to stop at a different restaurant, this one called the Feedmill. *God help me*, she thought. The next sign she noticed just read, STOP HERE. GOOD STUFF. *I don't think so.*

That's when things started to sound not only Texan, but German—which made even less sense to Sydney. Oma's Haus and Garten? The Vogel Orchard? Becker Vineyards?

Texas possessed vineyards? Syd's Jersey lip curled. Well, if barley and hops could make beer, and potatoes made vodka, then she supposed . . . hay . . . could make wine.

The German influence continued as she approached Fredericksburg. The road she was on, Highway 290, became Main Street as she passed the intersection at Goehmann, and Sydney tried very hard not to be charmed.

She failed. The curl in her lip relaxed without permission or warning into a delighted smile. Through her window yodeled the sound of country music: "Why don'tcha luv me like you used to do? Why do ya treat me like a worn-out shoe?"

*You've got to be kidding me.* But she grinned at the sheer hokiness of it, and rolled down her window to hear more. The tune blasted from the truck ahead of her, driven by a man in a bona fide white ten-gallon hat. *He must be one of the good guys . . .*

Bemused, she drank in the vista before her. Main Street was lined solidly with shops: wood and stone cottages with big picture windows and welcoming porches, carved cedar benches and urns of flowers.

She drove slowly, taking in the galleries, gift shops, cafés and bars. A wine market, several jewelers and

25

countless antique stores surprised her. What were they doing in the middle of Nowhere, Texas?

The NASCAR place, Forever Texas Souvenirs and a quilt shop were more along the lines of what Sydney had expected. She was tempted to stop at the Uptown Visitor Center, but frowned at the impulse. She was there to talk sense into her sister, not be a tourist.

She panted along in the Ford, looking for Orange Street where Marv's Motor Inn was located. There was Crockett, which according to her map meant Orange was the next one. Aha. A right turn and there it was, a squat, ugly, no-frills building painted in Marv's familiar brown and mustard yellow. To complete the aura of bad seventies welcome, a giant neon arrow pointed to the COME ON INN sign, of course underscripted with their father's famous tagline: COUNT SHEEP FOR CHEAP.

Sydney winced and parked the car. She emerged, stretched her legs and took a deep breath of the murderously hot Texas air. August had never been this grim in New Jersey. Not even close. The oxygen seemed to clog in her nose before she could breathe it.

Sure the sun was adding dozens of freckles per second to her unfortunate skin, Sydney hurried to the door and hauled it open to find Julia.

Blinking to adjust her eyes to the dim interior, Syd

locked eyes immediately with her younger sister, who sat behind the registration desk, her petite blondness dwarfed by a veritable mountain of fat, glossy bridal magazines. *Uh-oh.*

Julia's mouth formed an astonished "O" before she jumped to her feet and surged around the counter to hug Sydney. "Syd! What are you doing here? Oh my God, it's so good to see you!"

Same old sunny Julia. You had to love her. Syd hugged her back, inhaling a snootful of blond curls and J'Adore perfume. She was sure she herself smelled far less enticing after her day of traveling— and specifically the hour or so spent stuck to the vinyl seats of the rental car while she tried in vain to lower the temperature.

Julia danced her around in a crazy, upbeat circle while Sydney laughed and stumbled.

"Syd, you Wild Thing! I can't believe you came down here! It's so impulsive . . . so not like you! Let me guess! You came to tell me congratulations in person, didn't you?" Julia's eyes sparkled guilelessly.

*Uh. Not exactly.*

"I am so excited! You'll *love* him. Roman . . . isn't that a sexy name? Makes me think of those buff warriors in the body armor—"

*Oh, yeah. Those guys who conquered, killed and enslaved entire populations. What a turn-on, Jules.*

"He's a dream . . ."

27

*A nightmare.*

". . . and I have to show you a bunch of dresses . . . there's no way I'll be able to decide on only one . . ."

She rattled on, and though Sydney wanted to interrupt, take her by the shoulders and shake some sense into her, she found herself unable to rain on Julia's parade. She looked so happy, so pretty, so very *Modern Bride.*

Syd bit her lip against both a rush of affection and an unwelcome coil of—but no, ridiculous. She'd never dreamed of a big white wedding. Well, very rarely. There was that one fantasy she had with the tiara, but it could double easily as your average, run-of-the-mill control-freak vision. It didn't have anything to do with being swung into the arms of a handsome devil who promised to love her 'til death did them part. Really. In her dream, she was just the center of attention and everyone did what she told them to do. Not at all unreasonable.

During her musings, Sydney caught a blinding flash of light somewhere in the vicinity of Julia's left hand. Holy cow! She grabbed her sister's wrist. "Is that a fallen star or a three-carat rock on your fourth finger?"

Julia blushed, made a brief pretense of modesty and then threw it to the winds. "Isn't it gorgeous?" The ring was new enough that her tones were still awestruck. "It belonged to Roman's great-grandmother."

"And most likely a czarina before that," said Sydney. The ring blazed, even under Marv's cheap fluorescent lighting and against the lovely faux wood–grain of the reception desk. It was absolutely flawless. And it was completely without color. Syd had never seen such a perfect stone—almost too perfect, for a well-worn, antique ring. Roman's great-granny—or great-gramps—had been either loaded or an accomplished thief.

"Julia, I've never seen anything more beautiful." *Ugh.* There it was again—that tiny, shameful green coil of envy.

Her sister lowered her voice. "I know, I can't believe it. And apparently Roman's sister is going to be royally pissed that I've got it. She's still mad it was left to Roman and not her."

Sydney shrugged. "Welcome to the dynamics of your new family. They can't be weirder than the old one, can they?"

Julia laughed nervously. "I haven't met them yet. I'm going to dinner at Roman's parents' house tonight."

"How can you not have met them yet? This town almost fits in the palm of my hand."

Julia's blush appeared again. "Well, they were visiting Roman's sister and spending time in New York for a couple of weeks. And then we were kind of, um, occupied for most evenings."

Sydney raised a brow. *Ah. Making like bunnies, in other words.*

29

"Don't look at me like that!" Julia said it defensively.

"Like what?"

"Like you're made out of fine china and have no physical urges or bodily functions." The crack was a warning that Julia's emotions were turbulent at the moment. *Uh-oh.*

"Excuse me?" Syd tried to neutralize her expression. Had her face really been that sour?

"You know, The Look. You've perfected it over the years." Julia ran a hand through her perfect tousled curls and retreated behind the registration desk. "Your nose goes up, your eyes narrow, your mouth pinches. It's the do-I-have-to-put-a-leash-on-her-again look."

"I didn't give you any such look," said Sydney, who did indeed feel the urge for a leash.

"Yes, you did." Julia's pink lips flattened mulishly.

"Did not." And just like that, they'd regressed to ages five and three. Except that three-year-olds didn't usually get engaged.

"Roman is different—he's the most amazing man I've ever met," announced Julia.

Sydney dropped her heavy leather bag and sank into a mustard velour club chair. *Step carefully.* "Jule, you said that about Santiago. And that Somers creep, too."

Her sister's eyes flashed and she folded her arms. "Why did you *really* come all this way, Syd?"

30

*Avoid the question or this will flare into ugliness.* There was a *looong* history between them of Sense driving Sensibility crazy. And vice versa. Syd said cautiously, "I want you to be happy."

"I'm happy."

*Deep breath.* "I want you to be careful."

"Caution is overrated, in my opinion, and this is real. Roman is The One."

*Don't let this escalate into an argument.* Sydney counted to three. *But I've got to say what needs to be said. Otherwise, what was the point of coming down here?* "Aren't you afraid you're rushing things? Riding some crazy romantic high?"

"I knew you didn't come down here just to help me celebrate! That would be completely out of character for you. No. I am *not* riding some crazy romantic high. I mean I am, but I know what I'm doing! And it really ticks me off that you just assume that I don't! Did Marv put you up to this? Is he out there in the car?"

Syd shook her head. "Pop doesn't know. Trust me, if he did, he'd be down here throwing a fit."

The phone interrupted their uneasy chat. "Marv's Motor Inn, may I help you?" Julia sang. "Yes, sir." A gurgle of faux laughter. "Where you count sheep for cheap, exactly, sir. We *absolutely* have a room for you on the nineteenth and twentieth. Will that be smoking or non? Double, queen or king? And would you like turn-down service?"

Syd blinked. *Turn-down service? Since when?*

"You get turned down all the time already? Well, sir, that's a shame. You sound like such a *nice* gentleman." Julia rolled her eyes at Syd.

"Well, no, sir, I couldn't do that. I just got engaged and my fiancé would not appreciate it. Yes, well, we do look forward to seeing you on the nineteenth, sir. Thank you!"

"You're just scary," Sydney said. "I would have hung up on him."

"And that's why you're not in customer service. You stay on the numbers side, okay? He's just a lonely old geezer and he thought he was being incredibly witty. Besides, Marv wants this location's receivables up twenty percent, and I'm not going to accomplish that by being rude to potential guests."

True. "Okay, whatever. To return to our discussion, how exactly did you meet this Roman guy? What do you know about him and his past?"

"Oh, here we go. The Syd Spinelli Inquisition! Forgive me, Boss, for not asking your permission before getting engaged. Pardon me for falling in love—I know, it's just so impulsive and ill-advised!"

Syd tried to interrupt, but Julia forged ahead.

"Before I agreed to marry Roman, I should have extracted some of his DNA and had it tested for genetic mutation, had him fingerprinted and run through the criminal justice system, made him get a physical, and drawn blood for analysis of any irregularities. Let me guess, I also should have run a financial check on him and hired a private investigator to dig into his past!"

Sydney winced. She *had* been thinking along the lines of at least a blood test and a PI.

Furious, Julia glared at Syd and folded her perfectly tanned, moisturized arms over her trendy Juicy Couture top. Her nails were healthy, shiny and polished, too.

Sydney told herself to keep control of her temper and sat on her bare, ragged, unbuffed nails, reminding herself that she didn't have time for such frivolities. Yep, that was it. Nothing to do with gnawing. She took a deep breath.

"I'm not trying to put you through an inquisition. All I asked was how you met him, okay?"

"I met Roman because he's renovating the place next door," said her sister, calming down a bit.

"Mr. Three-Carats actually performs manual labor?"

"Sydney, stop it. He likes doing that stuff—it relaxes him. Anyway, it was a Sunday, and I was laying out in back by the pool . . ."

*That explains it. One look at Julia in her tiny bikini and it was all over for the poor son of a bitch.*

". . . and I hear this deep voice saying that he's never wanted so bad in his life to count sheep for cheap." Julia giggled. "So I open one eye behind my shades, just to see where the voice is coming from, but there's nobody around.

"And then there's a big hearty laugh, and the voice says, 'Yeah. And Jack, my cabinet guy, would love for her to spill out of that top.'

"At that point I got mad. The voice was coming from an open window at the house next door. So I walked over there to tell him I didn't appreciate the running commentary, and this heart-stopping, shirtless hunk in a tool belt opens the door! Tool belts are *beyond* sexy, don't you think?

"Well, I gaped at him and he gaped at me, and he said into his cell phone, 'I gotta go,' and that was that."

*Huh? They'd smushed into each other, like chocolate and peanut butter?* "What do you mean, 'that was that'?"

Julia shrugged. "I told him that I was nowhere near falling out of my top, thank you very much." She smiled, all innocence. "And he said, *very* respectfully, 'No, ma'am.' He said he could see that, and he apologized most humbly for making me feel uncomfortable and he was really sweet about it."

*I'll just bet he was.*

"Then he dropped this monster cordless drill right on his toe and we had to come over here and get some ice for it."

*What a coincidence.*

"We just started talking and never stopped until morning. We talked through a pizza, some sundaes and even donuts at seven a.m. And don't look at me like that, I did not sleep with him. Not that night," Julia said, looking a little guilty.

Sydney didn't want to think about her baby sister sleeping with anyone. She shuddered. It was almost as bad as imagining her parents doing the deed.

There were some things in the world too grim to be contemplated, such as Marv chasing Myrna around a heart-shaped bed. Syd closed her eyes and blinked the image away.

In a tone that came out harsher than she'd meant it to, she said, "So your relationship with this Roman guy is based on great pecs and pizza?"

Julia snapped a *Bride* magazine closed and stood up again. "I should have known you wouldn't understand! You don't have a romantic bone in your body—"

"Oh, thank you very much." Stung, Sydney wasn't about to admit the accusation hit close to home.

"It's true, Syd. I still remember you asking David Whatshisface to your senior prom just because he was tall enough!"

"That's a total lie."

"Oh, really? You're going to tell me that you were madly in love with that dorky bag of bones? Have you ever even been in love, Syd? Are you capable of it?"

*"Julia!"*

"Or are you just a human calculator?"

"That is beyond insulting. You have no right—"

"Because I also remember you dating that law student freshman year because he'd be able to help you on some paper. And—"

"You know what," Sydney yelled, "we weren't talking about me!" And unfortunately her mouth just took over. What was it about siblings that they could get you to screaming point within one minute? "No, Julia—we're talking about *you* and snap judgments and basic flightiness—"

"Oh!" Julia stamped her Stuart Weitzman–clad foot.

"—and screwing up your life for the sake of some jackass in a tool belt! Julia, I don't care how well-heeled or well-hung he is—you don't need to marry the guy. Marv would be all too happy to buy you a ring with even more bling than that one if it'll blaze some *sense* into your head!"

"Sydney, you can take your high and mighty tone and shove it—"

A male throat cleared behind them and both sisters spun around. "Ladies! Ladies, what's going on here?" He set a small cardboard box down on a nearby mustard-colored chair, nodding at Julia. "Service with a smile: your bud vases from my Aunt Susie."

*Bud vases*, at a Marv's Motor Inn?

Julia snapped her mouth closed and blushed a disgustingly becoming shade of rose. Sydney narrowed her eyes upon her target. How much had he heard?

He was obviously amused. The deep grooves at the corners of his eyes, the jaunty tilt of his mouth told her that. Even the dark stubble at his jaw seemed to vibrate with humor.

Sydney swallowed as she took in all six and a half feet of him. Shoulders broader than Marv was tall. A chest wide enough to easily seat three naked vixens. Legs that would practically span the panhandle.

The guy was made to model snug denim, born to command, and could likely seduce the sun from the sky. Roman Sonntag was one hundred percent smiling bad news. No wonder her sister was one smitten kitten. Sydney felt a meow rising in her own throat.

"Nothing's going on," said Julia unconvincingly.

"What's going on," said Sydney, deciding to take the bull by the horns, "is a frank discussion of how crazy this snap engagement is! You two barely know each other—"

Sonntag opened his mouth to say something but she overrode him.

"—and Julia has a history of—"

"Sydney! Don't you go there—"

"—rushing into things without thinking very hard about them—"

Sydney had to pause for breath and Sonntag had

a chance to say something. "Jersey, you are waaaay outta line, here."

"What?"

"Calm down."

"I can't calm down, okay? And I am not out of line. If you're going to be a member of this family you may as well get used to me right away—"

He held up a big hand and talked over her. "Are you proposing to me, darlin'?"

Sydney blinked at him. "Huh?"

"You've got the wrong guy. I'm not Roman. My name is Alex Kimball." His eyes danced.

"Not Roman," Sydney repeated. *Oh, shit.* Her face caught fire. "Julia! Why didn't you tell me?"

Her sister put her hands on her hips. "You didn't give anyone a chance to tell you anything!"

Syd took a deep breath. "Sorry." She met the man's mocking gaze reluctantly. "Um. Nice to meet you?"

"Oh, the pleasure's all mine," he drawled, and clearly meant it. Pleasure at her expense.

How to recoup from here?

But it appeared she wasn't the only plainspoken one in the crowd. "So, you don't seem to have a very high opinion of my friend Roman."

Syd felt the heat in her cheeks flame impossibly higher. What had she said? Well-heeled and well-hung? She raised her chin. "I don't even know the guy."

"But you've already formed a negative opinion of him. 'Jackass in a tool belt,' I believe you called him."

*Oh, yeah. That, too.* She groaned inwardly while Julia aimed a vaporizing glare in her direction. "There's no need to, er, share that opinion with him," she said cautiously.

"Roman's not stupid," Kimball told her. "He'll pick up the nonverbal cues. Not that you seem shy about the verbal ones."

Sydney put her hands to her cheeks. "Can we just start over?"

"That might be a good idea." He stuck out his hand. "I'm Alex Kimball, a friend of Roman's since grade school."

She touched her fingers to his and felt a weird spark shoot up her arm and then down her spine. "Sydney Spinelli, Julia's sister."

"You got a cute Northern accent there, Jersey."

Indignation rose to join her blush. "You're making fun of *my* accent?"

He just grinned.

*Oh, don't do that. You're impossibly hot with your mouth closed. You're lethal when you smile . . .* Sydney might not have a romantic bone in her body, but she had to acknowledge some ninety-proof lust and a shameful spiral of relief that Alex was not, after all, her sister's property—so she didn't have to feel guilty basking in the supremely male wattage of that grin.

"Oh, stay down here long enough and we'll teach you the right way to talk. So when did you get in?"

"I just drove here from the Austin airport."

"Decent flight?"

She nodded.

"Good. Listen, if you'd like to meet Roman, I'm on my way out to the Sonntag place and I'd be happy to take you."

Julia looked alarmed. "I don't think that's a good—"

"I'd love to, thanks." Sydney smiled.

Alex turned to Julia and said reassuringly, "I'll keep things under control, don't worry."

"I'd come with you, but there's nobody to cover for me right now . . ." Julia bit her lip.

"It won't be necessary for Alex to keep anything under control," Sydney said stiffly.

"Probably not," he said. "After all, Roman might really enjoy being called a jackass in a tool belt."

*Hateful man.* And Julia didn't have to smirk like that, either. *I flew all the way down here to talk to her and this is the thanks I get! What's in store for me next?*

# Chapter Four

Alex winked reassuringly at Julia, whose big blue eyes were troubled. Then he held the door open for the Difficult Sister. Accent and meddling notwithstanding, Difficult had a flawless ass. Who knew Jersey turned them out so shapely? Neat little waist in that tailored, if damp, white blouse. Then the hips flared gently into cheeks curved like the bowl of a good crystal wineglass. Proportion was everything. Size didn't matter nearly so much—he was indifferent to whether a derriere was a size fourteen or a size four, as long as the specs were correct.

"Mmmm, mmm," Alex said under his breath, then quickly averted his eyes as she turned. "Do you smell brisket in the air?"

She shook her head. As he led her to his dusty Suburban, Alex took in her sensible two-inch heels and leather bag. "We've got to make a stop on the way," he said. "Hope you don't mind. I've got to drop something off at my uncle's ranch."

*Ranch?* Sydney grimaced. "No problem." But she couldn't say that she looked forward to being surrounded by cows. They were very large and probably smelly. Did they bite? She'd just stay in the comfort of the Suburban while he did whatever it was that he had to do.

Alex opened the door for her—at least these Texas guys knew their manners—and she managed to scramble without much grace into the truck. The heat inside hit her with the force of a blow. Sydney gasped and wilted. *So this is what a lobster feels like, when it's lowered into the pot.*

The Suburban wasn't much for creature comforts. It was an older model and the springs in the bench seat were shot. It tilted drunkenly, lower on the driver's side. She told herself to hang on to the door whenever they took a left, or she'd be sitting in Kimball's lap. Not that the idea was altogether unappealing, but the embarrassment factor would be high.

Alex swung in and started the ignition and AC, thank God. It spewed a stream of suffocating, musty heat at her and she felt sweat overrun her deodorant like a barbarian tribe. Any remaining makeup she may have had on her face dissolved and oozed down her cheeks. Her hair hung limply, gel and spray defeated.

Great. She was sitting next to the most gorgeous man she'd ever beheld, and she looked and smelled like something beyond fermentation. She cast a side-long glance at him. Exactly three tiny beads of sweat dotted his lip. Other than that, Kimball showed no signs of being affected by the heat.

They drove through town and turned down several dusty roads until they reached a big aluminum gate set over what Alex called a cattle grill. Alex swung out of the truck, opened the gate, got back in, drove through. Then he got out and closed it behind them. As they approached a wooden farmhouse, Sydney saw an older woman in a colorfully embroidered Mexican dress, squatting with a paintbrush in front of a huge, dark green egg. What on earth laid an egg that big? A pterodactyl?

The egg perched in a wrought iron stand apparently made to hold it. As they got closer, Sydney could see that the woman had painted an intricate design on the egg and was now layering gold pigment onto it.

Alex blew a kiss to the woman, who waved, and they continued along the gravel drive past the house. Sydney saw a couple of horses, but no cattle. They rounded a stand of mesquite, and her jaw dropped.

There in a pen of wooden boards and wire was a group of strange, giant birds. The adults were five to six feet tall and had to weigh as much as she did.

Alex glanced at her expression and laughed. "Emu," he said.

"E-*what*?"

"Emu. They're ratites, a cousin of the ostrich and the kiwi. People are starting to ranch them as an alternative to beef."

"Ratites? What's that, a rat of great height? I thought rats were rodents and birds were birds and kiwi were fruits." Sydney stared at the odd-looking birds, which looked right back at her. One of them yawned. Another bit at its long, bony leg. Yet another ignored them to walk along the fence, emu plop dropping behind it. *Eeeuw.*

Two young males tried to bite at each other over a barrier, grunting and hissing and flapping their wings. In a pen beyond them, another emu couple seemed to be getting romantic. As Alex rolled down the window, she could hear a sort of drumming sound from one, punctuated by grunts from the other.

Alex gestured toward them. "A hot date," he said. "She's showing off her neck feathers and her voice. He's complimenting her."

Sydney raised a brow. "Before you know it, they'll be planning a wedding."

Alex shot her an assessing look, but said nothing.

"Can they fly?" Sydney asked.

"Nope. Their wings are underdeveloped for their size. Look at the huge breastbone on them—it's often referred to as a keel."

"Why? Do they float?"

Alex frowned. "Good question. I don't know. I

don't think they're big on swimming, though. Look at the feet: They've got three toes. The ostrich only has two."

She inspected the bird closest to them, and it did indeed have three gnarled and funky toes. Julia would say they were badly in need of a pedicure.

Syd marveled again over the sheer size of the bird. "You're telling me that people really eat these things? As in emu steak?"

"You bet. There's emu steak, sausage and even jerky. You can get the meat ground, too—emu burger is tasty."

Syd wrinkled her nose. "Is it like chicken?"

"It's really closer to beef, but lower in cholesterol and fat."

Sydney looked at the bird herd and chuckled. "So they're becoming the other red meat?"

"We sure hope so."

"You don't see a whole lot of shrink-wrapped emu in the supermarket," said Sydney.

He nodded. "Which is precisely the problem. People like my Uncle Ted know it's a great product, but we're still trying to figure out how to get the word spread and increase demand." He passed a hand over his jaw. "Keeps me busy when I'm here."

He reached behind his seat to get a jar of something thick, brownish red and muddy-looking. "Here. Wanna taste?"

Sydney regarded the jar warily. "What is it?"

45

"My fabulous, chipotle-based, Hot 'n' Sweet Emu Sauce."

Sydney tilted it and watched the red brown sludge crawl toward the neck of the jar. "I think I'll pass. What's a chipotle?"

"You don't know what a chipotle is? A chipotle is a pepper. I thought you East Coasties up there were all cultured."

"We don't grow things like chipotle or emu in Jersey." *Not men like you, either,* she added silently. "You've heard the 'radioactive garbage' jokes. We specialize more in third arms."

He cocked his head. "Oh, so there's a sense of humor in there somewhere."

"Buried somewhere in the morass of officious, bossy older sibling, yes, there's a funny bone."

"I didn't say any of that, Jersey."

"You didn't have to. It was written all over your face. Look, I'm just worried, okay? What would your reaction be if your sister announced she was marrying someone she'd only known a month?"

Alex thought about it. "I don't have a sister. But my brother was engaged for two years before his marriage, and that didn't help hold it together."

She bit her lip.

He would have been glad to do it for her. The thought surprised him vaguely, and he shifted on the lopsided old seat. It dipped down on his side, which caused her to slide toward him. She grasped the door handle and pulled herself back in the other direction.

"I'm a little overprotective when it comes to Julia," she admitted.

"Roman's actually quite a catch. Especially since he got paroled—"

The look of horror on her face was priceless. "—and had that hunch-reduction surgery."

Realization dawned on her and she looked as if she might hit him. "Do you make fun of everyone?"

"Let me think about that for a minute," he said, actively enjoying the wrinkle in her forehead and her lowered ginger brows. "Yes. Any further questions?"

She blew out a breath and shook her head.

"Excellent. Now twist the lid off that jar and taste my sauce. It's your transportation and tourism fee."

Sydney tilted the jar again suspiciously.

"C'mon. There's nothing poisonous in it. And I need another guinea pig before I give it to Ted."

With visible reluctance, she tried to twist the lid off, but didn't have enough strength in those soft white hands of hers. "Oh, too bad. It's stuck."

He took it from her and removed the lid easily before handing it back to her. "Mmmm, yummy."

She sniffed it cautiously and wrinkled her nose. Then she dipped her index finger in the stuff and popped it into her mouth.

His gaze rested on the plump curve of her nude

47

bottom lip, so much softer than the stubborn chin below. She sucked the finger, lips surrounding it, and he felt a distinct twinge in a region that shouldn't be twingeing. He forced himself to look away.

"Not bad," she said, sounding surprised. "In fact . . . I like it a lot. It's sweet, hot, tangy and spicy. It's got both kiss and kick to it."

*Just the way I like my women.* Alex's eyes returned to her mouth again, and he half wished she'd left a drop of sauce there so he'd have an excuse to slick it away with his thumb. Hell, what was wrong with him?

"I do believe that's a vote of confidence. Thank you, Jersey." He took the jar from her and replaced the lid. "This one's for Ted to try, if the poor sonuvabitch can get hold of some emu meat."

"What do you mean?" Sydney gestured at the motley flock in front of them.

Alex chuckled. "He's not allowed to hurt them. Aunt Susie said she'd take a hike if he became a bird murderer."

Sydney's confusion was evident. "Didn't your aunt and uncle talk before he decided to become an emu rancher?"

Alex shook his head. "I don't think so. Ted's a real impulsive guy. He did it all in a single afternoon— had the idea, bought a battalion of emu, and showed up to take delivery still reading the how-to manual."

"I wonder if your Uncle Ted is related to my sister Julia," she said.

Alex chuckled and opened the driver's side door. "C'mon and meet him. He'll be in the barn over there."

The barn in question was on the other side of the emu pen. Sydney gulped. "Do those things bite?"

"No. They're actually very docile. Just don't crowd them up against the fence or they may flatten you, trying to get by. And don't hug one or you may get kicked."

"Believe me, it never crossed my mind." Syd scrambled out of the truck and picked her way gingerly over to him. Her heels might be "sensible" for an office, but they didn't do much for her on a ranch.

Alex opened the gate and she swallowed, then followed. The birds stared at them curiously but didn't gallop toward them or hiss. Sydney stuck close to Alex anyway.

"Uncle Ted grabs 'em by the wings and drives 'em like a wheelbarrow," Alex said, shaking his head. "I haven't tried that, yet."

Uncle Ted sounded like a character. She looked forward to meeting him more than this Roman guy, whose persona was confusing her more and more. Who was he? She'd now combined Sicilian alley cat, German officer, and a sweaty torso in a tool belt. Oh, and a freakin' three-carat rock. Nothing about him added up. Schizophrenic, she decided, and possibly psychotic since he'd developed a "keeper" instinct for Julia in only a month. Sydney sighed and passed a damp palm over the gruesome mess that now constituted her hair. She concentrated on keeping her footing in the dusty, rocky dirt. It smelled ripe out here, among the musky birds and their rather pungent by-products.

*Step, feet together. Step, feet together.* Sydney watched as the little initial "A" on each of her sling-backs lost its shine and went from gold to dusty brown, then disappeared. She took another step and focused on two enormous, nasty, three-toed feet that were most certainly not human. And they were *waaay* too close. *Uh-oh.*

Sydney looked up from the feet to muscular, alien legs—wow, this critter gave a whole new meaning to the term "drumstick"—to a breast-span Pamela Anderson would envy, and then up an insanely elongated, rubbery neck to a pair of inquisitive liquid eyes. The emu cocked its head and peered at her over a beak that reminded her of the nose of her calculus professor in college.

Her tonsils seemed to lob the breath back down her throat, which volleyed it forward again in the form of a screech. Sydney lurched backward into something squishy just as Alex reached her and took her arm. The bird scanned her and appeared to give her about a B, just like the calculus professor. Then it stalked away.

Heart palpitating, Sydney closed her mouth before she swallowed a fly or something. "What," she then asked Alex with trepidation, "did I just step in?"

His lips twitched. In a masterfully grave tone he said, "I don't think you want to know."


Uncle Ted told her that emu poop was great fertilizer, just like any other kind of poop, and that it had probably moisturized her toes more effectively than any salon treatment.

Sydney listened in disbelief while she sat on a bucket—a bucket!—and Alex ran water from a hose over her feet. As his nephew squirted dish soap onto her toes, Uncle Ted also informed her that the bird she'd met was named Snoopy, and he had a natural curiosity for anything foreign that entered his pen. He'd encountered Alex before, but she'd obviously smelled different.

Syd jerked in reflex when she felt Alex's hands on her skin, moving in circles to cleanse her foot. *Oh, my. Oooooh.* She closed her eyes.

She forgot to wonder exactly how Big Bird could smell anything when he didn't have a nose. Alex's hands were big and gentle and—oh, God—very sensual at poop removal. Wow, if he'd continue like this it would almost be worth taking a flying naked leap into a compost pile.

51

She opened her eyes to find Alex borderline-smirking at her. She pulled her foot out of his grasp.

"But honey, we haven't finished the rinse cycle yet." He calmly took it back and ran the hose over it before starting on the other one.

He completed the operation and dried her feet off with Uncle Ted's hankie. Then he turned to her shoes, which also got the dish soap treatment, but with an old kitchen scrub brush.

In the meantime, Uncle Ted set about trying the Hot 'n' Sweet Emu Sauce. "Damn, that's good stuff!"

"Think we can push that off on some unsuspecting tourists?"

"Oh, you bet. Even on suspecting ones. Mmmm, mmmm, that is a winner, A."

"Good. Now we need to come up with some packaging. And I still need that marketing plan from you."

"Yeah, yeah. Haven't gotten around to that yet."

Alex sighed. "Right. How about next week?"

"No problem."

"That's what you said last week."

Uncle Ted flapped a hand at him. Sydney wiggled her toes. "You know," she said, "I might be able to help you. I have a good friend in New York who's a graphic designer. She could probably come up with a label for you."

Alex straightened, frowned and started to say something, but Ted brightened. "Yeah? I was thinking of a cartoon emu, a rear view. And she's slapping her tushie. The caption could read, 'Put it right here!' "

Sydney blinked. "Uh, sure. That's a . . . great . . . idea. I'm sure Donna could sketch that right up for you."

Alex shook his head firmly. "Thanks, but we wouldn't want to trouble you or your big city friend. I'm sure we can handle it from here."

Sydney shrugged. "Suit yourself."

"Come on, Jersey," he said. "Let's get going. I'm sure you're all fired up to meet your future brother-in-law."

Sydney grimaced and wiped sweat from her brow with the back of her hand. She swept it off her forehead and into her hair. This matted her bangs into wet clumps that she could feel sticking to her forehead. Yuck.

"Uh," she stalled, "I'm kind of a mess. I should probably shower. I can meet him another time." She plucked her damp blouse away from the skin at her chest and made a woeful attempt to fan herself. *Useless. Damn this heat.*

Alex waved a hand in dismissal. "Oh, Roman's seen hot women before, Sydney." He shot her a look too bland to be innocent.

Syd narrowed her eyes at him. There was no need for him to mock her. "Really, I'd rather—"

"You don't need to primp for your sister's fiancé,

53

do you? Especially since you have such a high opinion of him and all." Alex's teeth flashed white.

She clenched her own. "No, of course I don't need to primp." She cast about for another out. "But my shoes—"

Again he rode right over her protests. "Aw, we hosed 'em off. They're good as new. And Roman won't care a bit. The Sonntags' place is just a little ole farm in the country, so don't you fret." He patted her arm.

She jerked it away and took a step to the side, opening her mouth again.

"Besides," he added before she got out one word, "you're not gonna make me drive all the way back to town first when I've got a delivery to make out there. Are you?"

She met his gaze resentfully. He had her, and she knew it. She'd invited herself along and the only gracious thing to do now was hang in there for the ride. Not that Sydney specialized in grace, especially, but she didn't want to be actively rude. She sighed and scrambled back into the truck.

Alex was going to have some fun introducing the Difficult Sister to Roman Sonntag. It wasn't only that she was a little worse for wear this afternoon, thanks to him; Roman wouldn't be what she was expecting.

As they went up the long, tree-lined drive to the Sonntag Winery, he saw her face change as she took in the vineyards and picturesque limestone walls, the large amorphous pool with a planted rock waterfall, and the gorgeous landscaping.

What had she pictured? That Rome lived in an ancient mobile home, a converted barn or perhaps out of his Chevy?

He bit back a smirk as Sydney whipped out a compact and took a horrified gaze at her face. She blotted some powder over that cute freckled nose and smeared some ginger brown lip gloss on her mouth. She dragged a comb through her hair.

He didn't have the heart to tell her about the damp patches under her arms or the fact that her skirt had molded like plastic wrap to her shapely rear end. As for the shoes . . . despite his earlier words, no amount of scrubbing would completely eliminate that smell.

He just stared ahead impassively and helped her down from the truck when they rolled to a stop. She cracked her neck, squared her shoulders and strode forward like a colonel—spoiling the effect a bit by clutching her purse like a security blanket.

Alex had to lengthen his stride to overtake her and open the door, since she was a lady. *In Jersey they don't open doors for ladies?* Not that she looked like a lady—she looked more like something a dog had gnawed on.

She swept into the winery like a queen anyway, though one in shoes that squished salaciously. They made disgusting, almost sexual slurps with each step she took, and she was obviously mortified by this. He repressed a grin. *Ooh, Roman, you're in for a real treat.*

The interior of the place was kept cool by thick limestone walls and warmed visually by oak flooring. Bottles of wine lined two walls and stood artfully displayed with various other Texas Hill Country products: peach jam, raspberry vinegar, a selection of crackers and dipping sauces.

To the rear Roman had constructed a charming little outdoor area. Wrought iron café tables and chairs dotted an open porch filled with hanging baskets and urns of flowers. Customers could sip wine and gaze out over hundreds of rows of neatly planted, carefully cultivated vines.

The door clicked genteelly closed behind them, and Alex called out, "Hey, Rome! Got a surprise for you."

His friend strolled leisurely from his office, a cell phone clamped to his ear, and nodded coolly at them, holding up a finger. *"Si, si. Ma quale? Quante bottiglie? E quando? Non, saranno pronte prima di Settembre. Si. Le vuole encora? Okay. Grazie. A piu tardi."*

Oh, excellent. Roman had changed from the jeans of this morning and was tricked out in actual linen pants, an Italian silk tie knotted at his throat over an Egyptian cotton shirt with a thread count of something like five thousand. Alex's guess was that Julia'd called him to warn him, so he'd armed himself.

Sydney blinked and tried to unstick the fabric of

her skirt from her thighs. Her gaze went from Roman to her shoes and back; she looked as if she might burst into tears. Alex almost felt sorry for her.

Roman's ice blue gaze traveled over her as he snapped the cell phone closed and slipped it into his pocket. His left eyebrow rose maybe half a millimeter. Then he adopted a polite smile and held out his hand. "You must be Julia's sister. How nice to meet you."

Sydney nodded and actually wiped her palm on her skirt before extending her hand.

*Tsk, tsk. You shouldn't let him see you sweat, darlin'.* Though Alex figured it was a little too late for that, since she was a walking puddle.

He slapped Rome on the back and tugged on his tie, pretending to choke him. Then, despite his stirrings of sympathy for the girl, he gave in to a wicked impulse and turned to the Difficult Sister with a one-hundred-watt shit-eating grin. "Yeah, Jersey. This is Roman . . . the jackass in the tool belt."

57

# Chapter Five

Sydney froze and closed her eyes. *I can't believe the rat bastard just said that.*

Was there any recovery from here? Any road back to civility? She opened her eyes, shot Alex a look of loathing that appeared to delight him, and lifted her chin, though she wished a few of the oak floorboards would magically slide open so she could drop out of sight. "I . . . I . . . uh." *Oh, very articulate, Syd. Impressive.* Her face flamed.

Roman's raised brows and stunned silence disintegrated at last into a polite laugh. And, unbelievably, he let her off the hook. "Alex has called me worse than that. We've been friends for many years." He directed a glance at his friend, who merely grinned.

Roman slid three wineglasses off a wooden rack to the rear of the bar. "I think maybe we could use a drink, no?"

*Drink? How about a bottle?* She cleared her throat

and clamped her arms to her sides, praying she didn't have visible sweat circles. "That would be great, thanks."

"So what brings you to Fredericksburg, Sydney?"

There were any number of bland answers to this question, but she decided not to prevaricate. "Julia's big news, of course."

"So you flew down to congratulate us."

"She flew down to make sure you're not a serial killer," Alex said helpfully.

Syd eyed the corkscrew lying on the bar and indulged in a murderous thought or two herself. But at least Alex's dark humor saved her from having to either offend Roman or lie.

"Ah, of course." Roman nodded. "And you've reassured her that I'm only a drunk and a womanizer?"

Alex looked regretful. "Well, Rome, I admit that I did. I know it's a touchy subject, but she's got the right to know."

"Thanks a lot, A." Roman assumed an expression of mock concern and hissed at his friend in a stage whisper, "But you didn't tell her that I fathered your secret love child, did you? I mean, that could screw up *everything*."

Sydney folded her arms. "You two are a regular comedy show."

"We got into a lot of trouble back in school," Roman agreed. Seeing that she wasn't all that entertained, he switched the subject. "So you're what, a year older than Julia?"

"Two." She waited for him to make the inevitable comment.

"You don't look anything alike."

There it was. Syd bit her lip. "No, we don't." *I'm the homely, redheaded stepchild.* "Julia looks more like our mother's side of the family." *I got the dog's features.*

Roman gestured to a couple of ladder-back barstools. "Have a seat. Do you prefer your wine red or white? Sweet or dry?"

She took a step toward the bar, even though she didn't feel much like staying. *Squiffle, schlursh.* God, her shoes! "Um, white," she said. "Dry. And preferably cold, thanks."

Roman looked at her footwear. "Alex, what did you do, drag her through a creek?"

"She had a close encounter with an emu pile out at Uncle Ted's," said the Rat, ever helpful. "Then we had to break out the hose."

"So *that's* what the smell is. And here I thought it was just Kimball's rotten character." Roman smiled at Sydney as he selected a bottle of pinot grigio and went about uncorking it.

It was her turn to smirk—but not for long.

"Hey now," said Alex, leaning on the bar. "It's *your* character that Miz Spinelli, here, is interested in.

I personally don't believe she flew down here just to say congratulations. Did you, Jersey Girl?"

Sydney accepted a glass of wine from Roman and debated whether to down it in one gulp or throw it on her tormentor. She turned to him, visibly restraining her temper. "You know, this is between me and Sonntag. I can do without your interference."

"Actually," Roman said in mild tones, "it's pretty much between me and Julia."

Sydney downed half her wine, pretending she hadn't heard the polite rebuke. Roman had drawn a line in the sand. Well, too bad—she was about to step over it.

"You like the wine?" Roman asked, reverting back to host. "Light, hints of peach and walnut, yet crisp at the finish."

"Yes, it's very nice. Thank you."

"My apologies," Alex said in wry tones, "for, er, interfering with your . . . interference, Sydney." He toasted her with the glass of red his friend had passed to him.

Syd could feel her ears heating, which they did in response to alcohol. They'd be bright pink within two more sips. Her mother's did the same thing. Unfortunately her chest and neck flushed when she got angry, and she could feel that happening, too, so she was seconds away from being fuchsia. She'd clash with her own hair.

She set her glass down with a snap. "I'm not here to interfere," she said. "I'm here to ensure my sister doesn't make a huge mistake."

Roman's blue eyes met hers evenly. "And you think I'm the huge mistake."

"Did I say that?" Sydney shook her head. "I did not. I'm not sure if you're a mistake."

"He was," Alex put in. "Just ask his parents."

Roman shot him a rude gesture, and Sydney ignored him. "You may be the greatest guy in the world," she continued. "But Julia doesn't know you very well, and marriage isn't something to be undertaken lightly."

"I agree with you," Roman said.

"At least his intentions are honorable." Alex nodded toward him. "Mine *never* are."

Sydney rolled her eyes at him and turned back to Roman. "How can you be certain, within a month, that you want to marry my sister?"

"I was certain within a day," said Roman.

"How? Because she's gorgeous? Because you saw her in a bikini?"

"He's not as shallow as he looks," Alex informed her.

"I don't know how I know," said Roman. "But I do. And it's not due to infatuation with her looks. I've seen lots of beautiful women in bikinis, but I haven't asked them to marry me."

Sydney blew out a breath. "Let me be blunt."

"Like we could stop you?" asked Alex, and Roman's lips twitched despite his polite demeanor.

"Julia needs to stand on her own two feet for a while. She doesn't need to be swept off of them. She needs to know she can make her own way in the world. She thinks some big wedding will solve all her problems, but it will only compound them."

Roman swirled the wine in his glass. "Why can't Julia be married *and* stand on her own two feet? I wasn't planning on binding them, Sydney. I won't chain her to the wall, either." He cast a sidelong look at Alex. "That's more something my buddy Alex would do."

"Nope," Alex said decisively. "I only chain my women to the bed."

Sydney felt her blush get hotter.

"And only when they're very bad—or mouthy."

It was a deliberate reference to her, and she knew it. But Sydney turned back to Roman. "Look, I'm not trying to be some kind of ballbuster. I just really worry about Julia." She stopped, not wanting to say too much. How could she explain the impact that Marv had had on his younger daughter's self-esteem?

*I worry that my sister's whole identity is caught up in getting married, and you're just a bridal accessory.* Nope, she couldn't say that.

Or *I'm afraid that her whole identity is caught up in getting married, and you're going to disappoint or hurt*

63

*her as soon as the birdseed hits the ground.* She couldn't say that, either. There was blunt, and then there was just plain rude.

Sydney evaluated Roman surreptitiously. Of course she didn't think he was a serial killer. But he could easily be a crook, a womanizer or a drunkard—and what better occupation for a drunk than running a winery?

But worse yet, he could just be a golf-playing, cigar-smoking, country-club asshole who wanted Julia as his trophy wife.

And Julia was all too ready to be a trophy: beautiful, golden and a status symbol. Marv had trained his daughters well: Julia, because of her looks, as a clotheshorse and Sydney, because of her lack of them, as a workhorse. And try as they might, they still hadn't quite escaped the Spinelli stable.

Roman held his glass to his lips and looked at Sydney over the rim as he drank. "I think it's nice that you worry about your sister. But you don't need to. Julia is bright, energetic and talented. She can take care of herself—and if that's ever in doubt, then I'll take care of her."

*Julia is bright, energetic and talented. But she doesn't realize it. And the worst thing that can happen is for her to never discover it. For her to just be taken care of so that she's beautiful and useless and unhappy.*

Sydney watched Roman swallow another mouthful of wine. *You're too good-looking, like your obnoxious friend Alex. You wear expensive clothes. You're into wine. If there's a country club in Fredericksburg, I'm sure you're a charter member. I don't trust you.*

"You don't trust me, do you, Sydney?" he said.

She looked down, into her glass.

"That's all right. It's understandable."

"Rome's a good guy," said Alex. "A great friend. After all, here he is getting you drunk so I can take advantage of you." He waggled his eyebrows at her and leered.

"Like hell," Sydney said, but this time she laughed at him. *As if a guy who looked like Alex would want me.* "Are you ever serious?"

Alex's mouth twisted at the question, and he stared out to the vineyard, no flip answer at the ready.

"Kimball's been a little too serious these days, believe it or not." Roman turned to rinse his glass in the stainless steel sink behind the sales counter, leaving Sydney to wonder what he meant.

Alex's gaze was far away and he, too, finished his wine. But soon he reverted back to form. "Y'all are doing this all backwards, you know. You've tackled the heavy stuff. Now you need to have some polite conversation, avoiding sex, politics and religion, of course. Sydney, you should ask Rome about the vineyard. Rome, you should ask Sydney what she does for a living. Ask whether she's got a pet or a favorite houseplant or a big charitable cause."

While Sydney choked on the last of her pinot

grigio, Roman said dryly, "Thank you for the coaching, A. Why don't you focus on rounding me up some investors for the Beaujolais nouveau, and leave the small talk to me?"

*Investors? Did Roman need money? Why?*

Alex shot him a mournful glance. "Ah, the humanity. You only keep me around for the money."

"Damn straight, I do."

"Are you a banker?" Sydney asked, curious.

"I'm what they call a venture capitalist," Alex told her. "I match up developing businesses with various sources of funding."

She nodded.

"Rome, here, wants to plant a bunch more grapes of a different variety. And he won't even let me stomp 'em the old-fashioned way. A guy can't have any fun these days. It's a shame."

Roman pointed to a corner that held a dusty wooden device with a metal crank. "That's an old-fashioned press for crushing grapes. Before those were developed the grapes were literally stomped with bare human feet."

"The rest of the human was bare, too," Alex noted.

Roman rolled his eyes, but admitted this was true. "Believe it or not, it was for hygienic reasons. People didn't change clothes every day like they do now. So the fear was that the dirty fabric might contaminate the harvest and spread disease."

"Listen to this. This is *beautiful* small talk," said

Alex. "Rome, take her out back and show her the machinery. The big stuff. And if she still doesn't like you in a few days, you can threaten to put her through that five-ton bladder press."

"Good plan."

Sydney found herself following the two men outside, behind the retail space. The heat hit her immediately, and within thirty seconds dampened the blouse that had begun to dry inside, in the blessed air-conditioning. A huge stainless steel object shimmered menacingly under the sun. "Roman, I never said I didn't like you—"

"What'd I tell ya?" Alex clapped him on the shoulder. "She's already whistling a different tune. We're classier in Texas than those Soprano people, though. They show you a meat grinder. We show you a winepress. They freeze a body and dump it in the East River. We take it and make a nice cabernet sauvignon. Wild West? I think not."

Roman demonstrated another piece of equipment that looked as if it contained a giant corkscrew. This, he explained, was a de-stemmer and crusher. And the final monster machine was a filter. The grape juice was filtered five times throughout the process of making wine. He showed Sydney the big steel storage tanks in which the stuff fermented, too. They weren't the wooden casks of the past. Like every other industry, the wine business had been modernized.

Sydney left Sonntag Vineyards with a new appreciation for Roman's knowledge and charm, but also the realization that every aspect of winemaking was expensive. The guy had never asked another woman to marry him, and yet he'd proposed to Julia within a month. Roman had mentioned that he was looking for investment capital for his new grape. He'd demonstrated an obvious passion for the business. But in spite of his appreciative words about Julia and his promise to take care of her, he'd never once told Sydney that he loved her.

# Chapter Six

What she needed was a shower and a good think and then a plan—in that order. What she got, after another Suburban steam bath before the AC kicked in, was a ride back into town with Alex Kimball.

Alex drove in silence, looking serene and stubbly and unfairly un-sweaty. She supposed that if you lived down here in the Wild West long enough, your glands got baked.

He broke the silence after a few minutes. "So, I told you Roman was a catch. He's a nice guy."

Sydney unstuck one miserable thigh from another and shot him a level look. "Yes, he was very nice. Professionally nice."

"Jersey, you're a tough one, aren't you? Considering that he'd probably just gotten a tearful phone call from your sister describing your harassment, I'd say he deserves a gold medal for hospitality."

"Harassment? Excuse me? And if he thinks I'm bad, just wait 'til he meets my father," she exclaimed.

"Your father being the Marv in the Motor Inns?"

"You got it."

Alex looked as if he were debating whether or not to say something.

"What?"

"I think I remember hearing about him. In fact—" Alex snapped his fingers. "Didn't he originally try to buy Sonntag House, next door to the existing Inn? And then they backed out of the deal?"

Sydney got a sinking feeling in the pit of her stomach. "I don't know." If true, Marv would be even less delighted about the impending nuptials.

"Yeah. They got wind of his, um, renovation plans and decided to hang on to the property."

"Meaning the mustard and brown, the neon sign, and the whole count-sheep-for-cheap thing?"

Alex shrugged.

"Don't worry—we're very much aware of my father's hellacious 1970s taste."

Alex laughed. "Yeah. Well, this must have been fifteen years ago, so Rome and I had other things— mostly beer—on our minds, but I do remember a stink. And Rome's dad was furious when your dad bought the place next door on Orange just for spite— and doubled the size of the neon sign. It impacted the view and the charm just a little."

The sinking feeling in her stomach was now turning to active nausea. Was Julia aware of this?

"So what you're trying to tell me is that we're not actually in Fredericksburg—we're in Verona?"

Alex lifted an eyebrow. "Could be. Here we are, Miz Capulet." He made a hard left into the Marv's Motor Inn parking lot, with interesting results, since Syd wasn't hanging on to the door handle.

She flew helter-skelter along the drunken, tipped seat and landed in Alex's lap.

He instinctively blocked her head from slamming into the driver's side window; the result was that his left hand spanned her face just like Chucky Malone's had, that day he'd thrown her into the lockers.

She could get over that. But Alex's right hand gripped her buttock. Heat flashed through her, especially when he showed no sign of letting go.

She lifted her face from his palm and struggled for dignity. She had to turn toward him to extricate herself, and this brought them nose to nose, iris to iris, mouth to mouth. His warm breath fanned her cheeks and she fixated on the curve of his lips, the cleft in his chin. Just as she thought, *No, don't think it*, she did: What would it be like to kiss Alex Kimball?

She inhaled his scent of sunshine and mesquite and red wine, laundry detergent and a faint sandalwood fragrance that might be aftershave or might be shampoo. The heat had blended it all with a little male musk that made him smell irresistible.

Those melted-chocolate eyes of his held definite sensual promise, the black lashes veiling but not completely disguising more than a hint of wicked intent. Was that mouth useful for anything but one-liners and good-natured insults? The moment stretched on.

Just as she was sure he'd touch his lips to hers, but not sure how she'd respond, he leaned forward and whispered in her ear instead. "Jersey, you've got one hot little body, but you sure do stink!"

Pure mortification propelled her out of his lap and up the steep tilt of the seat to the passenger door. Her sunglasses dangled by one earpiece, and she fumbled with them, her hand shaking, before she jammed them onto her nose again. Then she grabbed her purse, unlatched the door and leaped from the Suburban.

"Aw, come on, don't be that way. I meant it all in good fun." Alex regarded her from behind his Oakleys, not a drop of perspiration on his forehead, damn him.

*Of course you did. And I wish you the sweat glands of a Budweiser Clydesdale.* "Thank you," she said between clenched teeth, "for the ride."

*"De nada."* And Alex's oversized jalopy roared away in a cloud of dust.

\* \* \*

Sydney stood in the narrow, beige plastic shower under freezing cold water and soaped herself three times before uncontrollable shivering forced her to shut off the tap and step out. Even then, she enjoyed the way her teeth rattled in the air-conditioning, much preferring being chilled to being steamed and smelly.

As she dried off with a horrid, sandpapery towel, she made a mental note to inform Marv that if he didn't install rubber stick-ons in his tubs he was endangering his customers and opening himself up to hundreds of lawsuits. Of course he would resist the expense, so she'd have to research the statistics and costs and map it all out on paper for him. Ugh.

Speaking of Marv, she was going to have to call him on her cell phone and give him some good reasons why she wasn't around. She couldn't betray Julia's secret—he would go nuts and be on the next plane.

*Hi, Dad. I'm on the trail of Betty Lou Fitch and it turns out that she's a dangerous drug lord. The polyester double knit and the off-kilter lip liner were only a disguise, and she can kill a man instantly with an acrylic fingernail through the jugular.*

*Yup. So, anyway, she's onto me and I'm hiding out in a Mexican cave after a high-speed car chase during which I barely escaped with my life . . .*

If she managed to catch him right as he was on his usual good tear about the quarterly tax payments, he might actually buy it, since he'd be cussing a blue streak and not paying attention. If Marv ever went to jail for anything, she was sure it would be for tax evasion—which was another reason she wanted to get the hell away from his books.

Sydney closed her eyes and sprawled on the cheap polyester bedspread—adorned, of course, with pregnant brown and mustard flowers—and channel surfed.

From her window she saw Julia, looking divine, trip blithely out the door on Roman Sonntag's arm. They disappeared into a navy blue Jaguar and a cloud of Texas dust.

Today, Syd had "met" the Professionally Nice Roman's sister, Kiki. Julia had actually "introduced" all of her bridesmaids in cyberspace. She was in full wedding-planning mode already, which was very scary. Syd opened her laptop and glared at the e-mail again.


Subject: MY WEDDING!!!!!!!!!!!!!!
Date: XXXXXXX
From: CrownJule
To: numbersgeek, kiki@misstexas95.com, vshelton@kleinschmidtbelker

Okay, girls, I PROMISE I won't be one of those super-needy brides that inundate her bridesmaids with every little thing (well, I'll try not to, anyway) but I wanted y'all to meet, even if it's in cyberspace. (Did you notice the y'all? I'm practicing being a Texas girl!)

Anyhow, Syd and Viv, you two already know each other. So, Syd and Viv, meet Kiki, Roman's sister and my third bridesmaid. Kiki, I'm dying to meet you in person, too. Roman tells me we'll get along great. I guess we read a lot of the same mags. So you know, Syd's my big sister, and Viv is the absolute best friend a girl could have.

You guys can do the getting to know you thing later, but right now, we need to get down to business. We're doing this wedding so whirlwind (isn't it exciting!) that I've had to toss out all the bridal guides because the timelines just don't work. So RIGHT AWAY send me your dress sizes and shoe sizes. And any colors you want to veto off the bat (like if it makes your skin look sallow—Syd, don't worry, I'll take care of nixing colors for you). And if you have a favorite flower, let me know that, too.

I'm sure there are a hundred things more that we need to talk about, but I wanted to make this short and just put the three of you in touch with each other. I can't wait until you all get here. Viv, the German food here is to die for.

Love you bunches,
More soon, J

And now there was a response from the unknown Kiki.

Subject: Re: MY WEDDING!!!!!!!!!!
Date: XXXXXXX
From: kiki@misstexas95.com
To: CrownJule, numbersgeek, vshelton

Hi Girls,

I've heard of quick weddings (Britney Spears
and Nicky Hilton come to mind) but this is ridiculous. Of course, I'm happy my brother has found
his first wife, but why put such an important day
on the fast track? Is there something I don't know?
Should I pick up the shower gift from Bergdorf's
baby department?

If I sound bitchy, it's only because the timing
couldn't be worse—for me, that is. I'm already in
four weddings this summer, not to mention on the
audition track to land a new acting gig. Now I
have to endure fittings for another bridesmaid
dress? How will I get it all done?

Wish me luck,
Kiki

*First* wife? Bergdorf's *baby* department?! Oh, very
nice. Syd refused to acknowledge that similar
thoughts had run through her own mind. She hadn't
put them in an e-mail to everyone!

Forget about Kiki Sonntag. Her brother was the
person concerning Sydney. Who the hell was he,
really? Did she need to hire a private investigator, or
should she leave that honor to Marv?

Marv would have a coronary when he heard. Of course, he'd also feel that he had to show Roman a thing or two, like his swagger and his gold medallion, an inch or three of chest hair and his custom Mercedes SL. She groaned inwardly, preferring to focus on Roman rather than Marv.

What did they know about Roman's past? Nothing. *Was* he a womanizer or a drunk, no joke? A sadist? A control freak with a jealous streak? Did he lie, cheat, steal? Set dogs on fire for fun?

What if he was a drug runner, a megalomaniac, a perverse pervert? A bigamist, a bag man, a wife-swapping, pill-popping, bed-hopping horror? Did he possess a secret harem, ties to terrorism, fourteen aliases and a getaway jet?

The possibilities were endless and hideous. And the specter of a pregnancy . . .

Sydney didn't want to think about it. Had sweet, innocent Julia taken precautions before tumbling into bed with this creep and his tool belt? *Was* she pregnant? Was that the reason for all the rush with the wedding? Sydney swung her legs over the edge of the bed and headed for her suitcase and her emergency stash of Doritos. She needed to talk to her sister again, immediately.

# Chapter Seven

Sydney probably didn't choose the best time or place to ask her: in a local Dunkin' Donuts next day. But she had to know.

Julia actually spit out her coffee and then looked around to make sure nobody had heard. "Are you crazy? *No!*"

She fumbled for a tissue to wipe at the tiny dimple on her chin, now painted with Folgers' finest. She stared at Sydney.

Sydney gripped her own coffee cup. "Have you seen the e-mail from your future sister-in-law? I just thought that might be the reason for the instant engagement."

"Well, it's not! What e-mail?"

"You'll have to read it. Are you *sure* you're not pregnant?"

"Oh, for God's sake, Sydney. What are you really asking?" Julia lowered her voice and hissed.

"Whether I'm a virgin? Whether we've had unprotected sex?"

Syd looked away. "I, uh—"

"It's none of your business. Do you get that?"

"Do you need a napkin, Jules? I think I need another napkin. Maybe some more cream, too." Sydney pushed away from the table.

"No, I don't need a napkin. I think I might need a hit man. Jeez!"

When Sydney returned to the table, Julia gestured her close. With her head almost against her sister's forehead, she said, "Syd. I know you think you still have to wipe my nose for me and help me tie my shoes, but here's a news flash: No, I am not a virgin. Yes, I know how babies are made. Okay?"

A woman with orange hair was staring at them from across the place. Sydney ignored her. Julia gave her a polite smile.

Syd asked, without moving her lips, "Are you on the pill?"

Julia's pretty mouth tightened. "Again, *so* none of your biz! Can you admit that?"

Sydney hesitated, but then nodded. "I'm sorry. But I'm your sister. I worry about you."

"Thank you, but there's no need. And yes, I'm on the pill, okay?"

"Did you know that it's not one hundred percent effective?"

Julia threw up her hands, knocking over her coffee

Karen Kendall

in the process. They both jumped up to mop up the spill.

Over the napkin dispenser, Syd continued to push the issue. "Did you know that?"

"Yes!"

"So are you *positive* you're not pregnant?"

"Oh, why won't you leave me alone?"

"You should get a test done."

"Aaaaarrrggghhh!"

"Will you get one?"

"No!"

"Come on. I'll go buy the kit, if you're too embarrassed."

"You know what? Fine. If it'll make you happy, you freak, then I'll do it. Now let's get back to the Inn—I need to get some work done. Go act like a tourist or something. Try on cowboy hats. Drink some beer. Just go away!"

Sydney had won. After ducking the spiked Jimmy Choo Julia threatened her with, Syd left her in peace.

She walked over to Main Street and poked into some of the shops, hunting vaguely for a baby gift. Speaking of being pregnant, she still couldn't quite believe her friend Donna was—Donna the junk-food addict who drove like a bat out of hell and was never functional without at least two quarts of coffee in the morning.

This same woman, whose body had now been

snatched by a small human seedling that directed her to eat horse-sized vitamins, had become a scarily chipper caffeine-free morning person, and craved not ice cream but raw bell peppers. Bell peppers! She now ate them by the truckload, sometimes smeared with dressing or cream cheese.

All Sydney knew was that this was one very strange child sprouting in Donna's womb, and she missed her old friend. But two months from now, she'd become a three-letter word: MOM, and never sleep soundly again.

Sydney wanted to buy her several adorable outfits that she could coo over for at least thirty seconds before the tot drooled on them, puked on them or worse.

She found a yellow outfit with ducks on it, and a white one with little jungle animals in primary colors. Both came with tiny matching socks. Sydney had them gift wrapped and continued walking. Even at ten in the morning, heat blanketed Fredericksburg and seemed to toast the tops of her toes. She passed a custom boot place and couldn't resist going in.

Boots of every color and size greeted her, from pink with embroidered yellow flowers to bright turquoise with peridot green shanks; from burgundy with brown inlays to black studded with silver. She liked a pair in soft, supple chestnut brown, and found when she looked at the price that they cost a great deal less than Julia's Manolos. But she pictured herself, bowlegged and boot-clad, walking into the dry cleaners or A&P in South River, New Jersey, and saying, "Hi, y'all." Nope, probably not a good look for her.

She took a last, wistful look at the boots and exited the shop. A few doors down stood a hair salon that seemed to be frequented by an older clientele.

The last voice she expected to issue from the open door was Alex Kimball's.

"Please, Mama. Put them on."

"I don't *want* to."

Sydney looked in to find him, his back to the door, with a beautifully coiffed older woman. She'd obviously just had her hair done. She stood barefoot in white capri pants and a black-and-white embroidered blouse.

"I don't want to," she repeated. "It's hot."

"Yes, it is," Alex agreed. "And if you don't put your shoes on you're gonna burn the soles of your feet. Plus it's dirty out there on the pavement. You don't want to step in somebody's gum, do you, Mama?"

"No." She said it vaguely, looking past him at Sydney.

"Okay, then. Let's put them back on."

"No."

Alex sighed and picked up her mules, prepared to carry them.

Sydney stood there awkwardly. "Hi," she said.

He'd been entirely focused on his mother, and hadn't seen her. He turned and stiffened immediately. "Hi."

The grinning, wisecracking bastard of yesterday had vanished. Sydney had never seen a grown man look so lost, so helpless—especially not a man who looked like Alex. His aura of power and command had taken a hiatus, and dark shadows hung under his eyes, black crescent moons in the constellation of his face.

He dangled the mules by two fingers, looking from her to them and back. He shrugged and dredged up the ghost of a smile. "A sale. I couldn't resist."

Sydney smiled back. "They're you."

"Hot," his mother sighed. "It's unbearable." She began to unbutton her blouse and Sydney's eyes widened. She'd had a gut instinct that something wasn't quite right with Mama—that she wasn't just eccentric. Now she was pretty sure what was going on. She'd been all too familiar with erratic behavior in her grandmother before she'd died two years ago of Alzheimer's.

Alex whirled just in time to see his mother's lacy violet bra wink from between the plackets of her blouse. "Mama, *no!*" He put out his hand to stop her, but she smacked it away.

The salon's clientele looked on with great interest

as Alex tried to hold his mother's blouse together with one hand, restrain her with the other, and not hurt her in the process.

"Mrs. Kimball," Syd interceded.

Alex shot her a black look born of humiliation and dark pride. "We're fine," he told her.

"Mrs. Kimball," she said again. "That is such a beautiful blouse you're wearing!"

The woman stopped struggling and peered at her as if trying to remember her name. Alex did his best to button one-handed, but she elbowed him in the chest, making it difficult. "Nell," she said finally.

Sydney nodded, still operating on her hunch: that Mrs. K had early-onset Alzheimer's. If so, then frankly, it wouldn't be kind to correct her, and it was likely she'd forget the information within five minutes anyway. "The embroidery on your blouse, Mrs. Kimball—was that done by hand?"

"Oh, this?" She twisted out of her son's grasp and looked down at it.

He stood helpless and mortified and not pleased to have an audience—not the salon customers, not the staff, not Sydney.

"It's so intricate. Such tiny stitches. Do you embroider yourself?"

Mrs. Kimball nodded again.

"Is that your work?"

She beamed. "Yes. I made a matching skirt, too,

Nell. But I decided it was too much pattern, worn together."

"It looks so nice with your capris and black shoes."

"Thank you, honey. It's been such a while since I've seen you . . ."

"I've been traveling," Sydney told her, not missing a beat.

"Well, that would explain it. You've been away so long that Alex is all grown up now! Alex, say hello to Nell."

Though clearly taken aback, he reluctantly stepped forward and kissed Sydney on the cheek as if she were an old friend. She restrained herself from asking him if she smelled better today.

The dark stubble along his jaw scraped her skin, plucking tiny nerves like guitar strings and dispersing goose bumps along her neck and shoulders. Though the contact was brief, she detected the same sandalwood essence of yesterday. It had to be his aftershave.

Jerk or not, the fragrance made her want to weave herself through his legs like a cat. But at the moment, they were busy playing accidental roles on a strange stage. They were thespians in his mama's alternate reality.

Sydney smiled again at Mrs. Kimball and made small talk for a few moments before addressing the problem at hand. "Oh, look—your top buttons have come undone by accident. You know, I have a blouse with silly buttons like that." She reached out and touched the woman's shoulder. "Can I help you with those?"

"Oh, dear. Yes, thank you. I don't know how that happened."

"Most likely," Sydney said, buttoning away, "the holes here are just a little oversized. There! Now you're all decent."

"Yes." Mrs. Kimball winked. "We wouldn't want to get the boys excited, now would we?"

Alex looked horrified, but the muscle at his jaw stopped jumping and his shoulders relaxed visibly.

The overly made-up girl behind the reception desk looked disappointed, and Sydney disliked her for it. She hadn't moved a muscle to help, just sat there chewing her bubblegum like a Holstein with highlights.

"Where are you two going next?" Syd asked, just to make conversation and transition them out the door.

"Well, this is Mama's Saturday morning out," said Alex. "We get her hair done, and then we go and have coffee and a Danish, and we might do a little shopping. Then I take her to Mrs. Baumgarten's for a swim and lunch."

"How nice."

"Nell, would you like to come and have coffee

with us, dear? We'd love to have you." Mrs. Kimball patted her hand.

Alex looked less thrilled.

She could see protectiveness and wariness written all over his face. The flip, sex-charged guy she'd met yesterday was nowhere to be seen.

He didn't want her help, and yet he was crying out for it. He obviously didn't always know how to handle his mother and her disease. "Nell is very busy, Mama," he said. "I'm sure she's got things to do—"

"I'd love to join you for coffee," said Sydney with a smile. "Thank you."

They went to a pretty little coffee shop with white lacy café curtains, and Mrs. Kimball seemed to take a great deal of pleasure in ordering a white mocha latte with cinnamon and cocoa powder sprinkled on top. Alex glowered at Sydney before ordering plain black coffee, and she guiltily chose a tall cappuccino swimming in cream and sugar.

Mrs. K, in her charming Southern accent, asked the college-aged waitress if she could hang on to her menu a little longer to "contemplate" a pastry. She then launched into tales of a recent trip to Hawaii while Alex looked perplexed. Sydney guessed that the trip had actually taken place long ago.

"And we took a sailing trip up the Na Pali Coast, dear, which is the most beautiful stretch of shoreline you could ever imagine. Remember that television show, *Fantasia Island*?"

"*Fantasy Island*," Alex said. "Mr. Roarke. And Tattoo. De plane, de plane . . ."

"Exactly." Mrs. Kimball nodded. "That was filmed in Hawaii."

"And so was *Jurassic Park,* Mama."

"Which park?"

"The movie with the dinosaurs," Alex reminded her gently.

"Right." The little wrinkle in his mother's brow gave away the fact that she had no idea what he was talking about. She paused. "Now, where was I?"

"Hawaii," prompted Sydney. "You sailed up the Na Pali Coast."

"Yes, of course."

"Was this a trip you took with your husband, Mrs. Kimball?"

"My husband?" Alex's mother laughed gently. "No, dear. The distressing truth is that I've never been married."

Alex's jaw dropped and his pupils widened.

"Oh, I see," Sydney said diplomatically.

"I was engaged to a prince once. But he exhibited some ugly qualities before the wedding, and I broke it off."

Alex developed a fascination with the Dutch boy—and–girl salt and pepper shakers on the blond wood table. He began to switch boy with girl repeatedly, always moving them counterclockwise. Poor Alex. Trying to make sense of his world—order it by repetitive motion. Again he switched boy with girl. Parent with child?

"So when did you have Alex?"

Mrs. K blinked. "Why, March 4, 1969. The summer of love."

Alex's lips twisted. "So I'm your love child, huh, Mama?"

"Exactly."

"And how about Jake?"

Sydney guessed that Jake must be the brother he'd spoken of.

"Who?"

The tiny muscle in Alex's jaw was jumping again. "And when did you fall in love with Dad?"

"Oh, darlin'. You know we're just roommates."

It was Alex's turn to blink, and Sydney could see the tension ratchet up a notch in his posture. She put a hand on his arm.

She felt awkward, participating in what was essentially a private drama: a woman rewriting her past to suit Puck and Alzheimer's. What made Mrs. K do it? How did snippets of fiction and celluloid meld with past conversations and memories? At least she hadn't written Alex out of them entirely, as she had his brother, and as Grandma had with Marv. No, Mrs. K had just erased one child and her own wedding—at least for today.

The waitress brought their coffees over on a tray, and set Mrs. Kimball's down first.

"What is this, dear?" she asked the girl.

"A white mocha latte, ma'am."

"Oh, honey, I couldn't possibly drink that. It's loaded with calories and fat."

"But ma'am, that's what you . . . ordered?" The girl's voice trailed off into a question.

"I'd never order such a thing. Only black coffee, dear."

"Here, Mama, you can have mine." Alex took the latte and replaced it with his own coffee, while the waitress stared at his mother, confused.

The temptation to explain to the waitress tugged at Syd, and probably at Alex, too, but confusion for her was preferable to humiliation for Mrs. Kimball. Syd had experienced this type of situation many times with Grandma. Except, she reflected ruefully, Grandma wasn't nearly as nice as Alex's mother. In her, the disease had wrought a personality reversal. The grandmother who had clucked and fussed over Sydney and Julia while they grew up began to simply fuss. "Cantankerous" had been a kind word to describe her, before she died.

Alzheimer's was cruelest to the caretakers, really. The patient remained largely unaware of changes in her personality.

Mrs. Kimball sipped at Alex's black coffee, oblivious. Alex took a mouthful of her latte and did not appear to enjoy it. Too sweet and girly for him, Syd decided.

"Did you want a pastry, ma'am?" the waitress asked Mrs. K.

"Why, yes. I believe I'll have a blueberry Danish, thank you."

The waitress looked at her as if she'd sprouted another head. Her thoughts were clear: Hadn't the woman just been going on about calories? But she said nothing, just took the menu and walked away.

Alex exchanged a glance with Sydney as his mother powdered her nose from a small gold compact. Eventually the Danish was consumed—Mrs. K had two bites, Alex the rest—and they made their way out into the sunshine.

"Are you ready to go see Mrs. Baumgarten, Mama?"

"No, I never did care much for her."

Alex looked as if he wanted to tear out his thick brown hair. "Dorothy's your best friend, Mama."

"Dorothy? Oh, yes, she is. Are we going to go see her?"

Sydney touched Alex's shoulder. And then, because of the worry lines in his forehead; because of the softening of his mouth whenever he looked at his mother; because of the graceful way he never corrected her in a way that would mortify her— because of all those things—she stretched up on her toes and gently kissed his cheek again.

It wasn't something she knew him well enough to do. But she had a feeling that he needed it. This big, strapping five o'clock–shadowed man was out of his element, out of his comfort zone, but wasn't backing down. Alex Kimball was muddling along as best he could, with his mother in the grip of a bizarre, unstable disease.

# Chapter Eight

Sydney discovered that Julia had a surprisingly puritan work ethic, but managed to pry her away from the Motor Inn and take her to lunch the next afternoon.

They went to Der Lindenbaum but had salads. Neither of them was up for heavy German food in the middle of the day.

Julia was still irritated with her sister; she told Syd conversationally what a pain in the ass she was, and how much she'd disliked trying to pee on a tiny plastic stick. And no, she was not pregnant!

Pointedly changing the subject, Julia then asked, "So how's Ma doing?"

"Same old, same old. She floats around in her own private little Ma fog."

"Coffee, listen to Marv nag, coffee, knit, then lunch and organizing drawers all afternoon before fighting Marcella for control of the stove?"

Syd nodded. "Yeah, that pretty much sums it up. You just forgot the daily trip to the A&P."

"Right. And the bunko group on Wednesday nights."

"Plus visiting Mrs. Santini and Mrs. Walkowsky in the nursing home every Friday morning."

"Who's walking Humphrey these days?"

"Humphrey doesn't get walked. Marv lets 'da damn dohg' out 'da back doh' before work every morning. Then poor Humph stays out there until Ma feeds him or Marcella decides to vacuum him for fleas."

"Poor thing," Julia said around a slice of tomato.

"Yeah. Now that I've figured out the extent of Betty Lou's sticky-fingered retirement plan, I think I'm going to take Humphrey back home with me. Maybe get him a cat for company instead of the Home Shopping Network. The hound has got to be a walking catalogue of tacky jewelry by now."

Julia laughed and attacked a slice of cucumber.

Sydney wished, not for the first time in her life, for Julia to develop a craving for fried food, ice cream, and baked goods. She sighed and sipped at her iced tea.

Julia excused herself to go to the ladies' room, and Syd took advantage of the people-watching. At a nearby table sat a man in Wrangler jeans so tight that she wondered where he'd fit the Reuben he was stuffing into his face. Maybe the large silver belt buckle would help to flatten it out. Or maybe, like a pelican, he'd store the sandwich in his prominent Adam's apple.

At another table sat a couple gnawing on baby back ribs, sucking the marrow from the bones. They were going to need some wet wipes, about a truckload.

In the corner sat a table of ripened sorority girls, dressed by Harold's and perfectly made up. They all had flawless manicures, gold coin rings from Mexico, and white wine for lunch. A circle of shopping bags surrounded them. Sydney spotted logos for a couple of interesting stores and took a gulp of iced tea. She stared again at her own short, unpolished nails and ragged cuticles. Maybe she should ask Julia for the name of a salon?

Her sister stormed over then, threw some cash on the table and said abruptly, "We're leaving now."

"What? But I haven't finished—"

"*Now*, Syd." Julia's eyes blinked furiously. What was wrong with her?

"I was going to pay—"

"We'll figure it out later."

Sydney grabbed her purse and followed Jules, who was practically running from the place, though how she could run in those spiked heels defied imagination.

Julia didn't stop until she'd slammed into her car. "What is the matter with you?"

*"You* are the matter with me. I was in the bathroom and two women came in. You want to know what they were discussing?"

*Uh-oh.*

"They were saying how somebody named Thelma Lynn had heard that blond Yankee girl's sister ask her if she was pregnant! And how that explains why the Sonntag boy got engaged so quickly—he knocked her up!" Julia actually banged on the steering wheel.

While Julia searched in her pocketbook, most likely for her sunglasses, Sydney put a hand over her own mouth.

Julia yanked Chanel shades from her bag and fumbled them onto her pretty nose, which she then blew with an amazingly loud honk. "Thank you very much, Sydney! One of these days maybe you'll learn to mind your own business."

So much for sisterly détente.

Alex yawned as he reviewed the pro forma financial statements for a start-up company that was looking for an infusion of capital. The numbers looked overly optimistic to him, and his gut told him that his money would be safer elsewhere. The kid at the helm had a lot of big white teeth and very little business experience.

The phone rang as he reached his decision and slapped closed the file. Alex picked it up and idly watched his mama move normally about the kitchen she knew like the back of her hand. No short-term memory problems in the kitchen: She'd stored her things in exactly the same places for the last thirty years.

"Yeah," Alex said into the receiver, and touched his cheek, thinking about Sydney's sweet, reassuring kiss the day before. After the way he'd baited her mercilessly, he *so* had not deserved that. It disarmed him; embarrassed him; made him grumpy because he didn't know quite what to think about it—or her. Was she a bossy, meddling pain in the ass, or a sweetheart?

Jersey hadn't stunk, either. That gorgeous copper bronze hair of hers, clean and shiny and dry, had glowed in the sun and carried the fragrance of a hundred flowers. Her pale skin smelled of Dove soap—the same kind Mama bought—and soft, sweet jasmine perfume tinged with vanilla.

Though he hadn't wanted her help, Sydney Spinelli had handled Mama beautifully this morning.

"Hey, Rome. What's up?" He listened for a few moments. "*No.* She didn't really make Julia take a pregnancy test, did she?" He laughed. "You're kidding . . . Well, big guy, you *do* have Papa written all over you . . . okay, okay." Alex stretched out his legs.

"It's not funny, you're right. Well, she's worried

about her sister and this snap engagement. For all she knows, you paid your way through college as a street hustler. She's all right, man."

Alex listened. "You want me to *what*? How? Kidnap her, tie her up and throw her on the railroad tracks? . . . My charm? What charm? Oh, man, you are laying it on thick. I'm gonna need waders, here." He listened some more.

"My good looks and my hot car, huh. Yeah, the Suburban is the ultimate chick magnet, you're right." Alex sighed.

"Rome, I don't want to babysit this girl. I said she wasn't that bad. I did *not* say I wanted to ride into the sunset with her."

Alex groaned. "That is very low and underhanded of you, Roman. Yes, I do owe you one, you bastard. Fine. Goodbye."

He ran a hand through his hair and tried to crack his neck. Distract Sydney? Keep her away from Julia? Fabulous. Just great. *All I need is another crazy woman to take care of.*

He was ready to hit his father's bourbon, or his mother's cooking wine. Or both.

His gaze went to his mother again, humming as she chopped vegetables in the kitchen. Now in familiar surroundings, in her element, she seemed entirely normal—as if she'd never not recognized him or threatened him with a knife.

Alex wondered when the hell she'd acquired a violet bra, and decided he didn't really want to know. She could wear red lace, as long as she didn't try to take off her shirt in public again . . .

He thought again how lucky they were that Sydney had been there, and had seemed to know exactly what to do and how to handle the situation. She might be bossy to her sister, but bossiness often translated into leadership skills.

The question was, would she keep her mouth shut? He didn't want the incident all over town, though he supposed it was far too late to worry about that, since Mama had done her striptease in the middle of the damn beauty parlor, facing the damn sidewalk, so that any damn tourist or local could see her. Alex scrubbed a hand over his face.

He didn't know what to do with his mother. He and his father weren't about to hide her away and keep her confined to the house. It wasn't the 1800s, for God's sake. But they also didn't want her to become an object of pity and ridicule.

She'd been a prominent social figure in Fredericksburg, even in San Antonio and Austin. She'd headed every charity ball and fund-raising steering committee in the region.

Mama was well-known and she had been well-liked and respected. He knew how utterly humiliated she'd be if she'd been truly conscious that she'd displayed her bra on Main Street this morning. She would never knowingly make a spectacle of herself that way.

The Kimball men neither needed nor accepted help—not from anyone, friends or strangers. But however much he hated the necessity of doing so, he needed to call Sydney and thank her for her unsolicited interference.

Though it might be impossible to stop the gossip from spreading around town, his primary concern was that his father not find out about his wife's flashing her lingerie in public. Weak heart that he had, it might just kill him.

Irrelevantly, Alex wondered what color Sydney's unmentionables were. With that dark red hair of hers, she'd look amazing in forest green satin. Tantalizing image. In his mind, she tossed her hair, shimmied her hips, and hugged herself seductively. She spun and aimed a naughty look at him over her shoulder. The soundtrack: Joe Cocker, "You Can Leave Your Hat On."

Alex headed for his father's bourbon, shaking his head. *This is the woman that you just refused to "babysit" until Roman guilted you into it. Nice, Kimball.*

His thoughts turned to his brother, who'd popped in for a quick visit a month ago and hadn't even called Mama since then. Damn Jake. He didn't seem to get it. Of course, Mama hadn't had any bad days during his weekend visit, so Jake figured that they were all exaggerating. He didn't seem to believe that with early-onset Alzheimer's, Mama might have only six months to live as a relatively normal person—six months before she might not recognize any of them, ever again.

He splashed a healthy amount of bourbon into a cut crystal double old-fashioned, and knocked some back.

Jake was busy in Dallas, running his nightclubs and sleeping until noon. It must be nice. Alex knocked back some more bourbon and picked up the phone.

Some kid, not Julia, answered at Marv's Motor Inn and connected him with Sydney's room.

"Jersey," he said. "It's Alex Kimball."

"Hi, Alex." Her voice sounded a little different on the phone, but the faint huskiness he found so attractive still traveled along the wire. "How's your mother?"

"She's fine." Alex paused. *Just get it over with.* "And one of the reasons I called was to thank you for what you did. I hate to admit it, but I don't know what I would have done without you."

"Don't worry about it," she said. "It was nothing."

"My mother undressing in public is not 'nothing.' And I never would have thought of doing what you did . . ."

"My grandmother had Alzheimer's," Sydney told him. "That's what you're dealing with, isn't it?"

Alex sighed. "Yes. Early onset. Her behavior's not predictable and I don't always know what to do. But it's not like we're going to keep her locked up in the house."

She made a noise of sympathy. "Nothing about the disease is predictable. My grandma went through a personality reversal. She used to be such a darling, and never said a harsh word about anyone. But right before she died, I'd have sworn they fed her vinegar for breakfast and battery acid for lunch. And she told these outlandish lies—not that she really knew they were lies, the poor thing."

"Yeah," Alex said after a long pause. "Some of the things Mama said—well, they're not true. I'm looking at a silver-framed photograph of my parents' wedding as we speak."

It had been 1966, and Mama, fresh-faced and glowing, wore a sweetheart-cut white gown with little cap sleeves. A white satin ribbon bisected the gown, Jackie O style, culminating in a flat bow at her tiny waist.

His father wore a goofy grin and heavy black-framed glasses of the überdork variety with his tuxedo and white rose. They'd been so in love. And Alex had never seen any sign of that love waning.

As he talked to Sydney, his father's BMW sedan pulled down the long drive and Dad parked. He got out, rubbed absently at his bum knee, and came inside with a small bag of groceries for Mama. She stopped, onion in one hand and knife in the other, and looked up with such an expression of love that a lump formed in Alex's throat.

His father walked into her arms, onion and all, and planted a big smacker on her lips.

*That's the only kind of love I'll ever settle for. That perfect, amused synchronicity—and the passion still there after thirty years.*

"The things she says—they're not meant to hurt you. You know that, right?" Sydney's voice interrupted his musings.

"Yeah. I know."

"She's living in an interior world half the time, her brain trying to send signals through synapses that aren't always connected anymore. The blessing is that while she may be confused about why she can't access certain information, she's also flattening out emotionally so that it doesn't upset her like it does you. And a few minutes later, she forgets the troubling incident entirely."

"You've done your homework, haven't you?"

Sydney paused. "Yes. I have several books. I can write down the titles for you, if you'd like."

"What are you doing tomorrow?" Alex asked her, half because of Roman and half because he wanted to. "Do you have big plans?"

"No, why?"

"If you'll put up with a few errands, I'll show you around Fredericksburg and the Hill Country."

She seemed shocked. Then, to his amusement, she asked, "Why?"

"Jersey, you kill me. What d'you mean, why? You were nice. I didn't deserve it, particularly. Let me at least be hospitable, okay?"

"But—"

"What else do you have to do?" *You can't spend all day following your sister around, talking trash about Roman.*

"Um. Okay, sure."

"I'll even bring a different vehicle, just for you," he said with a chuckle, thinking about his accidental grab of her goods.

She must have been thinking of it, too, because she said, "That'd be great. I don't want to end up in your lap again."

"Hey—women fight to sit in my lap."

"You know, Kimball, one of the things I like about you is your modesty."

"And one of the things I like about you is your grace. Not to mention your tact." He wondered how long she'd badgered her poor sister before she'd agreed to take a pregnancy test. That took nerve. He couldn't really blame Roman for being annoyed.

She cleared her throat. "So. I'll see you tomorrow."

"Yep. Around nine, okay?"

"Nine it is."

# Chapter Nine

Sydney woke up early with a feline stretch and a yawn. She made coffee in the dinky little excuse for a pot with which Marv outfitted each of the Motor Inn's rooms. Knowing what it would taste like, she added both the flimsy filter packets, decaf and caf. Maybe then the stuff would be strong enough to be drinkable.

Syd thought again about what kind of story she'd need to fabricate for Marv. She was hot on the trail of Betty Lou, wrapped in a trench coat and dark shades? She'd tracked her to a nudist colony or a racetrack or a casino boat? Something along those lines.

She was definitely not going to tell him that his younger daughter was engaged, and that Syd herself was half playing hooky.

Running around with Alex today held definite appeal, since Syd was fast discovering that she had inherited even fewer of Ma's girly genes than she thought. Julia was full of BS these days—short for "Bridal Syndrome." If she heard another debate over white vs. ivory, pearls vs. sequins, or hat vs. veil she was going to throw a saddle on one of Uncle Ted's emus and ride screaming into the hills.

Sydney checked e-mail to see if there was anything urgent requiring her attention and groaned when she saw another one from Julia, with a reply from Kiki, and a brief two lines from the extremely busy Vivien, a divorce attorney in Manhattan. Syd wondered sardonically what Viv thought of all this.

Subject: Re: MY WEDDING!!!!!!!!!
Date: XXXXXXX
From: CrownJule
To: numbersgeek, kiki@misstexas95.com, vshelton@kleinschmidtbelker

Hey, girls!

Ha, ha, Kiki, you are too funny. No, there's no bun in my oven, don't worry. 4 other weddings!!!!! That's a lot, but you'll agree that Roman's & mine is the most important!  ☺

I know you've been dying of curiosity, but I finally decided (well, 98.7% sure) on the primary flowers for the spray that will be behind the minister on the dais at the ceremony. (I'm still debating other flowers, but these, of course, are absolutely KEY.) Anyhoo, I'm going with South American orchids. Only trouble is, they're impossible to find here in Fredericksburg. Kiki, could you be a dear and tell me who in town you think could track these down? I don't have a clue who to ask, and when I mentioned it to your mother, she didn't answer. Just asked what I had against traditional roses.

Roses! Sure, a few, maybe. But as my primary floral focal point? I don't think so! Roses are so last millennium!

Thanks ever so!
J

Subject: Re: MY WEDDING!!!!!!!
Date: XXXXXXX
From: kiki@misstexas95.com
To: CrownJule, numbersgeek, vshelton
  Hi, Girls,
Consider the problem of how to handle ALL the wedding details solved. The answer is Breckin Andrews! He runs an event planning business called With This Ring right there in Fredericksburg. This man had a chance to work full time doing floral arrangements for Elton John, but he chose to stay in his hometown and impart his impeccable taste on potentially tacky Texas brides. It's the ultimate in gay self-sacrifice. Think of this as QUEER EYE FOR THE STRAIGHT BRIDE.

Thank me later,
Kiki

Subject: Re: MY WEDDING!!!!!!!!
Date: XXXXXXXXX
From: vshelton
To: CrownJule, numbersgeek,
kiki@misstexas95.com

   Julia, darling, you always were an incurable romantic. Congratulations.

   Syd, how are you?

   Kiki, this IS a touch awkward, isn't it? No hard feelings about me representing Walter in your divorce.

xoxoxo, Viv


A horrified laugh escaped Sydney. Julia's best friend had represented Kiki's ex-husband? If she couldn't talk her sister out of this, it was going to be one interesting wedding.

Syd showered quickly. Then she got out, snatched one of the sandpapery towels that Marv purchased by the truckload and loofahed off the water with it. Damn, the thing almost had teeth instead of fabric nubs. She could just about comb her hair with it.

Julia had argued with their father recently about the towels, but he dismissed her complaints by saying that the crappier his towels were, the less likely it was that guests would take off with them. That was Marv for you—all about comfort and marketing.

She strode purposefully to her suitcase. Errands,

huh? This time, Alex was not going to be able to laugh at her in a skirt and heels. Errands probably meant milking a couple of matronly mammals, or shooting their lunch.

Sydney chose a pair of shorts, a T-shirt and her hiking boots. She didn't bother with jewelry at all, and stuck her shoulder-length hair in a ponytail. Though she didn't want Alex to think she was primping for him, she did apply eye makeup (waterproof this time) and lip gloss. Anything else would doubtless melt off her face in the heat.

She headed out of her room and down the elevator. Maybe Julia would have bottled water somewhere.

Unfortunately her sister wasn't at the front desk, and wasn't picking up the phone in her room. Sydney figured she could get Alex to stop for a bottle of water somewhere on their way to do his mysterious errands. She peered out the smoked-glass door, but saw no sign of Alex, just some yuppie guy in a beautiful dark green Mercedes.

Sydney took another look. *No way.* But the guy who opened the door, the guy who got out in pressed khakis and a shirt with a collar—was indeed Alex.

*Shit!* Sydney couldn't meet him looking like this. She turned tail and fled down the hallway, only to be stopped by his deep drawl. "Jersey, where you hightailin' it off to?"

*Double shit.* "I, uh, forgot my sunglasses," she lied.

"Really. You need two pairs?"

She looked down to find them hanging by an earpiece from her shirt. *Triple shit!* "Oooohhhh. There they are. I looked for those things everywhere."

He lifted a brow and jingled his keys. "You ready to go?"

She looked him up and down, from his neatly parted hair to the expensive loafers on his feet. Where were his boots?

"Um. Yeah." Reluctantly she walked toward him and out the door with him. She sank into the buttery leather passenger seat of the Mercedes and let the expensive German air-conditioning flow over her.

Alex got in next to her, smelling better than any man had a right to, and Sydney stared disconsolately at her hiking boots. "So what kind of errands are we running?"

"Today," Alex said, "we are going to make some attempts to market Emulsion, my aunt's homemade emu-oil face cream."

Sydney absorbed this. "Emu oil in face cream? Why?"

"It's great for skin. Heals burns, moisturizes and et cetera. It's in lots of skin care products now. You'd be surprised."

"Wasn't it just the other day that you were going to market emu barbecue sauce?"

"Yep." Alex started the car.

"And now face cream. Can I ask you a possibly rude question?"

"Shoot."

"If it's your uncle's emu ranch, why do you get stuck doing all the marketing?"

"It's complicated," Alex told her, as he waved to a familiar-looking lady with flaming orange hair. The woman peered intently at Sydney, who crossed her arms over her chest and stared right back.

"Who *is* that woman?"

"Thelma Lynn Grafton is not just a woman, Sydney." Alex lifted a brow. "Thelma Lynn is the high priestess of Fredericksburg gossip. She is a grapevine with legs."

"So that's where the rumor started," Syd muttered. "She didn't look like a person who was up to any good."

"Rumor?"

Sydney cleared her throat. "Uh, yes. For some reason there's this crazy rumor flying around that Julia is pregnant and that's why Roman's asked her to marry him."

"I wonder how that got started?" Alex sounded pensive.

Syd felt her cheeks heating. "I have no idea." She changed the subject. "So back to this marketing stuff. How is it complicated?"

Alex shot her an amused glance. "You Yankees are nothing if not direct, aren't you?"

Sydney shrugged. "Sorry."

"No, no, don't apologize. The complications with the emu operations arise because although it is, technically, my uncle's ranch, he's invested family funds in it. Yes, we reluctantly gave him permission, but let's just say that all the Kimballs have a vested interest in seeing the venture pay off."

"I see," said Sydney, though she didn't really see at all. If the rest of the family had thought it was a bad idea, why had they agreed to back it? "So what exactly is in this emu face cream?"

"Emu oil, which is known for healing skin conditions and burns. And other natural ingredients like lavender and honey."

"I'm not even going to ask how you obtain emu oil."

"So anyway"—Alex avoided that topic—"we're going to drop in at a couple of salons and spas and offer them a free sample."

"Can I see some of this stuff?"

"Sure. It's on the backseat."

Sydney turned around, and sure enough, there was a shallow box of twenty squat little jars. They'd been hand-painted, and lengths of grosgrain ribbon encircled their lids. She reached back and plucked one out of the box.

"Alex," she said suspiciously, "is this a *baby-food* jar?"

"Yes, I believe it started life that way, before Aunt Susie transformed it."

*Shut up, Sydney. Don't say it.* But her mouth opened of its own accord and told him, "They're, uh, cute. But you're not going to get anyone to take you seriously this way. They look too homemade."

"People around here like homemade," Alex said, after a pause.

"Maybe so. But you're going to want to sell this stuff outside Texas, right?"

"Eventually."

"Then you need better packaging. Professional packaging that will work in New York or LA. 'Cute' won't fly there, and the rest of the country follows the trends set in those two cities."

"I thought you were a numbers geek, not an advertising executive."

She shot him a dark look. "I've worked with clients who are small business owners. I have a client who owns a chain of salons and spas, for example. And I'd be happy to put in a good word for you, but I'll tell you right now that she won't touch anything that's packaged like this."

There was no mistaking the tinge of annoyance in Alex's voice now. "Well, I do appreciate your input."

Thinking that before she'd spoken, she should have at least looked at the stuff, Sydney twisted off the lid and peered at it.

Emulsion was a light, whipped substance that smelled of lavender, rosemary and lemon. That was good. The color was a little off-putting, though: a yellow taupe. Gingerly she poked an index finger into it and rubbed it against her thumb. It didn't feel greasy—another good sign. She scooped out a small amount and rubbed it into the back of her left hand. The stuff absorbed fairly quickly and did seem to soften her skin.

"Okay. In addition to packaging, you're going to have to change the color."

Alex's mouth dropped open and a short chuckle emerged. "More advice, huh? And why, Miz Sydney, do we need to change the color?"

"It's not attractive. You want women to open this stuff and fall in love with it. The 'emu' angle may already be a tough sell. You don't want anything else to make them hesitate."

Alex looked over at her, brows raised. "Wait a minute. I have seen women smear the most disgusting things over themselves in the name of beauty. Green goop, brown goop, white goop, grainy oatmeal-looking goop. Pink goop, too—and blue, sticky goop in their hair! Then there's the red goop on their lips and cheeks, purple and black goop on their eyes, and that so-called tanning stuff that turns 'em orange! And you're telling me that this *yellowish* stuff is bad?"

Sydney, laughing at his outrage, said, "Again—it

depends on the way it's marketed. Green is fine if it's an avocado- or cucumber-based product. The 'oatmeal-looking goop' you're talking about is probably a skin scrub or exfoliator, right?"

"Yeah."

"Well, yellow is fine if you're playing up the lemony aspects of something, but I think you want to avoid yellow if you're talking about something that's been squeezed from part of a bird."

Silence. Then, "Big Bird is yellow," Alex reasoned.

"Big Bird is for kids. Big Bird does not appeal to harried women who are looking for something to renew and maybe spoil themselves with."

"Huh."

"Trust me. I'm one of those harried women. We work too hard, we worry too much, we want to relax. We want products that will make us feel young, free and pretty."

"Why can't something in a baby-food jar make you feel that way?"

"Alex." Sydney put a hand on his arm and leaned toward him earnestly. He sucked in a breath, disliking the fact that he liked the feel of her hand far too much.

"A baby-food jar is not enticing, even disguised. It's an everyday reminder of drudgery and drool and laundry. We want exotic, mysterious, elegant packaging that promises an undiscovered elixir, a beauty secret that can be exclusively ours . . . for a price."

"Oh, please. Does that mean I should package my barbecue sauce in some kind of genie bottle?"

Syd shook her head and removed her hand. He missed its warmth immediately, irritating as that was.

"Absolutely not," she said. "For the most part, you're marketing barbecue sauce to men. You guys are different animals altogether. You'd want flames, peppers, action colors, maybe even an explosion."

"Half-naked women?" Alex asked.

"I'd draw the line at that," Sydney said, frowning.

"Why? They use sex to sell beer and car wax— even the cars themselves. Scantily clad women sell sports equipment, coolers, fishing rods, boats and even vacations."

"Okay, I get the idea."

"So why not barbecue sauce?"

"Fine. I'll see if I can get my friend Donna to draw your sauce bottle nestled between a giant pair of breasts. The vixen they belong to can be ducking her head to rip off the top with her teeth."

"Now *that* has possibilities," Alex said thoughtfully. "And it shows that she's limber." He grinned.

Syd shook her head in disgust. "See? Women want mystery—the keys to the universe. Men just want sex."

"Absolutely. Because for men, sex *is* the universe." His eyes gleamed and his teeth flashed very white. "So, Sydney, have I told you that you've got very cute knees?"

Alex thought she had cute knees? No—he was kidding around. She rolled her eyes at him. "To return to the baby-food jar problem. I think we should talk to Donna right away."

"I've never even met this Donna person or seen her portfolio. Besides, she sounds expensive, and the biggest benefit of baby-food jars is that they're cheap."

"Are you sure about that? How long does it take your Aunt Susie to paint and pretty up each one? Her time is money."

"Aunt Susie likes doing it. And her time is free."

"Donna is a genius with degrees from Parsons and RISD."

"Well, she sounds entirely too big-city for the likes of us," Alex drawled.

"Not at all! She—"

"Jersey, has it ever occurred to you that you're just along for the ride, and that we might not welcome your med—uh, help?"

Sydney compressed her lips. He'd been about to say "meddling." She should never have opened her mouth, and while he had every right to rebuke her, it still stung. She'd only been trying to help.

"Well, I'm sorry," she said. "I just call things like I see them, and 'being along for the ride' is not really my personality."

"I'd never have guessed that." Alex's tone was dryer than Texas dust.

"You know what?" she flared. "Passivity never got anyone anywhere. Passivity is apathy, which shares a Latin root with 'pathetic.' "

"Whoa. Where's all this coming from? Who are you mad at, Sydney?"

"I'm not mad at anyone," she muttered.

"Oh, I think you are. Somebody in your life is passive and lets you compensate for it. Who? Julia?"

"No. My mother," she finally admitted. "She never stands up to my father, and Marv walks all over her while she retreats to la-la land. She never stuck up for us when we were kids—*I* always had to stick up for *her*. And it's still happening! Marv has her locked in a ridiculous castle and terrorized by a maid. He's decided that Julia is beautiful and useless, and deserves the same fate. And that I'm—" She broke off.

"You're what?" Alex prompted.

"I'm supposed to keep his books for the rest of my lonely spinster days."

"You're kidding, right?"

She shook her head. "I wish I were."

She wondered if her mother's life would have been different if she hadn't been a sweet, shy girl, one with little self-esteem and even less sense of belonging anywhere. When she'd met brash and demanding Marv on a double date right out of high school, she'd probably been grateful to be propelled in any direction at all. And since he'd propelled her to the altar, she'd happily picked out a dress and veil along the way.

"So that's the reason you're so dead set against this wedding of your sister's. I didn't fully understand when you were talking with Roman."

"I'm not dead set against—"

"Yes, you are. But it's Julia's choice to buy into your father's image of her."

"There's been no choice. She's been brainwashed!"

"Those are strong words."

"True ones."

"And they give you the excuse to meddle?"

"What you seem to think of as meddling, I think of as being proactive, okay? I just want Julia to be happy," Sydney said.

A long pause ensued before Alex finally spoke. "And what makes you think you have any control over that?"

Sydney opened and then closed her mouth. "I can stop her from making a mistake."

"No, you can't," he said. "Not really. What are you going to do—drug her and kidnap her? Tie her up until Roman falls in love with someone else? You'll be waiting decades. I've never seen Rome like this. Up until now, he's been an extremely dedicated bachelor, and he's enjoyed every minute of it, too."

"Aha!" said Sydney. "So you're saying he's a hound dog." She mentally apologized to Humphrey.

"No. I did *not* say that."

"Well, what do you mean? Tell me about him."

"You know what, Jersey? I'm not going to tell you squat about Roman." His smile took some of the sting out of the words. "You don't want to hear anything nice, and you'll use anything else as ammunition."

She opened her mouth to deny it, but he shook his head knowingly at her.

"I'm gonna let you get to know him for yourself." He reached out and turned on the audio system, releasing a torrent of ZZ Top into the air. "Now where was I?" He drummed his fingers on the steering wheel. "Oh, yes. Wasn't I saying that you have awfully cute knees? They almost make up for your meddling."

# Chapter Ten

Alex grinned as Sydney stiffened and said, "I really think we should leave my knees out of the conversation."

"Why?"

"Because it's . . . flirting."

"No!" Alex exclaimed, in mock horror.

Sydney glared at him. "And people—guys—flirt with Julia, not me."

Alex peered at her, a puzzled expression on his face. "I didn't realize it was an either/or situation."

"You know what I mean. I'm the Brain and she's always been the Beauty."

"Sydney, that's ridiculous. Those are labels, not mutually exclusive qualities. Julia's not brainless, and you're not ugly."

"Gosh, thanks so much for the compliment."

"You know what, you're impossible," Alex said. "I try to flirt with you, and you won't allow it. I don't flirt with you, and you get offended." He turned off the highway and down a long drive that led to a large, pretty, white-columned house. A sign outside proclaimed it the HILL COUNTRY SPA.

"But do you *want* to flirt with me?" Sydney asked, in a small voice.

"Hell, yes!" Alex growled. *God knows why.*

"Why?"

*Of course she had to ask.* "What do you mean, why? I just do."

"Well, is it some kind of . . . blind instinct? Primal urge? Or is there something specific that makes you want to flirt with me in particular?"

*God Almighty!* How did she expect him to answer that? But he softened at the vulnerability in her eyes: vulnerability she'd deny was there to her last breath; she'd cloaked her voice in scientific interest.

"Sydney, I'm not a single-cell organism. Yes, there are specific reasons I want to flirt with you. One, you've got a mouth on you that just won't quit. Two, you've got those knees, darlin'. And three, you don't expect me to flirt with you, which is refreshing.

"Now, before you open those pretty lips to ask me if there isn't anything else, let me tell you that yes, there is. But those are private, very appreciative thoughts that I'm sure you'd interpret as offensive. So I'm not going to tell you about them." He grabbed a jar of Emulsion. "Okay? I'll be right back."

He closed the car door, amused at her expression, and headed for the entrance of the spa.

"Wait!" she yelled, scrambling out. "I'm coming in with you."

He admired the long, fluid grace of her pale legs in those shorts, and couldn't help wondering what she looked like without them. In fact, the green satin lingerie came forcibly back to mind.

"When you said 'a mouth that won't quit,' " Sydney asked, as she reached him, "what did you mean, exactly?"

Alex shook his head, repressing a grin. "What are you fishing for?"

"I am not fishing," Sydney said. "I am only asking for clarification."

"You are *so* fishing. You want to know whether I was referring to your irresistible lips"—he put his index finger right in the middle of the plump bottom one—"or the fact that you say things you shouldn't say and keep on saying them. Admit it!"

Instead, she seemed frozen, held in place by his finger. Reluctantly he removed it, and she licked the lip. He was positive she hadn't meant the gesture to tease, but it was seductive. *No, Alex. Don't go there with the Difficult Sister.*

He gestured toward the front door. "Shall we?"

Inside the Hill Country Spa they found mood lighting everywhere, along with white wicker furniture padded with floral cushions in soft pastels. Staff in white lab coats and immaculate makeup attended women in white waffle-weave robes and no makeup.

Behind the reception desk, long, shallow, mirrored shelves held dozens of jars, bottles and boxes of beauty products. Alex squinted at them. The packaging was simple, sleek and sophisticated for the most part. The items looked as if they'd been produced by a very elegant science lab. *Hmmmm.*

Alex looked down at the painted, beribboned baby-food jar in his palm. Sydney could be right, damn it.

"May I help you?" The woman behind the counter was a walking mannequin. She wore a gold nameplate engraved with the name TESSA.

"Nice place you have here," Alex said, smiling at her. She dimpled and tucked a strand of shortish blond hair behind her ear.

"Thank you."

"Have you been open long?"

"About a year." She openly scanned the length of his body, paying special attention to his biceps.

"Well, I'm marketing a new product and I thought maybe I'd leave a sample with you to try." Alex placed the jar on the counter.

"Is that a baby-food jar?"

"Well, we are just starting out. Emulsion is a wonderful face cream. It's made with emu oil—"

Tessa wrinkled her nose. "Oh, God, those stinky

birds again. Everyone is trying to push them these days!"

Behind him came a definite snort from Sydney.

"—and lemon juice, rosemary and lavender." Alex smiled at the mannequin, and watched her eyes widen and then assume a slightly glazed expression.

"I'd love for you to give it a try personally," he purred, pressing the unfair advantage of his looks. "Would it be okay if I gave you a call in a couple of days to see how it worked for you?"

Tessa practically fell down in her rush to supply her phone number. Was that a gagging noise behind him from the Difficult Sister?

"Thank you, Tessa." Alex gave her a wink before heading for the door. Underhanded tactics, maybe, but he'd bet she'd take a half dozen jars off his hands next week.

Outside, Sydney told him, "That was just disgusting. She practically lunged for that pen to give you her number."

"Well, that was the plan." Alex didn't mention that Tessa, while nice to look at, left him cold.

"Are you going to ask her out?"

"Now, is that really your business?" But he smiled. Silence.

"Your baby-food jars will not work," Syd continued, undaunted. "If you're not there personally to flirt and seduce the managers—and believe me, they're not all female—you'll never sell this stuff."

"Thank you for your vote of confidence."

In the car, Sydney whipped out a calculator. "So what's your aunt's cost per unit?"

"It's really pretty much just her labor and the cost of the lemons. She grows the rosemary and lavender on the property behind the house."

"How long does it take her to whip up a batch? How many jars does she get from one batch?"

"Syd, are you double-checking me to make sure my pricing's correct? Because, yes, I have figured in costs of marketing, distribution, manufacturing, and product liability insurance. But for right now, I'm pricing the stuff based on limited production with only local distribution in mind."

"Well, like I said, the key to beauty products is to price them high and package them gorgeously. I'm telling you, my friend can design what you need . . ."

Alex shifted the Mercedes out of reverse and back into park. He turned to face Sydney, removed the calculator from her grasp and took her chin in his hand. "Sydney. Which part of 'no' don't you understand? We Kimballs like to do things our own way, without much help—if any. Now, I appreciate what you're trying to do here, but *we're okay.*" Why was she trying so hard to help him, anyway? Alex had a hunch that she just couldn't help herself.

He gazed at those soft pink lips of hers, at the way they gilded that stubborn-as-hell chin. You could break rocks on her jaw. Reading both those features, without even looking into her eyes, he could see the thoughts going through her mind like goldfish in a bowl: her hurt feelings, her good intentions, her determination that she was right—that he was being backward.

Well, hell. Maybe he *was* being backward. But it was his right to be pigheaded, just as it was Julia's right to get married. This little redheaded Bonaparte wore her opinions like epaulets, and she needed to be stripped of her uniform.

*Bad metaphor, man.* He didn't need to think of Sydney and "stripped" in the same sentence—it started him wondering if she had freckles all over . . .

She didn't say a word, just turned to stare out the window. He actually appreciated the fact that she wouldn't apologize. She wouldn't have meant it.

Alex put the car into drive again. "Tell you what. We'll visit a couple more places with the Emulsion. If you're right, and the baby-food jars get the same reception, then I promise I'll think about hiring your friend."

The smile she rewarded him with was pure sunshine. "Promise?"

"Yeah."

"Then Donna's hired, 'cause you're going to get the same response."

And damn it, he did.

\* \* \*

Sydney tried to contain her smugness over lunch, she really did, but she had a feeling that it oozed out of her just like the barbecue sauce from her brisket sandwich.

Alex gazed at her sardonically and pointed at her with his pickle. "Don't look so pleased with yourself."

"It's not nice to point. And I can't help it—my friend Donna is pregnant and trying to establish a business on the side so that she'll be able to work at home after the baby comes. Bringing her a new client is the best baby gift I can give her." She took a huge bite of her sandwich and succeeded in smearing barbecue sauce across her cheek and onto the tip of her nose.

Alex thought she looked just fine that way. He tried to imagine the lovely Julia with food on her face and failed utterly.

But Sydney . . . Sydney was real, and funny, and very appealing when she wasn't being annoying. He'd like to handcuff her to his bed, paint some barbecue sauce on her with a brush and lick it off. He grinned.

"What?" she asked. "Talk about looking pleased with yourself: You're the cat and I can see canary feathers stuck in your teeth."

"Oh, I'm no common house cat, Jersey."

"And I'll bet you've never been offered up as a

baby gift, either." Sydney reached for another, much needed napkin.

"Can't say as I have."

"So what do you think your budget will be for the Emulsion packaging?"

"Eat your pickle."

"I just want to give Donna an idea of the scope of the project. And I don't like pickles."

"I will give *her* all the information she needs. Not *you*. Eat your coleslaw and your beans."

"I'm full." She stuck that chin out again. "So where are we going next?"

Well, since the Emulsion had been a bust, they'd move on to his Hot 'n' Sweet Emu Sauce. And nobody'd care what kind of jar it came in.

"You been to Rustlin' Rob's?"

Her eyebrows rose. "Rustlin' Rob's? What is that, a horse-thieving outfit?"

"Rustlin' Rob's is an amazing gourmet place. You'll love it."

"Gourmet? In Texas?"

"Yup. You just wait."

Rustlin' Rob's looked like an old Western saloon on the outside, complete with Lone Star motifs. On the inside, it resembled a general store, with merchandise stocked on rough-hewn wooden shelves.

Sydney looked around in amazement when they entered the shop. Thousands of jars of every kind of dip, sauce, vinegar, oil, soup or jelly imaginable lined the walls. And unbelievably, she could taste each one! She immediately wished she'd eaten only half the brisket sandwich, but she'd wolfed the whole thing.

She decided, however, that getting a stomachache might be worth it. Baskets of pretzels, Wheat Thins and bowls of the various concoctions called her name and stimulated her curiosity.

While Alex talked with the sales staff and then the owner, Sydney dipped and munched and marveled at what she found. Surreptitiously, she went back for seconds on certain items: Fischer & Wieser's Texas 1015 Onion Glaze, D.L. Jardine's Cowpoke Artichoke Salsa, and the Asian Sesame Oven and Grill Sauce from Robert Rothschild Farms.

She found pesto, flavored vinegar and herb-infused olive oil as good or better than any she'd sampled in Italy. And her true downfall was Rothschild's Raspberry Chocolate Pretzel Dip, where Alex found her grazing after he'd sold several cases of his Emu Sauce.

"I thought you said you were full, Jersey."

"I was." She chewed guiltily and swallowed. "But I never got dessert."

"Uh-huh. And what's that under your arm?"

She clutched a package of Hombres Foods' Cappuccino Chipotle Brownie Mix as if it were a brick of twenty-four-carat gold. "I thought I'd send this to my mother."

"Bull," Alex said. "You'll be sneaking into the Marv's Motor Inn kitchen with that in the dead of night. Here, get two." He plucked another package from the shelf. "My treat."

She wasn't going to argue with this. "So you sold a bunch of Emu Sauce, huh?" She followed him, never taking her eyes off his precious cargo.

"Yep." He grinned. "I'm even on the verge of talking them into sponsoring a big Emu Roast."

"You're kidding, right?"

"Nope. It'll be a huge draw if we can do it during the Fredericksburg Food and Wine Fest, Oktoberfest or the Mesquite Art Festival. I'll send you an engraved invitation."

"I'll probably be back in South River, unraveling another one of Marv's accounting nightmares," she said dolefully.

"Don't you have your own business to run?"

She nodded.

"Then why are you tied up with his? He's got motels all over the country—surely he can afford to hire someone."

"It's a long story, but he doesn't trust anyone outside the family."

Alex leveled a disbelieving look at her.

"I know—it sounds weak. But it's true."

"As long as you don't mind."

Oh, she minded, all right. She just needed to figure out how to tell Marv and cut the umbilical cord. Easier said than done. She heard her own words echoing in her head. *Passivity is apathy, which shares the same Latin root as pathetic.* Had she said that?

"Well," Alex said, "now you'll have to let me take you for a drink to celebrate my sale. Then I've gotta go whip up several batches of Emu Sauce."

"You don't have other plans?" asked Sydney, trying not to wonder how many more Tessas were out there for him.

"Now, when a woman asks you that she's either thinking you're too gruesome for words, or feeling you out to see if you've got a girlfriend. Which is it with you, Sydney?"

She flushed. Of course, she *had* been wondering if Alex had girlfriends, but she didn't like being read so easily. "You are pretty gruesome. Way too gruesome to have a girlfriend," she returned, "so I'm not worried about that part."

He laughed. "Yeah, I have this problem with small children screaming at the sight of me and running away. But what can I do?"

"Out of *pity* I might have a drink with you," Sydney said in a considering tone.

"You're all heart."

# Chapter Eleven

Alex took her to a "Biergarten," right on Main Street. It was an open, spacious place dominated by an enormous bar, behind which stood the huge copper and steel tanks of a microbrewery. Four-top tables sprinkled the left and rear areas, over which an enormous twelve-point buck presided.

He seemed to stare accusingly at everyone who entered, and the hairs on the back of Syd's neck stood up. Had the poor thing been an unwilling customer of Big Rack Taxidermist, the business she'd passed on the way into town?

To Sydney, most beer tasted like carbonated motor oil. But before she could tell Alex that she disliked it, he'd ordered two pints of the Biergarten's special.

Keeping her face neutral, she accepted the mug and they toasted to the successful sale of his Emu Sauce. She hoisted the stuff to her mouth and discovered that it was delicious, not bitter at all—smooth and rich and somehow caramel-y.

Alex cocked his head and reached out for a strand of her hair. She sat very still, her gaze flying to his, as he let the strand slide through his fingers and a tingle ran down her scalp.

"The beer's the exact shade as your hair," he said. "A deep red mahogany."

She lowered her gaze. "My hair used to be carrot-colored. I got it from my grandmother—my ma's ma."

"The same one who had Alzheimer's?" Alex asked.

"Yes. I hope I didn't inherit that particular gene."

Alex tipped half the contents of his glass down his throat in one convulsive gulp.

Struck a nerve, had she?

Alex changed the subject before she could pursue it, and they talked about what it was like to grow up in Texas, land of football, beef and oil. It occurred to her that this was an excellent time to find out more about Roman and see if she could dig up any dirt. How many beers would it take for Alex to get careless about what he said?

"So did you and Roman play football?"

"Of course. He played strong safety and I played defensive end. Another friend of ours, J.B., was the quarterback. He was the only one of us to go on and play college ball."

"You guys must have dated all the cheerleaders."

His eyes crinkled at the corners, and she noted that they looked lighter today, almost the shade of good brandy. "We went out with our share," Alex agreed. "There was the pep squad, too, of course."

"Of course." She smiled at him blandly and had another sip of beer. Now they were getting somewhere.

"But Rome had a pretty serious girlfriend," Alex said, disappointing her.

"What happened?"

He shrugged. "I don't know—it just fizzled out, like a lot of high school relationships. He and Melissa didn't have enough in common to keep it going. He wanted to leave town, go to college, see something of the world. She wanted to get married right out of high school and settle down. How many guys are ready to get married at eighteen?"

"Is that what your girlfriend wanted?"

Alex snorted. "Hardly. I was dating Roman's sister Kiki at the time, and she is hell on heels."

"What do you mean by that?"

"Kiki is something else. Let's just say she's a little high maintenance and leave it at that."

"Does she still live in Fredericksburg?"

Alex laughed out loud. "Uh, no. Kiki lives in Manhattan. She's not cut out to be a small-town girl."

Oh, right. Julia had mentioned something about Roman's parents visiting her in New York.

"And," Alex said mock seriously, "you should

135

never, ever forget that she was runner-up to Miss America in 1995."

Alex had dated a Miss America contestant. Oh, fabulous. *Why is he sitting here with me?* Sydney inhaled a large gulp of beer. "So . . . what does Kiki do?"

"Kiki's an actress."

"Broadway?"

"Nope. Soaps, commercials, that kind of thing. What is this, Twenty Questions?"

"Sorry," said Sydney sheepishly. "I'm just curious." Then, unable to resist, "So Kiki broke your heart in high school, huh?"

Alex settled back on his stool and ran his tongue over his teeth before his mouth settled into something half grin, half grimace. "Not exactly. Kiki fixed my little red wagon in high school, is what Keek did." Finally he laughed.

"Oh, come on. Share the joke," Sydney prompted.

Alex grabbed a few peanuts and tossed one into his mouth. "Kiki and I didn't always see things quite the same way, and we broke up every other day. On one of those occasions I decided that the breakup was final. She didn't agree, but I wasn't in a negotiating kind of mood. So Kiki got mad—and Keek mad is a dangerous thing. She spread it throughout the whole school that she was finished with me because I was such a dud in the sack."

Sydney pressed her lips together to keep from laughing.

Alex shot her a slant-eyed look. "Which is not true, and I still have her claw marks in my back to prove it."

*Claw marks?* Sydney blinked.

He cleared his throat. "Don't think she's evil: I probably deserved her payback. I was pretty impressed with myself back then."

She nodded, raised her beer to her mouth again, and decided it was time for a subject change. "Uh, this is good."

"You sound surprised." Alex leaned back in his chair and eyed her lazily. "I don't get the feeling you expect too much from Texas."

She cleared her throat. "Well, there are a lot of stereotypes."

"What did you expect to find, the Wild West or Southfork?"

"I wasn't sure."

"Did you think we were all backward and chewed on straws?"

"No, of course not."

"But you didn't expect to find emus and wine, high-tech companies and gourmet products."

"No. I thought more along the lines of big hair, cows, Cadillacs and rodeos."

"Well, I can show you all of those things and you'd have a ball. But there's a lot of diversity here. The universities bring in plenty of interesting people, and born-and-bred Texans are fascinating in themselves.

Don't ever make the mistake of underestimating them." Alex tipped back some more beer.

*Excellent. Keep on drinking, buddy. I need some dirt on your friend Roman.* Sydney wondered how she could steer the conversation back to him without being too obvious. She wanted to know more about this mysterious Melissa person, the high school girl-friend. Maybe she still lived around here. Maybe if she found out her last name, she could track her down. And maybe Melissa could provide information that would stop Julia from rushing into marriage with her ex-boyfriend.

"Let me get another round," Sydney said, signaling the bartender. "You're basically down to backwash, there."

Alex's mouth quirked. "I'll gladly have another beer, but I won't allow you to pay for it."

"Why not?"

"Because I'm old-fashioned."

"You're too stiff-necked to let a woman pay for your drink?"

Alex sighed. "Yeah. Just like you're too stiff-necked to accept either a compliment or a lousy couple of beers."

Sydney blinked.

"Besides," he continued, "it would bankrupt you to buy enough beer that I'd spill all about Rome's past. So don't bother." He grinned at her as her mouth fell open.

"I wasn't trying to do any such thing."

"You've got that righteous tone down pat, don't you, Jersey?"

"You know, I really wish you'd stop calling me that. I don't wear tight camel-toe jeans or have mall bangs."

"You trying to tell me that my conceptions of Jersey are as dated as yours about Texas?"

She nodded. "So how is beer made, exactly?" She gestured toward the huge metal tanks behind the bar.

"Well, it's a complex process, but basically a brewer combines barley, water, hops and yeast." He raised a brow. "Since your sister is marrying into the Sonntag family, I would think you'd be more interested in the winemaking process."

Sydney thought of Roman again and grimaced. She'd get some dirt on Mr. Professionally Nice if it killed her.

"Still being snotty about Roman, I see. Or are you being snotty about the idea of Texas wine? You seemed to like it enough the other day. Either way, you're making a mistake. Roman's a good guy—"

"Don't you think you're a little biased, being his best friend?"

"—and Texas wines are competing now with Californian and Australian wines in national tastings."

Yeah, yeah—a blue ribbon to the Beaujolais Rodeo and the Cabernet Saddle-On. She didn't know jack about wine, but again, she was convinced Alex was biased. What else was he going to say? He wasn't going to walk around commenting that his friend was making grape piss. She couldn't help it—a small snort escaped her.

"Is that considered ladylike in Jersey?" asked Alex. "Because you sound just like a mare with a horsefly up her nose."

Sydney's mouth dropped open and she actually raised a hand to push him, or maybe smack him—she wasn't sure which. But before she could follow through Alex caught it in his own, along with the other, and her breath hitched in her throat. His broad palms covered her knuckles, folded them gently down, and his fingers held her in calm but powerful captivity.

His expression was amused, but as they looked into each other's eyes and the moment of tension lengthened, his irises deepened from caramel to chocolate. His eyes were teardrop shaped, the outside corners tilting down slightly. Dark lashes framed them, added power and masculinity.

Sydney found herself looking at his mouth next—at lips that curved seductively, the line of them forming a sensual, sideways, scripted "E." E for edible? E for easy? E for erotic?

Alex's mouth came closer. *Oh, my God. He's going to kiss me. Why would he do that? Why—*

Her thoughts stopped, replaced by sensation as his lips touched her own. He brushed her mouth softly in exploration, then angled his head and returned for more contact. Her lips were still apart with the surprise of it, and he dipped between them to enter her mouth.

Sydney had never really cared for kissing before now. It had always been an awkward affair of rubbery, fleshy lips and excess saliva and alien tongues, never making much sense to her.

She'd obviously never kissed someone like Alex. And it dawned on her what she'd been missing: a slow introduction to sensuous languor that overrode the quickening of her pulse, the sharp surge of sexual electricity, the desire to consume and be consumed.

She could kiss Alex for hours. His mouth stroked her, excited her and soothed her all at once. He slipped into her mouth and melted something at her core.

He smelled of sandalwood and sunshine, Ivory soap and dark, sweet beer. He tasted unique. He was tender and rough at the same time: As the kiss deepened, she could feel that five o'clock shadow of his scrubbing at her skin like steel wool. It only heightened the sensations plucking at her nerves.

Sydney realized with strange clarity that Alex was the first *man* she'd ever kissed; he relegated the rest to boys. She understood at last what that overblown, vaguely ridiculous term "passion" meant: the completely primal response of a woman to a man.

Unfortunately, with all this clarity came fear. *I'm*

*kissing Alex Kimball, whom I've known for a day and a half. I'm kissing him like a desperate, drowning leech of some kind. He'll have to have me surgically removed from his face. What am I doing?*

Sydney jerked away from him, blinked in utter confusion and panic, and slid off her barstool.

"Why did you do that?" she blurted.

Alex gazed at her, the picture of calm. "Because I wanted to. Very much."

She swallowed and reached for her handbag.

"Should I apologize, Sydney?"

Her eyes flew to his. "I—" She twisted the ring on her index finger, a nervous habit. "I don't know. But I have to go. Thanks for the beer." She turned quickly and walked out, under Alex's perplexed gaze.

# Chapter Twelve

Sydney hurried along Main Street with her head down. What had just happened back there? They'd gone from verbal sparring to annoyance to a playful kiss on Alex's part—and she'd reacted like a match to a lighter. How mortifying. He must be able to see that she hadn't even been on a date, much less in someone's bed, for over a year.

Maybe it was time to get a battery-operated boy-friend so she didn't embarrass herself in front of human candidates. God, she'd stuck to the man like a kid's lollipop to a car seat. And he'd just been messing around!

She had a buzz from the two pints of beer and her face smarted from beard stubble. The man had more prickles than a cactus.

She passed the wide glass door of the beauty salon where she'd first seen Alex's mother, and a familiar face peered out from under a dark slather of evil-looking slime. Thelma Lynn Grafton's orange eyebrows furrowed and her mouth pursed like an overripe prune. She looked Sydney up and down, making her feel more uncomfortable than Marcella ever had. In fact, Marcella seemed positively friendly compared to this lady.

But the thought occurred to Sydney that Thelma Lynn Grafton, high priestess of Fredericksburg gossip, could be extremely helpful to her on her mission to uncover dirt on Roman Sonntag. So although she didn't feel like it at all, she forced herself to stop, turn and double back to the salon. She needed a distraction from thoughts of Alex, anyway.

She opened the door, smiled at Thelma Lynn and her gruesome slimy head, and said hello. *Whew, whatever is in that orange hair dye smells like Eau de Landfill.*

Mrs. Grafton stared at her for another long moment, nodded, widened her prune enough to crack a polite smile and then pretended to go back to her magazine while Sydney explained to the receptionist that she was visiting from out of town and wondered if she could get a menu of their services.

It was the same receptionist who had been there the other day, the Holstein with highlights. "Menu?" She looked blank and chewed her bubblegum like cud.

"Yes, like a price list."

"I'm sorry, ma'am, we don't have one of those. But I can tell you what we charge. Are you wantin' a haircut? Color? Highlights?" Her world-weary blue gaze and head-to-toe scan implied that Sydney needed all three, plus a new wardrobe and perhaps cosmetic surgery.

Sydney didn't really want anything, but she wanted to talk to Thelma Lynn. She noted that the two manicure tables were close to where the woman was sitting, and thought quickly of her ragged cuticles and scruffy nails. "How about a manicure?"

"That'd be twelve dollars, unless you're wanting a full set of tips."

"No, no, just a manicure, thanks."

"We have an appointment right now, if you want—Lindy can take you."

"Perfect." Now all she had to do was put Alex completely out of her mind and come up with some way to engage Thelma Lynn in conversation.

Sydney sat down across from Lindy, who was an obvious sweetheart. In her late forties, Lindy had soft dark hair, a wide, hot-pink smile and gentle, competent hands.

They chatted for a few minutes, especially about Syd's Northern accent, which meant explaining she was in town to visit her sister.

"The little blond gal that's gotten herself engaged to the Sonntag boy?" To Sydney's relief, Thelma Lynn joined the conversation without any prompting.

"Yes, that's my sister Julia." Sydney nodded and smiled. "I'm Sydney."

"I'm Thelma Lynn Grafton, and you tell Roman I'm expecting a wedding invitation."

Sydney blinked. *Well, all righty then.* "I'll do that."

"You and Julia sure don't look anything alike, now do you?"

Lindy raised a brow and looked up at Thelma Lynn from across the manicure table. Syd tried not to let the familiar comment hurt. God knew she was used to it by now.

"Uh, no. No, we don't. Julia looks a lot like my mother's sister, and they tell me I look like our great-grandmother on our father's side. She was French-Irish."

"And your other people?"

*My people? I don't currently own any, thank you.* "We're mostly Italian on our father's side, and—"

Thelma Lynn nodded, and a speck of her evil head-slime splatted onto her salon robe. "That would explain 'Spinelli.' " She pronounced their last name as if it were a foreign and particularly distasteful vegetable.

"—Scotch-English on our mother's side," finished Sydney.

"Roman's German," said Thelma Lynn, "like all the original founders of Fredericksburg." She ruminated for a moment, as if contemplating the fact that a combination of French-Irish, Italian, Scotch-English and German would make for a real nice Eurotrash baby.

But Sydney had her right on the very topic she wanted her on: Roman.

"So Roman's family has been here for a long time?" she asked.

"Hon, Roman's family practically founded the town. Old Ercel came over from Frankfurt with a bunch of laborers and the work ethic of ten men. He saw, he drilled, he conquered. Oil, that is." Thelma Lynn rubbed her nose with a scrawny, orange-tipped hand. "The Sonntags were rolling in bucks until recently, when the wells started to go dry."

*Oh, really?* Here was an interesting bit of information. The Sonntags were having money problems? And now Roman had suddenly picked the daughter of a motel magnate as his bride.

"When did the wells stop producing?" Sydney asked.

"From what I hear, it's been mostly in the last year or so. It was all hush-hush, but a few months back they sold some of Olga's fine antiques at one of them big auction houses. Now they're putting what they have left into this winemaking business. Sounds crazy to me, but you never know."

Lindy pushed back Sydney's cuticles with a strange tool and then began to buff her nails. "I got a bottle of their Chablis as a gift, and it was delicious," she said. "I don't know much about wine, but I know what tastes good." She brushed oil from a tiny bottle onto Sydney's cuticles, and told her to

147

go to the sink and wash her hands. "Then pick your color, sweetie."

Syd didn't feel very sweet at all as she thought about the fact that it took lots of money to launch a new business like a winery—money that the Sonntags didn't have, but Marv did. Was Julia Roman's collateral for a nice business loan?

The more Sydney thought about it, the more she was convinced: the linen pants and expensive shirt; the highbrow interest in wine and the tiny cell phone on which he was speaking to someone in Italy—forget the tool belt, this Roman guy had champagne tastes and needed an infusion of cash to support them. It didn't hurt that Julia was adorable and sexy and cheerful.

But how to confirm all of this and warn her sister before Roman hooked her? She needed to be able to show her proof. Suddenly Sydney thought of that honker of a diamond engagement ring, and how flawless and white it was for an antique. She thought of Thelma Lynn's words about the auction house. A horrid possibility occurred to her. What if . . . what if the stone wasn't real? She was almost ashamed of herself for wondering, but once the thought popped into her head, she couldn't banish it. How could she get the ring off her sister's hand in order to find out?

"What's gotten into you, Loverboy?" demanded Sam, Alex's favorite bartender at the Biergarten. "I haven't seen you kiss anyone like that since Spin the

Bottle in seventh grade, when we thought you'd swallow Kristi Snow's entire tongue." He laughed.

Oh, hell. Sam had been a witness to his impulsive behavior. Of course he'd just *had* to kiss Sydney in a public place, idiot that he was.

"Hi, Sam. Didn't see you come in for the shift change."

"So who is she?" Sam wiped down the bar with a clean towel and waggled his eyebrows like a wicked Groucho Marx. "I've never seen her before in my life, and I thought I knew every cute girl in town."

"She's an import," Alex said. He really didn't want to go into detail.

"An import." Sam began to restock the peanut bowls. "Well, that's descriptive."

"What d'you want me to say?"

"Well, for starters, she's a chick, not a Japanese car. Then there's the fact that she's not your usual well-endowed blonde. And finally, there's the hilarious twist that she just ran away from you, dude." Sam picked up the towel again and snapped it at Alex. "And I find that just . . . comical. Headline: Redhead runs from local Don Juan. What's that about? Was Kiki right, all those years ago, or is it your breath?"

Alex shot him the finger and laid some bills down to pay for their beer. "Guess I'm running low on animal magnetism today."

He ignored Sam's guffaw and headed for the door.

He looked up and down Main Street, only to find no trace of Sydney. He still wasn't sure why he'd kissed her, and it bothered him that he'd enjoyed it so much. She'd been first shocked, then tentative, then wondering—as if she'd never found pleasure in a kiss before. But once she'd started to enjoy it, her response had been volcanic.

Today Sydney'd smelled like his mother's favorite vanilla candles, chased by something floral. Was it her skin? Her hair? A perfume? Her scent had driven him crazy.

But what drove him crazier was that she'd run. What *was* that about? He wanted to find out.

Sydney Spinelli was a bundle of contradictions. She could obviously be a supreme pain in the ass— witness the hard time she was giving her sister. But her motivation seemed to be love and concern. She was also intelligent and funny. And she'd been so sweet and so warm with his mother.

She was aggressive both in her business thinking and in her desire to "fix" Julia's life, but had turned tail and run when he kissed her. He could have handled it if she'd slapped him—but nobody had ever run from him. Alex didn't really think of himself as a Don Juan, but since that brief Kiki-induced dry spell senior year, he'd certainly never lacked for a date. And not one but *two* women had actually proposed to him—one brazenly and one abashedly. He'd turned them both down.

Sydney's surprising vulnerability intrigued him, especially since she'd struck him as such a cynic.

Sydney returned to Marv's Motor Inn with clear polish on her short nails and a renewed sense of purpose. She hadn't gotten much more information out of Thelma Lynn, since the evil slime had to be rinsed out of her hair, revealing an even more terrifying shade of orange. But they'd parted with a vague date to have coffee sometime, so maybe she'd have another chance to pump her for information. Of course, Thelma Lynn's objective was the same—she wanted the inside scoop on Julia.

Syd said a tentative hello to her sister upon entering the motel. *Is she still mad at me for exposing her to the pregnancy rumor?*

Julia looked up from the computer. "Oh, hi, Sydney. Marv is looking for you—" She stopped. "What *is* that all over your face?"

"What do you mean?" Syd tried to see her reflection in the glass door, but the light wasn't cooperating.

"You've got some kind of rash or something around your mouth and on your chin."

"I do?" Puzzled, Sydney went around the corner to check in a large wall mirror. Sure enough, she looked like a kid with cherry Kool-Aid stains. *What is that?*

And then it dawned on her: whisker burn! Alex

had kissed her very thoroughly in the bar, and had left his mark on her. The rest of her face reddened, too, from mortification.

*I sat in the salon and had a manicure looking like this!* And nobody had said a word to her, probably out of politeness since they didn't know her well.

Julia followed her around the corner. "See what I mean? You know, that looks a lot like—"

"It's an allergic reaction," Sydney said quickly. "To, uh, this skin cleanser I tried."

Julia looked skeptical. "You only wash the lower half of your face?"

"Well, that's where I started, and then it burned, so I washed it off. I didn't realize it would get red like this."

Julia stared at her. "If I didn't know better, I'd say you've been making out with some guy."

"Don't be ridiculous. I'm not the man-eater that you are."

Julia put her hands on her hips. "Just because I've dated a few guys does not mean I'm a man-eater."

"True. You just chew on them for a little while before spitting them out. You've gone through dozens of them," Sydney reminded her, eager to move the topic of conversation away from her "rash."

"Roman's different! I swear it. I've never felt about anyone the way I feel about Roman." Julia's eyes shone and she grabbed Sydney's hand.

"Come on. I want to show you some of the dresses

I like. I'm thinking of ivory, instead of true white, with a full bell skirt and lots of petticoats. But I'm not completely sure, since I also loved that Narciso Rodriguez gown that Carolyn Bessette wore when she married JFK Jr. That's a whole different look: totally simple, body-hugging, very sexy and sophisticated.

"Of course, there's also the possibility of a really fun, short flapper dress with a dropped waist. So unusual and very chic. I'm thinking opera-length pearls for that, and a fabulous, accented sling-back sandal. Silver polish on my toes, in that scenario, since my ring is set in platinum . . ."

*Or so you think.* Sydney eyed the obscene rock on her sister's hand as she followed her to the reception desk, where Julia swept the invoices aside and replaced them with six different bridal magazines.

The emerald-cut stone sparkled madly under Marv's fluorescent lighting. Would a fake catch the light like that? Of course it would—cubic zirconia littered the country, and they were hard for even a jeweler to spot without a loupe.

How could she get the thing to a jeweler without Julia knowing? As her sister rattled on about fabrics and styles and designers and samples, Sydney briefly contemplated cat burglary. But Julia probably slept in the thing. She wouldn't be surprised if she showered in it, too. Hmmmm . . . that gave her an idea.

"So have you taken that ring off since you got it?" she asked, her voice teasing.

Julia looked sheepish. "No. Not once. I haven't wanted to—and to be frank, I'm afraid I'll lose it if I do. That mess with Somers taught me a lesson."

"It's probably covered in soap scum and hair spray," said Sydney. "Let me see."

Julia held out her hand and the ring for inspection.

"Oh, yeah—look at that. See, it's all cloudy on the sides. Do you want me to take it and have it cleaned for you?"

Julia gave her an odd look. "Syd, if you want to try it on, just say so. You don't have to come up with some elaborate scheme to clean it."

"I wasn't—"

Julia slipped the ring off her finger and dropped it into Sydney's palm. Sydney stared at it, heavy and winking in her hand.

*Nobody's ever offered me one of these, fake or not. I wonder if anyone ever will?* She pushed the thought away. She didn't want a tiny leash that meant she had to answer to some man. Who was she kidding?

All her married friends complained about their husbands: Donna's snored and left the toilet seat up; Cindy's was a scrooge with money and Lana's never did anything around the house. Who wanted a husband? She'd rather have Humphrey for company. Sydney hoped Marcella wasn't vacuuming him every single day.

"Go ahead and try it on," said Julia.

"No, no—that's okay. But it really does need cleaning." Sydney tilted it under the light.

Julia sighed. "Okay, fine. We'll go over to Jeep Collins on Main and see if they'll put it in their sonic cleaner thingy."

*Yes!* Sydney could have the jeweler there take a look at it while they had it in the back.

"Syd?" Julia said tentatively.

"Mmm?"

"Don't you worry. You'll meet the right guy some day soon."

Was it pride or defensiveness that sent the heat back into her cheeks? *You're one to talk, as the girl who's met the ultimate* wrong *guy.*

But she had the grace not to say it aloud. Sydney quickly returned the ring to her sister. "I'm not looking for Mr. Right. Not remotely. Marriage doesn't interest me at all—Marv and Ma provide enough dysfunction for one family."

"Just because Marv and Myrna have a warped 1950s marriage doesn't mean that we have to repeat the pattern, Syd. Don't you want kids someday?"

*Oh, sure, if I can hold a man's interest long enough to produce them.* Sydney shrugged. "I don't know. Right now I'm happy with my freedom. You can have the kids and I'll be the auntie who spoils them rotten." She smiled and changed the subject. "So show me these dresses you were talking about."

*  *  *

Jeep Collins displayed a treasure trove of beautiful baubles through huge plate glass windows and doors. Sydney couldn't imagine working in such a place—she'd never bring home a dime of any paycheck, and would end up selling her body for the pair of emerald and diamond dangle earrings she was currently drooling over.

Of course, selling her body required someone who wished to sample her meager charms, so maybe that wasn't a good option. Alex Kimball's face popped into her mind, but she knew very well he'd only been playing around. And she still couldn't figure out why—maybe just because she presented a challenge. He was probably seeing if he could get a rise out of her.

"Hi," she said to the saleslady, "I just spoke to someone on the phone about having my sister's ring cleaned."

The woman nodded, her eyes darting back and forth between Julia and Sydney. "Oh, yes, I remember."

Julia slipped off her diamond and held it out.

"My goodness, what a gorgeous stone! Yes, we'll clean this up for you right away. Would you like to see anything while you're waiting?"

The woman took the ring to a back room and gave it to an older gentleman. When she returned, Julia tried on a couple of bracelets and a pair of earrings that she thought might look fabulous with a wedding gown. She lingered over a dressy watch. She chuckled at an outsized cocktail ring that nobody but Elizabeth Taylor could carry off.

Sydney tore herself away from the emerald and diamond earrings and asked the saleslady if she could use the bathroom.

"Yes, of course. Come behind the counter, here, and go to that door in the back, hon. Then it's on the left-hand side."

"Thank you." Sydney did as she was directed and found herself in the working studio behind the retail space. The older gentleman looked up from his bench and fixed a kindly gaze on her. "Facilities are right there, ma'am."

Her heart beating faster and blood rushing to her face, Sydney said, "I actually came back here to ask you a favor. Could you possibly take a good look at that stone in my sister's ring? I think it might be a fake."

The gentleman's brows knitted and he stared at her. "Young lady, I know that ring very well. I've seen it dozens of times, on the hand of Olga Sonntag before she died. What you're suggesting is preposterous."

"I—I'm sorry," Syd told him. "I know you probably think I'm crazy, but please humor me. I need to know."

He shifted on his bench, which creaked, and just frowned at her. "Miz, uh, Spinelli, is it?"

This *was* a small town. They all knew her sister's name. She nodded.

"Miz Spinelli, the Sonntags are a very old, well-respected family around here. The ring has been handed down for generations. Your sister is an extremely lucky young lady, do you understand?"

*That remains to be seen.* Sydney said, "I'll be happy to pay you to do whatever testing you need to do."

"I'm telling you, I don't need to test that stone! I know the history of the thing. It came straight from Brussels with old Ercel's brother about a hundred years ago. Talk of the town, my grandfather said it was, when Ercel put it on his Helga's finger.

"After her death, it went to their son's fiancée, Olga—Robert's mother and Roman's grandmother. And she wore it 'til the day she died. She never offered it to Roman's mama, who was attached to her own ring from Robert anyway. So, young lady, that ring has been in a bank vault for years now, until young Roman signed it out."

*Uh-huh. And how easy would it have been for him to switch out the diamond for a nice CZ, using the proceeds to fund his vineyard?*

"That's a lovely story," Sydney told him. "And I realize that it's very unlikely that the stone is a copy. But please, will you just humor me?"

He pushed back from his bench with a creak and a grumble. "Does your sister know you're doing this?"

After a split second, Syd nodded. "Yes. She's the one who has doubts. You don't really think I'd have the gall to—" She coughed slightly and reddened under his piercing stare. These Texans weren't stupid, were they?

He limped a bit as he moved to the sonic cleaner which held the ring. "I'm going to take a look, Miz Spinelli, just to prove your suspicions are unfounded. As for your sister, I've never seen a girl more in love. So don't tell me any tales, hmmmm? You should be ashamed of yourself."

She gulped. "Yes, sir." And Sydney darted into the restroom, closing the door behind her with relief. She felt sick to her stomach.

She took her time, brushing her hair, applying some lip gloss, and patting the shine off her nose with a little powder. She was still stalling, reaching for a tube of hand lotion, when she heard the jeweler exclaim, "Well, I'll be a son of a gun."

She emerged quickly to find him staring at Julia's ring, an expression of disgust and surprise on his round, jowly face. He leaned both worn hands on the surface of his workbench, shaking his head.

Reluctantly he met Sydney's gaze. "I have never been more shocked than I am right now. This stone is a high-quality copy of the original."

# Chapter Thirteen

"So are you happy now? My ring is clean." Julia couldn't help admiring it in the sunlight and Sydney wanted to throw up. She'd achieved her objective: She now knew Roman Sonntag, Creep Extraordinaire, had given her sister a fake engagement ring. It confirmed her suspicions that he didn't love Julia, but just wanted access to her money and Marv's money.

But acting on the knowledge was a completely different ball game. Julia stared lovingly at the ring and tripped along blithely in her Claudia Ciuti sandals, the glowing picture of bliss.

How could Sydney pass along this information and explode her happiness? She felt like an ogre. True, she wanted Julia to reach her full potential and not lose herself in some man. But she didn't want to make her miserable—didn't want to see her break down in the tears of betrayal.

Anger began to rise in Sydney along with the nausea. She could kill Roman with her bare hands right at this moment. Choke him with that snooty silk tie of his, or with one of his precious grapevines. She could brain him with a bottle of his finest. Why should *she* be the one to hurt Julia, when he had orchestrated the whole catastrophe?

Her sister would go into total denial first. And then she'd hate Syd for being the messenger.

Syd's hands clenched into fists. No. Roman had popped the question. If she had to hold a gun to head, Roman, now, would take responsibility for bursting Julia's bubble. Sonntag would have the pleasure of explaining how and why he'd gotten down on one knee to give her a piece of glass, certainly an apt token of his "love." And he could explain his behavior to the entire town of Fredericksburg, too.

While Sydney dreaded making her sister cry, she now burned with the desire to confront Roman Sonntag.

"Sydney, what is wrong with you? The expression on your face is frightening." Julia waved a hand in front of her.

"What? Oh, nothing. I was just thinking about—" She cast about for something. She could hardly tell her sister that she was fantasizing about cutting off parts of her fiancé's body and force-feeding them to him, slowly.

"I was thinking about ways to market and distribute this Emulsion face cream that Alex Kimball's Aunt Susie makes. I'm going to put him in touch with Donna . . ."

Julia looked at her and laughed. "Syd, you never change. You've been in town now for what, three days? And you're already questioning my marriage, micromanaging my life to the point of making me clean my ring—and trying to run Alex and Ted's business. You are something else."

Stung, Sydney opened her mouth to refute her sister's words, but she couldn't. Honesty demanded that she acknowledge the truth. She closed her mouth.

"Syd, don't get offended. I know you're only doing it because you care."

"I *do* care, Julia. I'm not trying to come in and boss you around. I just want you to really think things through and make sure Roman is the right guy for you. Again, how do you know after only a month?"

Julia took a deep breath. "Syd, you just have to trust me. Roman and I click on so many different levels and we just *know* that it's right. I want to spend my life with him. He wants to spend his with me. That's all there is to it."

Syd bit her lip and twisted her ring. Her fingers had swollen with the heat, and the gold dug into her flesh. She forced herself to keep her tone mild. "Will you just consider delaying the actual wedding? You know, have a year-long engagement first. What's the rush?"

"Sydney, we are going forward with the wedding." Julia's smile was sweet and tolerant, but firm. "I'm telling you, I know what I'm doing."

*Yeah, just like a toddler knows what she's doing when she runs into traffic.*

Sydney sat on the horrid brown and mustard bedspread in her room, number 239, and put off confronting Roman by checking e-mail first.

To her surprise, there was a private one to her from Vivien, Julia's best friend.

Subject: Your little sister has gone crazy!
Date: XXXXXXX
From: vshelton
To: numbersgeek
    Sydney, I cannot tell you how concerned I am that Julia is marrying some cowpoke that she's only known a month. What is up? Have you met him? What's he like? Must fly. I have a deposition. Viv

*This electronic message transmission contains information from the law firm of Klein, Schmidt and Belker that may be confidential or privileged. The information is intended solely for the recipient and use by any other party is not authorized. If you are not the intended recipient, be aware that any copying, disclosure, distribution or use of the contents of this transmission is prohibited. If you have received this electronic transmission in error, please notify us immediately. Thank you.*

Sydney typed back immediately.

Subject: Re: Your little sister has gone crazy!
Date: XXXXXXX
From: numbersgeek
To: vshelton

Tell me about it! Yes, I've met him, and there's something fishy with the guy. What kind of Texan speaks Italian, wears designer clothes and has a vineyard??? And Viv, here's the really awful part: the ring he gave her is FAKE!!!!!!!!!!!!!! I think he's marrying her for the $$$. But I can't talk sense into her.

Syd

She closed down her computer and shut her laptop. She'd put this off long enough. Syd reached a shaking hand for the phone to dial Sonntag Vineyards. But it rang before she touched it, startling her.

"Sydney?" Alex's deep voice vibrated into her eardrum.

*Oh, shit.* What was she going to say to him? "Y-yes?"

"I just wanted to see if you were okay."

"I'm fine, Alex. Why wouldn't I be?"

"Well, you did leave Auslander's a little abruptly. I hope I didn't offend you."

"Oh, no, not at all." Sydney paused and then added, "I kiss strangers all the time in bars. Weekly, as a matter of fact. Sometimes biweekly."

"Is that so." Amusement tinged his tone.

"Yup." She waited a beat.

"So I'm just one of a crowd."

"Yup."

"But Sydney, I'm not really a stranger, am I?"

"You're definitely strange."

He chuckled. "Why?"

*Because guys like you don't go around kissing girls like me. You could be with a swimsuit model.* But she didn't say it.

"Sydney? Do you have plans for tomorrow night?"

Was he asking her out? *What is wrong with him?* She took refuge in sarcasm. "Actually, there's a formal ball here at the Motor Inn I have to attend."

"That's a shame, because I wanted to take you to dinner and then country-dancing at a place called Gruene Hall. Are you interested?"

"I can't dance."

"I'm going to teach you."

"No, I'm *really* bad." She turned her ring round and round, staring at the familiar, tiny scratches in the soft yellow gold.

"Sydney, can you walk? If you can walk, then you can do a little dance called the Texas Two-step. I promise. I'll pick you up around seven, okay?"

*Hey, wait a minute—I haven't even said yes.* Her mouth moved without her permission. "Okay," it said.

"See you then."

Sydney hung up the phone and stared at it. She had a date with Alex Kimball. She put a hand to her mouth and felt the still-sensitive area around her lips. She hoped he wouldn't kiss her again. Then she hoped he would.

Roman had an uncanny sense of timing, the jerk. Because when she got up the nerve to call the vineyard again, an older gentleman told her that he was out of town on business. Could he take a message?

Sydney thought about it. *Yes, please. Would you tell him that I'm going to personally come out there and put his body through that crusher/de-stemmer thing? That he is never going to get his hands on my sister's money?*

"Is he reachable by cell phone, and do you have that number?"

"Who's calling, please?"

No, she wasn't going to discuss this with the creep over a cell phone while he sat in some bar or café or limo. She needed to get in his face. "Uh, never mind. I'll just call him when he returns. When *is* he returning?" She supposed she could ask Julia, but she didn't want to arouse her suspicions.

Roman, the older gentleman informed her, would be back in just a couple of days. He'd be more than happy to take her name and number . . .

"That's all right. Thank you." Sydney hung up and reflected ruefully that now she really did need to call Marv. She just had to think of a good story—not her forte.

"Yeah?" he barked when he answered the phone. "Syddie, where da hell are you?"

"I'm in New Mexico. Santa Fe, to be exact."

"What da hell you doin' there?"

"Tracing Betty Lou."

"She take my money to some spa there, or what?"

"Well, she's been here. But now she's gone, apparently headed west. Maybe Vegas." *Yeah, stick close to the truth, Syd.* And the truth was that Betty Lou had checked into the Bellagio shortly after she'd disappeared. There were receipts from a tacky boutique, Sparkles, that indicated she'd bought three different evening gowns, and other receipts from an upscale beauty salon. It didn't take a rocket scientist to surmise that Marv wasn't ever going to see his money again—but Sydney didn't quite know how to tell him that. She'd turned expert at keeping ugly secrets these days, that was for sure.

*"Vegas!"* Marv screamed. The decibel level was enough to not only shatter her eardrums, but also to blow her eyeballs through the top of her skull at Mach 2.

*Well, I may as well prepare him.*

"You find her and you keep her outta the casinos, Syddie!"

"I'll do my best."

"You sure she hasn't been in Vegas all this time already?"

"I think she came out here to Santa Fe to visit her sister," said Sydney. *This story's kind of in reverse order, but I really don't want to go into that with you right now.*

"Drive, Syd, drive. Stay at Number Thirty-seven and Number Forty-six along the road. Keep those expenses down, you hear?"

"I hear. Are you sure you don't want to bring the police into this?"

*"No police.* Nobody poking through our books. Nobody but you."

*I am so washing my hands of the family business, before I end up in jail.* "Marv? You know I don't like to hear you talk like that. And if I find more bogus or duplicate receipts, that's it. I'm gone."

"Syd, sweetheart. Call me Pop, can't you? You're my little girl."

*No, I'm your little patsy.* "Marv," she said pointedly, "I will not play that kind of ball. I will straighten out Betty Lou's stuff, but after that you need to keep everything legit, hire somebody competent—an accounting degree would be a plus—and actually pay some benefits."

"Damn cell phones," Marv said. "You're breaking up. You find her, Syddie, and my money. And stick with the cafeterias, doll. No fancy restaurants."

"Am I allowed to buy gas?" she asked. "Or should I siphon it from parked cars?"

"Not a bad idea," said her pop. "Talk at ya later."

Sydney found herself wondering if her own mother's ring was fake.

# Chapter Fourteen

Sydney stared into the mirror the next evening and yanked her hair out of its ponytail for the third time. She should never have agreed to a real date with Alex Kimball.

Did leaving her hair loose only accentuate her long, narrow face? Or did it look more feminine that way, more appropriate for a date? Should she follow the when-in-Rome theory and try to spray and tease it into Big Hair?

For the ten thousand and three-hundred-thirty-ninth time in her life, she despaired over her nose, which she'd inherited from Grandpa Spinelli. Unlike Julia's adorable button, she'd gotten what she thought of as a long, Sicilian honker, and it made her look like a worried anteater. Her eyes weren't bad, a nice shade of hazel that tended toward brown, but her lips were too thin—she'd never have the plump, pretty pout that Ma and Julia had gotten from Grandma MacLaren. They'd also, quite unfairly, gotten her breasts, while Syd had been cursed with Grandma Spinelli's, and often could get away with no bra.

When she'd despaired over her body as a teenager, Ma had told her she had the build of a racehorse or a greyhound. Sydney felt more like a particularly awkward giraffe, devoid of anything resembling a curve.

What to do with her hair? What to wear? How to behave?

She was at the point of just crawling under the bed and standing Alex up when there was a knock on her door. She opened it to find Julia, lugging a pile of clothes, a makeup bag, and some kind of round, electric brush.

"I know you're going out with Alex," Julia said. "And I know you're standing in here trying to figure out what to wear."

"Alex who?" said Sydney, making a face. "And how do you know, anyway?"

"Roman told me before he left on his business trip. I'm going to help you look gorgeous, as long as you promise to come and sample wedding cakes with me."

Syd wrinkled her nose. "But I hate white cake. And you're going to make me taste nineteen or twenty, at least. Ugh."

"Do you want my help or not?"

171

Syd shifted from foot to foot. "Why would I care what I look like?"

Julia just shot her a look.

"Okay, okay. But it's just like you, Marie Antoinette, to tell me to eat cake. If it's gross, then off with your head."

Julia laughed, dumped everything in the middle of the bed and ignored her while holding various tops under her chin.

"Those are just fabric samples, right?" Syd asked. "Because none of them are actually big enough to cover a human torso."

Julia selected one about the size of a pocket hankie in a wild abstract print of greens, blues and creams. "Take off that rag," she instructed.

"Rag? This is a nice cotton top," Syd protested.

"Yes, if you're cleaning house. Take it off. You're going to wear this silk Pucci halter."

"Halters are slutty," Syd protested, "and I don't want to look poochy."

"Pucci the designer, Clueless One. Now put it on. It's not slutty, it's sexy."

"Maybe in Brazil. How am I going to wear a bra with that?"

"You're not. Now stop arguing."

Sydney sighed and obediently stepped into it, even though she wasn't used to taking orders from her sister. The silk felt wonderful against her bare skin, and the ends of the bow at her nape tickled between her shoulder blades.

But she shook her head at the *very* small jeans Julia seemed to want her to wear—fancy boot cut jeans with leather lacing along the thighs. "You're two sizes smaller than me. There's no way I can get into those, and they'll be too short."

"I wear them with five-inch platform sandals. We're going to put you in little kitten heels. And they're half spandex, so they'll stretch."

"Julia, those are bondage jeans! I can't possibly wear those."

"The idea isn't bondage, it's just a hint of easy access. It makes men drool on their shoes. Now come on." She shook them.

"Nooooo," whined Sydney. What had gotten into her sweet, malleable sister?

"Yes. You can show up here and order me around, insult my decision-making abilities and treat me like a twit. But you cannot question my fashion sense. Now get over here, young lady."

Sydney stared at her. "Yes, Miss Julia." She took the jeans and slid one leg into them, then the other. "I do not treat you like a twit."

"We can have this discussion later, okay? Now pull up those pants and stop waving your fanny around."

Sydney hauled the things up her thighs, eyeing the

173

leather lacing. "I feel like I'm putting on a wet suit," she moaned.

"Excellent. Now tie that leather thingy at the waist and let me see. Oh, yeah. He's going to be gnawing on his knuckles all night. That is for sure."

Sydney slunk into the bathroom to check out her new slut persona in the ugly Motor Inn builder's mirror.

"There's only one thing," Julia said behind her. "The panties have got to go. And those are really ugly, anyway—haven't you heard of Victoria's Secret?"

"I'm not going on a date without underwear!"

"Did you bring a thong with you?" Julia sighed. "No, never mind. I'm sure you don't even own one—"

"I do, too!"

"—so it's commando for you."

Sydney's mouth worked. "No."

In a voice appropriate for reasoning with a two-year-old, Julia asked, "Why not?"

"It's not . . . nice."

"Since when have you prized being nice, Ms. Tact?"

"That's different."

"Look. It's not like you're going to sleep with the guy, right?"

"Of course not. I barely know him!" But the thought of sleeping with Alex sent a hum through her body.

"Well, then he'll never know whether you have panties on or not. So what do you care?"

"*I'll* know."

"Yep. And it'll make you feel sexy." Julia grinned. "Very empowering. You should try it sometime."

"I never knew you were such a little vixen."

"Live a little, Syd. There's more to life than numbers." Julia folded her arms and leaned forward, her eyes dancing. "I double-dog-dare you to take off those panties, so nothing comes between you and your Cavallis."

"But they're *your* Cavallis. Ick."

"I don't want them back. I have two other pairs." Julia shut the door on her.

Sydney grimaced into the mirror. *Live a little*. With a sigh, she peeled off the jeans, shimmied out of her panties, and struggled back into the jeans again. She felt . . . weird. But it was kind of fun. Like she had a secret that nobody else knew about.

She turned around and checked out her rear view. Oh. My. God. These Cavalli things were painted on! But there was something amazing about the cut of them: They fit her like a glove without looking trashy.

Sydney opened the door. "Julia, I don't even want to know how much you paid for this pair of jeans, but they might have been worth it."

Julia nodded. "I know. Boy, I'm going to miss my

Nordstrom discount, though. Now, let's work on your makeup and hair. No grumbling."

By the time Julia was finished, Sydney almost didn't recognize herself. She had creamy, model-perfect skin and no freckles, thanks to some miracle in a bottle. On her mouth played a full, mauve, shimmery smile, her eyes were dark and mysterious, and even her nose looked smaller and more regal.

Julia even outfitted her with blue topaz dangle earrings and a matching bracelet. She used the electric round brush to turn Sydney's hair under at the ends.

The only issue was her shoes. Even Julia's open-toed mules were too small, and Sydney couldn't wear either her own brown sling-backs or her hiking boots. Julia thought for a moment and then made a phone call.

"Hi, Mrs. Sonntag, it's Julia," she said. "Fine, thanks. Uh-huh. So my sister has a hot date—"

Sydney made a noise of protest.

"—a hot date with Alex Kimball, and we have no shoes that work. Kiki e-mailed me that she's a nine, right? Wonderful. Is there anything in her closet we can borrow? Anything she might have left behind? I need a sandal with a low heel in silver or cream. If there's nothing like that, then a cowboy boot."

"Julia! I can't borrow the shoes of some woman we've never met!"

"Thank you so much. Yes, I'll be right over." Julia hung up and turned to Sydney. "Yes, you can. Mrs.

Sonntag said it was fine. Just don't step in any cow patties." She smiled.

Syd groaned. "Alex described Kiki as 'hell on heels.' What if she finds out I raided her closet and puts out a hit on me?"

"Kiki's not violent. She's just spoiled and high maintenance from what Roman says. She has a good heart."

"And she's got to be gorgeous—she's a soap star and she was runner-up to Miss America in 1995! Even worse, she used to date Alex in high school. Not that I really care," Sydney added hastily. "He's just taking me out because he's bored."

Julia walked over to Sydney and put her hands on her shoulders. "He is *not* taking you out because he's bored. Sydney, look in the mirror. Can't you see how pretty you are?"

"Ha," said Syd. "Yeah, that's why you're here doing an entire overhaul on me."

"Don't be a butt-head—if you didn't have the goods, I couldn't polish them."

Syd stuck her chin out. "But I'm talented at being a butt-head. It's one of my best personality features."

Julia rolled her eyes and put her hands to her temples. "I don't know what to say to convince you. It's impossible."

Her "diamond" flashed fire and Sydney averted her gaze from it. How could she possibly ruin her sister's happiness—and especially when she was being so nice to her? But how could she *not* tell her something this important?

Only a complete *jerk* would give his fiancée a fake ring. Syd couldn't let her marry him. And she'd bet Julia wasn't planning on signing a prenup.

Tomorrow. She would solve this problem tomorrow. And maybe she'd call Vivien. It never hurt to be armed with legal information.

For tonight, she'd pretend this was a real date and that Alex Kimball was actually interested in her, was even attracted to her. For tonight she'd pretend she was a fabulously sexy party girl, somebody like . . . Julia.

Alex hummed as he buttoned a white oxford shirt and tucked it into a pair of well-worn Wranglers. He added a Western-style belt and tugged on his boots. Though he never wore hats, he figured he looked pretty damned Texan for his date with the Jersey Girl.

He headed for the kitchen to say goodbye to his mother, who was snipping fresh parsley into a marinara sauce. "Now remember, Alex, you can't behave like a bachelor anymore."

He blinked. "Pardon?"

"You've got a wife, a family and a dog and they all need you, darlin'."

*I do? They do?* Alex tried to absorb the information. Who had he married? How many kids had Mama

178

bestowed upon him? Boys? Girls? A couple of each? And what kind of dog?

"So you can't be staying out until all hours and coming home drunk," his mother continued. "Nell won't put up with it."

Nell, aka Sydney. His mother had them married off! He was tempted to ask her about the wedding, but he didn't want to be late.

"I know, Mama," he said, in reassuring tones. "I won't be out too long."

"She's a good woman, that Nell." His mother waved the scissors at him, and Alex was uncomfortably reminded of the time she'd waved a knife at him. "And I like her, so you treat her well."

"Absolutely, Mama."

"Bring her flowers for no reason, and always compliment her dinners, even though they're not as good as mine. And massage her feet every once in a while. She'll love you forever."

"I'll keep that in mind," Alex told her, trying to hold a straight face. Keeping his eye carefully on the scissors, he kissed her cheek. "Dad?" he called. "I'm leaving now."

His father's voice rumbled back at him from the home office, and Alex closed the door behind him.

A welcome evening breeze fanned his face as he walked to the detached four-car garage. He'd take the Chevy pickup to round out the Texas atmosphere of the date. Cherry red and late model, it would look

179

just right parked outside the Gristmill and Gruene Hall tonight.

Inside the garage hung the old familiar pegs with jackets, parkas and hats that had been around since he and Jake were kids. There was the sweat-stained John Deere ball cap that his dad wore while cutting the lawn, and the goofy straw hat he wore fishing, and a golf hat. His father, like Alex, didn't own a cowboy hat, but he'd given a cream one to Mama one Christmas on a whim. Alex stood gazing at it for a long time, remembering the year she'd opened it and laughed and exclaimed. She'd put it on immediately and tilted it at an angle so she could kiss his dad. She'd looked good in it, even though she'd worn the hat with plaid flannel pajamas and terry-cloth slippers.

Alex picked it up and gently shook the dust off it. Then he opened the truck's passenger door and set it on the seat. Sydney should wear it tonight. She didn't seem to have her sister's flair for fashion—not that he cared—so he'd bring her an appropriate accessory.

He thought about Sydney as he drove the short distance to Marv's Motor Inn. "I kiss strangers in bars all the time," she'd said. *That dog won't hunt, sweetheart. I know a lie when I hear one.* But his lips quirked at the bravado of the statement. Sydney might not get out from behind her computer much, but she'd be damned if she'd admit it to the likes of him.

He wondered what she saw when she looked at him. Did she write him off as untrustworthy because he was a friend of Roman's and therefore the enemy? Was that why she'd run from him in the bar?

He decided it was the only explanation, since he'd clearly felt her attraction to him. So in order to convince her that *he* was okay, he'd have to convince her that Roman was okay—which he wanted to do anyway so she'd stop trying to interfere with the engagement. But now he had a little extra incentive.

Sydney made him laugh, and due to the situation with Mama, he hadn't felt much like laughing lately. What had she said, that she had a formal ball to attend at the Motor Inn tonight? Cheeky little thing.

Alex pulled up outside the squat brown and mustard building, which looked even more déclassé in the fading light. Sydney and her sister Julia didn't belong in a building like that. He quirked a brow at the familiar COUNT SHEEP FOR CHEAP tagline and headed inside.

Julia wasn't at the front desk. Old Abe Santos's pimply teenaged son greeted him instead, and called Sydney's room with a hastily repressed smirk. "Uh, Miz Spinelli'll be right down."

"Thanks, Hector," Alex said. After the obligatory "How's school" and "How's your dad" questions, he stared absently out the glass door, focused on nothing in particular.

"Hi, Alex."

He turned at the sound of Sydney's voice and the words in his mouth evaporated. She looked like garnished sin on a platter.

He hadn't seen her in anything formfitting until now. She wore the skimpiest of halter tops and absolutely no bra that he could discern—and he considered himself an expert at bra discernment. Someone had obviously sprayed on her jeans, because not a wrinkle or bulge of fabric marred the delicious long lines of her hips, thighs or calves. Leather lacing suggested that he could spring her from the denim at a moment's notice and tie her up if they were feeling kinky. And upon closer inspection, he didn't see even a tenth of a millimeter's room for panties. He felt sweat droplets form on his brow.

That dark red hair tumbled over her gorgeous bare shoulders, her lips looked wet and shiny and her cinnamon eyes were huge and alluring. They tried hard to be mysterious, too, but she was so nervous that she blinked approximately every two seconds. And it was that naked anxiety that reached out and tweaked his heart more than anything. She hummed with it.

Of course, she didn't know he saw it. But he noted that when she licked her lips it was for function, not provocation. And when she straightened her shoulders, thrust them back and lifted her chin, she did so as if remembering instructions, not to show off her breasts. And when she walked forward in the pair of cowboy boots she'd acquired and swung her hips like a pole-dancer, he discerned that the issue was the novelty of the boots and not sensuality.

The Difficult Sister looked a helluva lot easier than she had yesterday—he was sure those lace-up jeans were illegal in a lot of states. And she'd done it on purpose for him. For some reason he was touched. Of course other women had taken pains to look nice for him. But this was different, out of character.

Alex shut his mouth, which he'd left hanging open, and instructed Hector to do the same. "No drooling over my date, son."

Sydney, overhearing this, ruined her new diva persona by snorting. Then, perhaps remembering what he'd done after the last snort, her eyes flew to his and she blushed adorably.

Alex took her hand and set his mother's hat on her head. "I thought this might complete your outfit," he said.

She put a hand up to the hat. "Thank you."

"You look so beautiful." He stared at her.

Sydney flapped a hand at him. "You don't have to go overboard, Kimball," she hissed. "We both know this is a mercy date."

*Mercy date? Mercy date, my ass!* Alex, stunned, just stared at her before shaking his head. He glanced at

Hector, who'd had to take a call. Then he tugged her out the door so they could finish this without an audience.

"Sydney, honey, I don't know where you got that idea, but there's absolutely no truth to it. We are going out, you and me, because I think you're *hot*— and funny and smart, too. Not to mention kind and generous."

She looked uncomfortable and pulled her hand out of his so she could flap it again. "Look, I didn't say that for reassurance—"

*The hell you didn't. But it would kill you to acknowledge it.*

"—I'm just stating the facts. I'm not some beauty queen or calendar girl and everyone knows it. And I don't want you to tell me things just to make me feel better. That's happened all my life, ever since—" She stopped.

He didn't really have much trouble filling in the blank. *Ever since Julia was born.* But she wouldn't say it aloud, and he couldn't blame her.

It was one thing to admit to yourself that you were jealous of your sister. It was quite different to admit it to another person. Sydney Spinelli, Caretaker and Fixer, needed some care herself. And maybe some fixing, too. He knew just the man to do it.

# Chapter Fifteen

*I should never have let Julia talk me into wearing these clothes.* Sydney felt a blush burning up her neck and exploding into her cheeks as Alex opened the door of a red pickup—did the man ever drive the same car?—and stood behind her, seeming transfixed, as she climbed in.

*He can see! Oh, God, he can tell that I'm not wearing panties. I'm going to die of utter mortification.* Sydney refused to look at him as he shut her door. She folded her hands primly in her lap as he walked around the hood of the truck and got in himself.

"Are you too warm?" he asked.

*Oh, you could say that.*

"Because you look kind of flushed. Here, let me crank up the air-conditioning." Alex started the engine. For the first time, she noticed, his whole brow was damp, and she wondered if he was hungover or ill. The AC was just as much for his benefit as hers.

185

She prayed for it to kick in fast. Just the walk to the car and his obvious scrutiny of her backside had caused her to perspire enough to dampen her jeans, which meant they had to be even more revealing— if possible—than before.

Air-conditioning used Freon, right? And she'd heard that stuff was poisonous to cats. Maybe that was true for humans, too, and she could put a straw through the vent while he wasn't looking . . .

"Is that better?"

She nodded, not trusting her voice. *Or maybe I can hurl myself out onto the highway once we get moving.*

"Sydney?"

*No—then I'd end up in the emergency room with no panties, and what would Ma say about that?* "Yeah?"

"Why are you looking suicidal? Is it that much of a chore to go out with me?"

"I'm not sui— I just feel weird. That's all."

"Is it a good weird or a bad weird?"

She glanced at him. "I don't know. I guess I just feel like I'm not . . . me, right now. These clothes are my sister's."

"And the boots are Kiki's." Alex laughed at her horrified expression.

"Oh, God. You can just turn the truck around, now, and take me back. It was bad enough for *me* to know that I was wearing your ex-girlfriend's boots."

"You look great in them. Better than she did."

"Yeah, right."

"I'm serious. Kiki was never much into the whole Western-wear thing. She's high fashion, all the way. Shit-kicker boots were not her style. But they suit you."

"Uh-huh. They go great with my Northern accent. Alex, take me back to the Motor Inn."

"Nope. You've officially been kidnapped at this point. I'm holding you hostage until you learn the two-step."

"Alex!"

"Relax, Jersey. It won't hurt a bit. You cannot show up looking this edible and then blow me off. You got a hot date with ninety-pound Hector, back there?"

She had to laugh at that. "No, I already did him in the supply closet." Her answer got her a flash of white teeth.

"That's my girl." He reached over, slung an arm around her shoulders, and hauled her closer to him, looking impossibly gorgeous.

The concept of being Alex's girl was heady. Just for tonight, she'd live that little fantasy. His arm was heavy and solidly muscled, turning her on and making her feel safe at the same time. It was also warm, and his bare skin against her own felt heavenly, awakening every nerve ending she had.

His eyes glinted at her from behind a pair of Maui Jims and he said, "I love the way you look right now, but I do miss the freckles."

She put a hand up to her nose. "You're kidding, right?"

He shook his head. "No. I like them. I had freckles when I was a kid, and Mama used to tell me they were kisses from butterflies and ladybugs."

She smiled, delighted. "How is your mother today?"

Alex lowered his sunglasses and looked at her over the tops of them, eyebrows waggling. "She's great. She's decided that you and I are married, with kids and dogs."

Her breath caught in her throat, and she had a sudden image of them romping on a beach together with a dark-haired little girl and a carrot-topped little boy, playing Frisbee with a couple of golden retrievers who'd buried the suntan oil.

"Isn't that a hoot? She told me to treat you right and always compliment your cooking."

Sydney forced herself to laugh. "That's a pretty tall order, considering that I have to read directions to even boil water."

"What do you eat when you're all by yourself up in Jersey?"

"A lot of takeout. Why, do you cook?"

"Every night, when I'm at my condo in San Antone."

"You don't live here?"

He shook his head. "No. I just drive over a lot to be with—and to help with—Mama. My dad's got a weak heart, my younger brother's got his head up his ass, and I try to anchor things a little bit. It's the computer and cell phone age—it's not too hard for me to do.''

Sydney found herself swallowing a lump in her throat. She hesitated, but said it anyway. "It's going to get harder, Alex. Things . . . the stages . . . of early-onset Alzheimer's can go really fast."

He exhibited no reaction whatsoever, but his foot depressed the gas pedal and their speed increased.

"You're going to have to think ahead. About maybe a facility with trained staff—"

"No."

"—or the possibility of bringing someone in to care for her."

"No." He stiffened and removed his arm from her shoulders. She wasn't sure if she shivered at the finality in his voice, at the abruptness of his withdrawal, or at the sudden loss of his warmth.

While she knew she was right, she also knew that the time was not. If they were going to enjoy the evening, she needed to change the subject fast. "So where are you taking me?"

"The Gristmill. It's on the banks of the Guadalupe River. You'll like it."

"What kind of food? Let me guess: deep-fried roadkill on a bed of pinto beans?"

"Filets of armadillo stuffed with ground emu. Boiled possum with sauerkraut. Aged, marinated quarter horse with peach chutney. Will that work for ya, Jersey?"

"You bet. Tequila shooters on the side?"

"Now you're talking."

They drove in companionable silence for a few miles. Sydney wiggled her toes inside Kiki's boots and wondered what it was like to be a runner-up to Miss America. She wondered what Julia and Kiki would think of each other. And then she reminded herself that they'd probably never get the chance to meet, because once she let the cat out of the bag regarding the fake engagement ring, everything between Roman and Julia would be over.

The thought didn't bring her nearly as much pleasure as it should have, though, because she kept worrying about Julia's inevitable devastation and how she didn't want to be the author of it. Was there any way around it?

*Short of just not telling her, no.* And Syd couldn't in good conscience not give her the information, whether it came out of her mouth or Roman's.

*But you're lying to Marv,* said that good conscience. *You could just as easily mind your own business and pretend not to know about the ring. Let Julia make her own mistake—live her own life.*

But wasn't that irresponsible? An act of betrayal? And she wasn't really lying to Marv—she was just delaying having to tell him the truth, so that she could buy some time with her sister.

What if she did let Julia marry the creep, and learn her own lesson, but made sure her friend Vivien forced her to sign a prenup so that no lasting harm was done? Julia would get her big wedding, discover that marriage was no fairy tale, learn her lesson—but keep her money. And Roman would learn his lesson too—that he shouldn't have tried to marry a bank account. She, Sydney, could feel smug and . . . no. She, Sydney, was trying to get out of her position between a rock and a hard place.

She had a moral responsibility to tell Julia what she knew, whether or not her sister hated her for it and blamed her for destroying her happiness.

"You're looking suicidal again," said Alex. "That's not the expression of a happy date. I'm about to get downright insulted, here."

"Sorry. I've just got a lot on my mind."

"Want to share?"

She shook her head. *Yes, let me tell you what a low-down, belly-dragging snake your best friend is. Unless you already know that and you're in on it?* No. Alex was a decent guy. A guy who spent half his time with his parents because they needed him.

"Okay, then I'll just have to distract you." He stopped, an odd but fleeting expression crossing his handsome features. "It'll be my pleasure."

They turned off the highway and into the little town of Gruene, located about forty-five miles from San Antonio and very close to New Braunfels.

Gruene, like Fredericksburg, had been settled by German immigrants in the 1850s and was full of historic charm. Nestled on the Guadalupe River, the Gristmill Restaurant was built on the remains of the old Gruene cotton gin, and the facade could have been a set in a classic spaghetti Western. Sydney half expected to see Clint Eastwood emerge with the cast of *The Good, the Bad and the Ugly*.

Alex pulled into the parking lot, got out and opened her door. Syd was now going to have to walk several hundred feet in her painted-on, borrowed Cavalli jeans. She slid off the pickup's seat and out onto the gravel, firmly resisting the urge to tweak the denim out of her crack, even though it felt firmly lodged as high as her shoulder blades.

Chin up, she stepped out in Kiki Sonntag's cowboy boots and tried to enjoy Alex's mesmerized expression. She even tossed her hair—almost spraining her neck in the process, since she wasn't accustomed to it.

She'd be dancing a long mile in Kiki's boots. She winced, wondering if the beauty queen had ever worn them while putting those alleged claw marks on Alex's back. *Okay, don't go there. What does it matter anyway? This isn't a real date.*

Syd focused instead on the big rusty sign proclaiming the name of the restaurant. Underneath it sat whiskey barrels planted with impatiens in every possible color. A flagstone path led to the entrance, which was flooded with people.

The Gristmill was not a quiet eatery, but it had charm in spades. Inside, the flooring consisted of wide, polished wooden planks and the walls were a combination of cedar, stone and glass. Outside, wooden tables dotted the spacious grounds and the old paddle wheel that had once generated power for the gin was still running, courtesy of the cool, mossy green Guadalupe.

Alex requested the River Room, where they got a spot overlooking the water below. It was like sitting in an oversized tree house, and Sydney was charmed. Until, that is, she felt eyes on her back and looked around to see a giant longhorn glaring at her from the mantel of the enormous Lone Star fireplace. What was it with these Texans and their need to decorate with dead animals?

Alex noticed her shudder and laughed. "That's Lupe, Jersey. He's the king of the castle."

"That *was* Lupe," she said. Lupe the Longhorn? Nice. Lupe did not seem pleased with his perch, or the hundreds of customers below. He presided over everything with a bored, sardonic expression. He obviously needed a brewsky.

"Look, he's got your coloring. Lots of ginger on his neck."

"The similarities end there, Kimball. Last time I checked I didn't have horns or a tail."

Alex started to say something, his eyes dancing,

193

and then apparently thought better of it. Probably that Lupe and his horns had butted in anywhere he'd wanted, just like her.

She fought against the idea. She was not here to interfere for fun, as he'd accused her at the vineyard. She was here to protect her sister. There was a big difference.

He ordered frozen margaritas, no doubt to get her liquored up for learning the two-step. They arrived in gigantic, frosty beer mugs, and Sydney decided she liked the fact that everything was oversized in Texas. She started to make serious inroads into her 'rita, savoring the fresh lime and tequila. They didn't make them like this in New Jersey.

After looking at the menu, she asked in dry tones, "What, exactly, is chicken-fried steak?"

"You've never had chicken-fried steak? You've gotta be kiddin' me. Great stuff: comes with a beak and tail feathers on the side." He laughed at her expression. "It's country-fried steak, Jersey. Served with their famous white cream gravy."

He ordered a T-bone himself, while she decided to risk the artery-clogging white gravy and the fictitious beak. Alex also insisted that she try some Texas Torpedoes: deep-fried jalapeño peppers stuffed with cream cheese. The Cavalli jeans were definitely going to pop off her, revealing her panty-free state to the entire patio grove below. Sydney wondered if she could loosen the leather lacing before she had to dance in them.

Once the waitress had taken their order, Alex raised his margarita glass to her. "To our first date."

*And no doubt our last.* But she clinked her mug against his and drank.

"Which is not, by the way, a mercy date. You're a beautiful woman, Sydney. But more important, you're a fascinating one."

"Hey, don't forget about my cute knees, you professional flirt."

Alex leaned back and folded his arms. Dark hair emerged from the rolled cuffs of his shirt, and she wondered if he had much more on that broad Texas chest of his. "Jersey, I'm beginning to think you have a very low opinion of me."

"Whatever gave you that idea?"

"That sweet mouth of yours. The one that just won't quit." He stared at it, bringing heat to her cheeks again. "You're all about autumn, honey. Looks like God rolled you in warm milk and dipped you in cinnamon."

"You sure it wasn't cayenne?"

"Shhhhh." He actually reached across the table and put his finger gently on her lips. The gesture was bold and possessive and should have annoyed her. Instead it switched on a glow deep inside her.

Alex didn't seem self-conscious about it at all. He

trailed the finger down so it rested only on her bottom lip. "I have a challenge for you, Sydney. You have to listen to five compliments in a row without saying a word or deflecting them in any way."

"And what happens if I meet the challenge?" she said against his finger.

A slow smile spread across his face, rode like a bandito through all the five o'clock shadow. "Why, you get a reward." His voice was sex-drenched.

A tremor ran through her. "And if I don't?"

"Then we start all over again until you do." He trailed his finger from her lip to her chin, tracing the contours there before dropping underneath, making the lightest of figure eights against the sensitive skin of her throat. Then he was in the hollow, at her clavicles, and back up to her chin, which he took in his hand.

Her breathing had quickened, and every centimeter of skin he'd touched felt awakened, bathed in strong spirits. This guy was no mere professional flirt. He was a master manipulator. But she couldn't make herself care.

He withdrew his hand as the waitress approached with a platter of Texas Torpedoes, effectively separating them. She blinked at jalapeños and wondered how to get out of eating one, but she didn't have a chance. Alex plucked one and, after making sure it wasn't going to burn her, held it to her lips.

She grimaced and looked down at it dubiously.

"Jersey, you still look cute cross-eyed, but if you're not careful they'll stick like that."

Her eyes flew to his amused ones as he rubbed her lips with the hot pepper. Slowly she opened her mouth to take it in, then bit down. His pupils widened and darkened as she licked her lips, savoring the spiciness against the creamy filling. It tasted surprisingly good, and not as hot as she'd feared. But there was enough heat to make her reach for her margarita in short order, and she drained a third of it. Tequila and triple sec began to hum through her veins.

She looked around at the casual, boisterous crowd and felt herself relaxing, amused that even in jeans and cowboy boots, she was one of the dressier women there. The Pucci silk halter and dangling earrings set her apart, but nobody seemed to notice or care. She stopped obsessing about the fact that she wore not a stitch of underwear.

After signaling for two more margaritas, Alex bit the tip of one of the jalapeños and eyed her lazily. "Are you ready to meet the challenge?"

"I can't. You know I'm going to talk back." Sydney blushed and twisted her ring.

"You'll talk back to your own damn pallbearers, Spinelli. 'Hey, you on the front left corner! Higher, please. And you in the middle, pick up the pace— you're jolting me, damn it.' "

"I will not!"

"Bet me. It's one of the things about you I find irresistible."

"You're calling me a nag and irresistible in the same sentence?"

"I never said you were a nag. That's a demerit, Jersey. No extrapolating insults out of my compliments. See, we've got to start over."

Sydney rolled her eyes and finished off her 'rita. The waitress appeared conveniently, whisked away their empties and supplied them with new drinks.

"Your coloring and your brisk personality," Alex said, "remind me of October. Pumpkin pie with vanilla ice cream. French toast with butter and maple syrup. Red orange foliage, just touched by frost in the early morning. And good brandy in a crystal snifter, warmed by the palm of my hand."

His voice low and mesmerizing, he managed to say all of these things without being cheesy—how, she didn't quite know. She was still stuck on that last phrase: warmed by the palm of his hand. She could think of several parts of her that would greatly enjoy being warmed by his palms. She squirmed and reached for more tequila.

"What, no smart-ass comment? Are you falling asleep on me?" She shook her head. "Okay, then that was a good start. But those weren't actually compliments—they were just images to establish the right atmosphere."

"Lull me into compliance?"

"Yeah, pretty much. So here we go. You, Sydney Spinelli, have the most gorgeous, thick, red bronze hair I've ever seen, and I want to feel it on my bare chest."

Her eyes widened, and her tongue stuck to the roof of her mouth.

"Your eyes are full of warmth and wit, and they reveal more than you know. I particularly love seeing them go cloudy when you're turned on."

Syd dove for more margarita.

"Your nose is one of my very favorite things about you—nope, be quiet—because it's one of the keys to your personality. It begins with a high, proud bridge and it's long on character. It culminates in a very sensitive tip and small, private nostrils. You have a strong nose, Jersey, but it's pretty and vulnerable just where you'd least expect.

"We've talked about your mouth, darlin', but not about the two little arrows that form in your cheeks when you smile. They point upward to the sunshine. And then there's that dauntingly stubborn chin of yours, which you brandish out in front like a bazooka. Let's call it a charming chin."

Sydney wanted him to stop, yet she didn't want him to stop. She couldn't recall anyone ever seeing her this closely, much less sharing his thoughts out loud. These weren't your typical manufactured sweet nothings. Certainly nobody had ever told her that her chin was charming.

Her natural cynicism told her that he spouted a lot of bull. But an insidiously female aspect of her purred and stretched and twitched, curling around his words.

Alex wasn't done with her charming chin yet. "Your chin, sweetheart, is so stubborn that it refuses to dimple, even though it's got a clear indentation right there in the middle where the damn thing should go. Like you had a . . . dimplectomy or something."

She couldn't help but grin at that one.

"Yeah, see? Your eyes crinkle at the corners, your cheeks open up, the little arrows jump out and you glow. But no blasted dimple. Like your chin is too studious to join in the fun."

She ducked her head, blushing. "Stop!"

"Hush, or we start all over again, remember?"

"That was five!" she protested.

"Nuh-uh. You've got to let me *finish* five. I wasn't done with your chin."

"What else could you possibly have to say about it?"

"I don't know, but you interrupted my train of thought. This verbal stuff is tough for me. I'm a numbers guy, just like you. I see the world in columns and figures, not prose." He took a large swallow of margarita and settled back in his chair. "Now, where was I?"

After something about her shoulders, the crazy

man, he started up about how she was generous and sweet and a bunch of other crap. Thank God their entrées arrived and made him stop.

But Sydney sat up a little taller, unconsciously debating whether or not straightening her "fabulous" shoulders was worth the inevitable thrust of her breasts against the silk halter. What if he commented on those? She wouldn't put it past him.

Suddenly she realized that, though it was nice to hear the compliments, they didn't really matter all that much. She liked the fact that he found her attractive, but what seemed to engage Alex was her sense of humor and her intelligence, and the fact that she'd helped him with his mother. Alex liked her for herself. She didn't need to be a beauty queen. She didn't need to be a Kiki or a Julia.

She was touched that he was trying so hard to make her feel beautiful, though. More than his specific words, it was the caring gesture: He felt she needed to hear them. It made her warm inside.

With the posture of an empress, she sliced into the vast portion of chicken-fried steak before her to find it tender and mouthwateringly good. If she ate the entire thing, she'd no longer have shoulders, because she'd be the shape of a beach ball. Syd decided she didn't care. The cream gravy was nectar of the gods, and if the Roberto Cavallis blew off her thighs, she'd just shake her naked caboose and keep on eating.

"I do like a voracious woman," Alex commented.

She entertained embarrassment briefly, then decided it would ruin the taste of the food. If her plate had arrived with a beak or tail feathers on it, she would have used them to sop up more gravy.

"Would you like me to get you the recipe for that?"

"*No.* I'd have to be clothed by a tentmaker."

"Stick with me, kid. I don't care if you're clothed at all." Alex shot her another sex-drenched grin, and her blood heated and thickened to the consistency of Gristmill gravy. If the man continued to look at her like that, and make comments like that, she couldn't be held responsible for her actions, could she?

# Chapter Sixteen

Sydney almost cried over the fact that she had not a square millimeter of room for something called H.D.'s Chocolate Supreme. It consisted of fudge pie, two scoops of vanilla ice cream, chocolate syrup, whipped cream, pecans and a cherry. The dessert looked better than sex—well, maybe not sex with Alex, but sex with the average human male.

Sex with Alex was something that she really should not be thinking about, which meant that she couldn't *not* think about it.

She entertained him greatly by reading the bill upside down and instantly informing him what the tip would be at 18 percent, 19 percent and 20 percent. Testing her margarita-driven math skills, he asked for 18.5 percent and then 19.3 percent, and she impressed him by supplying each figure within ten seconds.

"I might just have to hire you, Jersey," he said.

"No, Kimball, I think I'll hire *you*."

"I wouldn't make such a great lackey."

"Oh, and with this chin, I would?"

They started for the exit and she preceded him down the wooden stairs. When she didn't hear his boot-steps following, Syd glanced behind her, only to find him at the top of the flight, mouth slightly open and eyes half lidded. "Alex? Are you coming?"

"It's a distinct possibility," he muttered, almost too low for her to hear.

Oh, God. The Cavallis and her commando state. She'd forgotten. But at this point, she'd had far too much tequila to blush. Instead she cocked a hip and placed a hand on it, arching her brows. This was . . . fun.

She searched Alex's face as he made progress down the stairs, and noted that his eyes were a little glazed. She experienced a small surge of wicked female power, and liked it too much.

She marveled at the effect a simple pair of jeans had on poor Kimball.

*Don't be silly, Sydney. With all the worries over his mother and marketing bizarre emu products, the guy just hasn't been laid for a week or two. It's just a simple seven-digit phone number that separates Tessa from his fly.*

But as they walked the very short, moonlit distance to Gruene Hall from the Gristmill and Alex actually took her hand in his, she found it easy to forget that.

Historic Gruene Hall, too, could have been on the

set of a spaghetti Western. As Alex explained it, just about anyone who was anyone in country or blues had performed in the place. Willie Nelson, Aaron Neville, Hank Williams III, Jerry Jeff Walker, George Thorogood, Joe Ely and Little Feat had all played Gruene Hall fairly recently.

Tonight, though, they would apparently see a band called Two Tons of Steel, and Alex was friends with the lead guitarist, Dennis Fallon.

Gruene Hall, Texas' oldest dance venue, was all about rough wood, neon beer signs, cheering fans and boot scootin'. Two Tons personified good-natured rockabilly with an infectious beat, and Sydney understood that she'd finally stepped into the heart of Texas.

Alex bellied up to the bar, dragging her by the hand behind him, so that she bumped hips and nuzzled ears with total strangers. They couldn't have been more affable, moving aside as best they could in the crowd.

The front room of the place was full of wobbly wooden tables, littered with pitchers of beer and bare elbows. Syd averted her eyes from a few more animal heads on the wall, but fell in love with the old iron pipe stove that must heat the room on cold nights—not that she could imagine a cold Texas night at the moment.

Gruene Hall stayed true to the times in which it was built and did not feature modern improvements like air-conditioning—just a few overworked, struggling ceiling fans. The noise level was impressive. Several hundred pairs of boots swaggered, clomped, two-stepped and tapped on the creaking nineteenth-century floors, punctuating the roar of conversation, shouts of laughter and lazy insults.

Two Tons of Steel played in the actual hall behind the front bar, accompanied by enthusiastic whoops, hollers and whistles. I-can't-dance Sydney felt her hips swinging of their own accord, and Kiki's boots forced her toes to tap.

"Hey, Red, let go o' that loser and come dance with me," said a rangy blond guy with a small hoop through his ear.

Sydney grinned, and one of Alex's hands tightened on hers as he swung around with two Shiner Bocks in the other. "You ditchin' me already, Jersey?"

She shook her head and shouted to the other guy, "Sorry—he's got beer!"

"Shallow wench," Alex said into her ear as she took a long draught of the beverage she'd once despised and found this flavor good, too. "C'mon."

They somehow threaded their way into the hall, where Two Tons presided over the party, looking like they couldn't believe they got paid to have this much fun.

Kevin Geil, vocalist, wore a plaid shirt with the sleeves rolled up to his biceps, a pair of ancient jeans over his swinging hips and a straw cowboy hat. He had a voice like liquid mesquite and he poured it liberally over the crowd.

Dennis Fallon's fingers shot lightning over the neck of his electric guitar, his infectious smile brighter than a West Texas moon. In shades and an old-fashioned fedora, he could have been a youthful 1930s mobster who'd lost his suit and gained a sense of humor.

The other members of the band exuded Lone Star energy and talent: Chris Dodds on drums, Ric Ramirez, upright bass and harmony vocals/lead vocals, and Denny Mathis on steel guitar. Two Tons' music was energetic, light on its feet, fast, full of life and just plain fun.

"We'd like to do a little song for you now. It's about a Cadillac," said Kevin.

The band broke into their signature song and the crowd yelled. A few of the dancers even went for the tabletops. "That's us in about half an hour," Alex shouted.

"Oh, no, I don't think so." Sydney had never danced on a table in her life, and didn't plan to start on a night when she had on no underwear.

"Well, I got a baby—she's so doggone sweet," Kevin sang.

*"I love to slip inside and caress her seat . . . I slip behind the wheel, ooh what a thrill, I got a baby made of two tons of steel! Shake it, baby . . ."*

The hall became a blur of swinging backsides, dipping torsos, big hair and wide grins. Sydney protested as Alex hauled her into his arms and began to sway, boot scoot and rock with her. All she knew how to do was shift her weight from one foot to the other and occasionally cock a hip. But that seemed to suit him just fine for now.

Being next to Alex or under his arm in the truck had quickened her pulse. Being flat up against his chest and pelvis completely undid her. That sandalwood aftershave, the breezy scent of detergent on his soft shirt, the leather of his belt—they all intoxicated her. And when he unexpectedly slid his hands from her waist and took one of her own, when he spun her out into the crowd and then reeled her in again, she was all his.

She forgot about embarrassment and ego and followed his lead, their fingers clasping them into one sinuous, graceful muscle. She felt her hair fly out around her, and tipped back her head and laughed as he dipped her. All that stood between her and the floor was his strong grip and one of Kiki's boot heels. Then she flew upward and he spun her into the crowd again.

Kevin sang about a pretty little rockin', rollin' redheaded girl and Sydney flushed with pleasure. Alex lip-synced along with him, looking straight into her eyes, and heat stole through her.

She felt that the next song was hers: "I'd Do Anything." *I'd do anything to keep you next to me* . . . but she wouldn't let her lips form the words. They were too needy, too revealing.

During "Sweet Elena," Alex brought her close against his body again, holding her tenderly and sliding a hand down to the small of her back. His other hand gripped hers and he rocked her into the simplest of rhythms. Step, back, step, turn. Step, back, step, turn. She did it unconsciously, laying her cheek against his chest. She felt his jaw settle over the top of her head, and nothing had ever felt so right.

His heartbeat filled her ear and told her, without a word, anything and everything she'd ever wanted to hear.

"See, you're an expert." His voice vibrated against her.

She looked up at him. "An expert?"

"At the Texas Two-step. You're doin' it right now, and you didn't even realize. See how easy it is?"

Of course the moment she thought about it, she lost the rhythm, making him laugh. "No, no. Don't concentrate. Just enjoy."

He pulled her close again, and his hips kissed her tummy, sending shock waves through her as the ridge at his groin sent a clear message. His hand on her back slid a little lower, until just his little finger brushed the bare skin under the low-rise waistband of her jeans. Just the slight, feathery movement made her ache with want.

His other fingers began to play along her spine in time to the music, and Syd breathed him in again. She knew a longing to feel his bare skin, too—just run her hand up under his shirt and along his back.

Evidently the band was partial to her coloring, because they segued into another song: "Redheaded woman."

*"It takes a redheaded woman to get a dirty job done . . .*
*Oh, sweet Mama, you were built for havin' fun . . ."*

Alex threw back his head and laughed at her expression as the lyrics got steamier. Then his hands were in her hair and he kissed her full on the mouth. She melted on the spot, feeling his tongue possess her and pluck secret strings deep inside. He was one hundred percent hot, Texas, turned-on male, and she still couldn't quite believe that she had done the turning-on.

But somehow she had, because there was no mistaking that denim-covered ridge hard against her stomach. And that wicked pinky of his plunged a little lower until it just barely caressed her tailbone and whispered of intent to go lower.

He made love thoroughly to her mouth with his, while her nipples pebbled against his chest and the silk against them became sweet torment. What would it feel like if his mouth were on those peaks?

Alex broke the kiss with a quick, playful nip at her bottom lip and caressed her jaw, hands then moving back into her hair and awakening every nerve ending in her neck and scalp. She shivered and the sensation crested between her thighs.

"We'd better go back to dancing, Jersey," he said in a thick voice. "Unless you want to be taken on a picnic table, with an audience."

The idea shocked and yet aroused her. Then she was immediately ashamed of the arousal. What was she, some kind of closet pervert? She tried to pull away, but Alex's hands settled firmly on her shoulders and his gaze was intent. Then he bent his head to her ear.

"That," he said with certainty, "excited you."

Startled, she shook her head and again tried to back away.

"Yes, it did," he purred. "You've got a little twist in you, don't you, darlin'? I like that."

Fire seared her neck, cheeks and ears. She opened her mouth to deny everything he'd ever seen about her and tell him he was wrong, wrong, wrong. But he ate the words from between her lips before she'd formed more than a squeak. He stroked her tongue and licked around the words and then swallowed them whole.

His perception burned her as much as the rough whisker stubble around his clever, seeking mouth.

But as much as she felt distress at what he saw, she also felt an odd joy that someone could read her. That *he* could read her.

"It's okay, Jersey. I've got a few fantasies of my own. And one of them involves you not wearing a stitch of lingerie under your outfit. How does it feel to be a walking fantasy, hmmmm?"

She couldn't breathe. She couldn't move. She couldn't speak. He pinned her with his dark eyes and caught his top lip between his teeth. Then he reached around her for their beer and held her bottle to her lips. She drank the entire thing without breaking eye contact or stopping for air.

Outside the breeze blew balmy under a lazy Texas moon, and an orchestra of cicadas hummed and chirruped while gravel crunched under the heels of couples exiting Gruene Hall.

Syd allowed Alex to back her up against a convenient oak tree that hid them from view, and he hungrily took possession of her mouth again. His beard stubble scraped her face, while tree bark scraped her back. She exclaimed as a knot dug into her flesh and he made a rough noise of apology, turning them so that he leaned against the oak's trunk. He slid a hand down her bare spine, caressing her, and then turned her so that he could see the injury, which he kissed. A deep tremor ran through her as his lips moved from the sore spot up to her bare shoulder, trailing fire along her skin. He made gentle love to the nape of her neck, holding her hair aside, and a small moan of pleasure escaped her. His warm breath sang along her nerve endings and his lips on her ear sent delicious shivers eddying through her.

She turned to face him again and met his lips, now doing some exploring of her own. She tasted his skin and touched her tongue to the rough stubble on his cheeks and chin. She teased his ear with the tip and felt his arms tighten around her. He separated her knees with one of his, propped the heel of his boot against the oak, and pulled her up, astride his muscular thigh.

One hand at the small of her back, he used the other to cup one of her breasts through the thin silk of her top, and rubbed a thumb lightly over her nipple. She gasped involuntarily and her thighs instinctively clenched around his. He smiled in satisfaction, passing a big, warm palm over both breasts and melting her sensually. He bent his head and closed his mouth over one nipple while she let out a low whimper of pleasure. The heat, the wetness, the suction of him . . . she hummed with need. He simply pushed the scrap of Pucci away from her other breast, and took it naked between his lips, torturing and teasing with his tongue until she could barely remember what her name was.

Another couple came stumbling out the dance hall's door, passing close to them and forcing them

213

both to their senses. Alex quickly raised his head and tweaked her top back into position. He set her on her feet and looked down into her eyes, his expression rueful.

"Jersey, I don't suppose you'd believe that I have a flat tire, or that I'm too drunk to drive?"

She fingered a couple of his shirt buttons, wanting to just rip the garment off and throw it in the bushes. "Depends on how skilled a liar you are." She smiled in the darkness.

He found her mouth again. When he raised his head, he presented another option. "I've been thinking about it since I picked you up. But I thought, she's pretty smart. She might see through either one of those fibs. So then I figured that if worse came to worst, I could walk right into a low-hangin' beam in there and give myself a good concussion."

She laughed.

"I mean, you're not heartless, after all. You wouldn't force a gravely injured man to drive you a long distance back home, now would you?"

"No, of course not. I'd just have to take his keys and drive *him*."

"Well, see, that's where the buckets of tequila were gonna come in. I'd buy you so many 'ritas that your blood would run green."

"That's a pretty dastardly plot."

"There's some awfully nice places to stay around here, Jersey. Bet you'd enjoy the Prince Solms Inn of

214

New Braunfels, or Accents of Gruene, or if you want a spectacular view, the Lodge at Turkey Cove on Canyon Lake."

He stood waiting for her agreement, this tall, powerful dream of a guy whose shoulders blocked the moon from her view. He wanted to take her, Sydney Spinelli, to bed. He probably knew that he could just sweep her along with the force of his personality and her desire, but he wanted a clear-headed decision on her part. She could eat him whole like a giant Godiva truffle.

Those dark chocolate eyes gleamed with humor and sensuality, but not a single promise of anything other than a good time tonight. Whatever else he might be, Alex Kimball was no liar.

The question was whether or not she was prepared, for the first and only time in her life, to have a one-night stand. Syd had never been able to eat just one truffle and sensibly push the rest away.

But as she stood there thinking about it, a new attitude swept over her. So she'd waited at least a month to sleep with a select few men over and over again until they began to treat her badly or bored her stiff. Had the smug exercise in morality given her satisfaction in any way? Had it given her multiple orgasms?

Live a little, Julia had said.

Maybe the Cavalli jeans made her shameless. Maybe she had a crazy, tequila-born urge to fill Kiki's boots with a vengeance. Maybe she didn't care since she didn't live in Fredericksburg and wouldn't hear any hurtful gossip.

But she couldn't *not* take her one chance to sleep with Alex Kimball.

# Chapter Seventeen

After a simple cell phone call to make a reservation, Alex took her to the closest bed-and-breakfast he could think of: Accents of Gruene. It was an intimate and charming little house of white Texas limestone, nestled among five acres of choice Texas Hill Country.

Alex rented the entire extra cottage on the property for complete privacy, and Sydney exclaimed over the gorgeous king-sized four-poster bed and the enormous Jacuzzi tub.

He shut the door, locked it and threw off his shirt, walking in just his jeans and boots to the tub. Her mouth went dry at the sight of his naked torso, those broad shoulders tapering into a beautifully defined, lightly furred chest and a lean, flat stomach. His skin gleamed golden in the low lamplight and she swallowed as her gaze swept down to the waistband of his faded, well-worn jeans. They rode low on his hips and sat snug, tantalizing her by molding exactly to what lay beneath. A long, solid bulge curved close to the left front pocket, and it grew under her gaze.

Alex leaned against the vanity and crossed his muscular arms over his delicious chest, spoiling her view. "You gonna return the favor?" he asked softly. "Or do *I* get to untie that criminal little scrap of fabric you're wearing?"

She walked to him, lifted her hair and presented her back. He untied the knot behind her rib cage, trailing his fingers over her heated skin. She shivered, goose bumps rising on her arms, and her nipples sprang to attention. The little piece of silk hung between her breasts, still dangling from her neck.

Alex made quick work of that knot, too, and the halter fell to the ground. She stood motionless with her back to him, still lifting her hair and clad in nothing but jeans and boots herself.

"My God," he breathed. "The lines of your body are so beautiful." He reached a hand out and caressed the contour of a breast, tracing it with wonder.

She let the hair cascade down her back again and felt his fingers in it. And then they moved to her waist and curled around to her belly. He pulled her back against him and she felt his erection clearly nudging the base of her spine.

Imprisoned by his arms, Sydney savored the feeling of his smooth, warm skin against her. The fur of his chest tickled between her shoulder blades as he buried his nose in her hair, inhaling and exhaling deeply.

He stroked her belly, brushed along her ribs, and finally moved up to cup her bare breasts. She let her head fall back onto his chest and gave in to the pleasure of his circling, seeking, kneading fingers. His palms covered the small mounds completely, dwarfing them. But for the first time in her life Syd didn't feel inadequate, because he seemed so happy with them.

He knew just what to do, just how to touch them: sliding her nipples along the canals between his fingers until they kissed the junctures between them; pinching lightly, rolling them under his thumbs. Her breath began to come faster and catch in her throat, and he let out a contented hum, bending his head over her shoulder to watch, scrubbing her cheek and ear with that lethal stubble once again.

She arched her back and Alex slipped his knee between her thighs again, rocking her slightly and forcing her legs wider.

He abandoned one breast, still toying with the other, and his hand dipped down into the front of her jeans, stroking the skin between her hip bones and smoothing through the top of her hidden curls. He groaned. "I knew it from the moment I watched you step into the truck. Not a stitch, Jersey. Not a stitch. Do you know you were killing me all night?"

She shook her head but savored the words. He'd really been wanting her for hours. *Her*.

He played in the curls and she squirmed, so desperate for him to go lower that when he did, touching her most sensitive spot with only a finger, she made an unintelligible whimper. He rubbed and circled until she thought she'd die, then plunged a finger inside her. But the skintight Cavallis would only stretch so far. He slid his hand out and fumbled for a moment with the leather lacing at her waist.

She went for the side lacing and together they achieved a puddle of denim within seconds.

His hands moved over her naked hips and buttocks, traced the cleft and the private smile lines where they met her thighs. She felt his teeth nip her shoulder and he wrapped his arms around her, as if to say *Mine*.

"I just want to eat you up, Beautiful." And he turned her to face him, giving her body a long, appreciative perusal.

She felt self-conscious as his gaze went to the juncture of her thighs, and she pressed her knees together. His response was a torrid, outlaw smile. Then he licked his lips.

He pulled her to him and kissed her deeply, while working his magic again on her breasts. She reached out a tentative hand and touched the impressive bulge in his jeans. His hand covered hers and clenched her fingers around it, then moved them to his fly.

Sydney undid the top button, then the next and the next, almost holding her breath. He sprang more or less free, though still hidden by the fabric of his boxers. She tugged them down and he broke the kiss to help her. He was heavy and thick in her hand, and beyond aroused. She fingered him with wonder and then looked up into his half-lidded eyes. "You need a third boot," she teased.

He grabbed her and set her on the marble countertop, which was cold, cold, cold under her backside. He spread her thighs and rubbed himself against her, his tongue caught between his teeth and his hands firm against her bottom.

She rocked against him, the wet heat at her core an erotic contrast to the chilly, dry marble under her. He teased her mercilessly until she felt wild and got uncharacteristically aggressive, hauling him by the hips until he slid, inch by inch, inside her.

The fullness in itself was erotic, and she paused to savor it. Then Alex moved within, slid and stirred, and she was lost, a slick, hot rider with no earthly destination.

After a minute or two, he pulled out of her with a groan, and she mumbled an incoherent protest. He smoothed the tumbled hair from her face and grinned down at her. "I know, but it's necessary, darlin'. First of all, I'm not going to last another thirty seconds at this rate, and then there's the fact that we need a condom."

The word blew away the sensual fog in her mind and her eyes widened. She'd just let him inside her without one—was she *crazy*? Was she born this stupid, or had the tequila killed off all her brain cells? Hadn't she just made her own sister take a pregnancy test?

She flushed, hopped off the counter and shook her head in disbelief. Alex tipped up her chin and kissed her nose. "See," he said, "I can't have you, too, spreading it all over town that I'm a dud in the sack." He fished his wallet out of his jeans and pulled from it a foil packet.

She dredged up a voice somehow. "Too late. Unless you wanna pay me to keep my mouth shut?"

He strode back to her. "No, Jersey," he said in husky tones, "but I'll pay you to keep it open." He kissed her and pressed the packet into her hands. When he pulled away he frowned at her and shook a finger. "Did I give you permission to get down from there?"

She squeaked as he picked her up again and set her back onto the cold marble. "Now, be good." He bent his head to her nipples and playfully bit one as he spread her legs and then knelt between them.

"What are you *doing*?"

"Hush."

"You can't"—she clutched at his hair—"oh, my God!" Rough bristle abraded her thighs and he played her expertly like a flute while she panted and whimpered, helpless under the assault of such pleasure. A final foray with his tongue left her poised on the brink of explosive climax, but he pulled away and then entered her fully sheathed. She'd dropped the condom somehow and he had to be a magician to have gotten it on, but he had.

He pulsed within her now, trying to restrain himself and not unleash his full power on her smaller frame. He slid in and out, perspiration filling his brow and trickling down at his temples. She was actually making the man sweat.

He picked her up bodily, the level of the counter all wrong for his height, and moved her back and forth along the length of him. The sensations within her, the hot, wet friction and the sight of his corded, muscled arms completely supporting her finally built to a peak, and she came apart with a cry. She disintegrated into a thousand particles of moonlight, and with a sound half growl and half shout, he came with her.

Alex sat in the oversized Jacuzzi tub with her later. She lay between his thighs, her hands draped over his knees, and he played with her beautiful, copper bronze hair. He started to count the freckles on her pale skin, and had gotten as far as number thirty-nine when she reached back and tugged on his tool. "Don't make fun," she said. "There's a whole galaxy of them back there."

"I wasn't making fun," he told her. "I happen to love every single one of these freckles. And you'd better not pull on that, 'cause you'll get yourself in trouble."

"What, this?" She tugged again. "I'm not sure what it's good for." It swelled and hardened in her hand.

"You're not, huh?" he growled. He yanked her hips back until she was sitting on it, breathless and laughing.

"It's good for this," he said, sliding into her tight, wet heat a little ways. "And this . . ." He slid out. "And this . . ." He plunged to the hilt, ground against her backside, and commandeered her breasts. She felt indescribably good.

"Oh, is that all," said Syd, around a moan.

"Nope." He lifted her off and turned her to face him. Then he pulled her down so that she straddled him and took her that way. "It's good for this, too . . ." While she rose up and down, he rubbed her intimately with his thumbs until she melted over him like warm butter.

"It's an old-fashioned kinda tool, Jersey, but it never," he panted, "goes out of style. A classic, you know? I doubt I'll ever hang it up for good."

"I hope not," she breathed. And then, "Oh, God. Yes. *Yes* . . ."

"You like that?" The sight of her giving in to pleasure undid him. The features of her face went all soft and dreamy: Her eyes clouded, her cheeks flushed and her lips got plump and sweet. He kept doing what he was doing. "Just . . . like . . . that?"

"Mmmmm-hmm."

"Okay, baby. Come to me, now. Come for me. There you go . . . good girl."

# Chapter Eighteen

*I've never, ever done anything this irresponsible in my life.* That was Sydney's first conscious thought after awakening to a physical glow in the big king-sized four-poster next to a sleeping Alex Kimball.

He sprawled beside her naked on the wildly tossed sheets, facedown and buns up. They were very nice buns, as taut and muscular as his thighs and arms—and pretty much every other part of him.

Even relaxed in sleep, his face was powerfully handsome, five o'clock shadow dense and black against his lean, tanned cheeks. Just looking at it made her thighs tingle and her throat go dry. Her cheeks burned, too, and the side of her neck, the soft skin of her breasts—she'd gotten the full stubble treatment last night, everywhere.

Every limb felt languorous and heavy, like the guilt she should be feeling for having a sleazy one-night stand. It was knocking on the other side of some mental door, but Syd refused to let it in. She couldn't, right at this moment anyway, cheapen what she'd shared with Alex last night.

*It wasn't cheap. It wasn't sleazy. But it's got no future. I'll fly back to the East Coast and brave South River and Marv's wrath one last time. I'll hire him someone competent and honest. And then I'll return to my own life, my own business. Alex will be here, whipping up new emu-oriented products and struggling with the realities of Alzheimer's.*

*And Julia? She'll head off to San Francisco, or maybe LA, and make a career for herself in fashion. Roman will use some other idiot woman to fund his vineyard, and this chapter of our lives will be closed. Maybe Mrs. Kimball will ask occasionally for Nell, and Alex will hazily recall what I look like and how he taught "Jersey" to two-step.*

She smiled ruefully and slipped out of bed. *He'll never have to pretend I'm beautiful again, and he certainly won't have to compliment my atrocious cooking . . .*

Her eyes misted and she sternly told the lump in her throat to deflate and get the hell out of there. She walked into the bathroom, folded her arms over her nakedness, and stared at their discarded clothing, the crumpled remains of passion.

The legs of the Cavalli bondage jeans splayed awkwardly, one bent under itself to the front and the other lying straight behind it, to the rear. It was the position of a hurdler, midleap. It told her to run, not walk, away from Alex Kimball before she got attached and therefore hurt.

She closed the bathroom door quietly and stepped into the shower, lathering and soaping the traces of Alex and sex from her skin. She shampooed her hair, trying not to think of how he'd stroked it and played with it in the tub. *You have the most gorgeous, thick, red bronze hair I've ever seen, and I want to feel it on my bare chest.*

She banished the memory of his compliments at the Gristmill, too, but not before she touched a finger to her nose. *Your nose is one of my very favorite things about you.*

She snorted and stuck her "charming" chin under the spray of water, since shampoo lather was running into her mouth. Kimball had a silver tongue, that was all . . . and he'd been trying to get into her pants, God knew why. She turned her back to the water and rinsed her hair.

Suddenly the shower door opened and he stood there naked and aroused in front of her, hands on his hips. "No fair showering without me, Jersey. I had plans to make you dirtier before you got clean."

"Hey, what happened to privacy?" she complained. The last thing she needed was to make love with him again. Her brain was already scrambled enough.

"No peace for the wicked, and no privacy for the

naked." Instead of climbing in as she half expected, he reached for her and plucked her out as if she weighed nothing, muttering about tying her to the bedposts.

"You cannot tie me to the bedposts! I am sopping wet, and you'll ruin the furniture. Besides, we have to go . . . my sister is going to wonder where I am this morning. She can't know about this!"

Alex silenced her with his mouth and deposited her on the bathroom rug, sitting on her with an evil grin and pinning her arms over her head at the wrists. "I'm not done with you, my pretty," he said in villainous tones. "*Mwah-ha-ha-ha . . .*"

And he began to tease and arouse her.

"You're insatiable," she protested.

"Yes, for you. Besides, I want to see your dimple again."

"You told me I didn't have one!"

"You don't . . . except when you orgasm. You get this blissful expression on your face, your mouth falls open—and just as you make that last gasp or whimper, the dimple appears."

"You make it sound like the little yellow button on a Butterball turkey."

"Exactly." He nodded. "Bing. You're done!"

She tried to get a wrist free to hit him, but he held tight, laughing. Then his mouth was on her breasts, and she ceased to care.

Later they showered again, and he suggested that

they go down to breakfast before driving back. Sydney took one look in the mirror and moaned. "What have you done to me?"

He cocked an eyebrow. "Well, I hoped that I'd made you happy."

"My face! It looks like it's been scrubbed with bleach and a household brush. I can't go anywhere looking like this."

Alex cupped her chin and grimaced. "It's not so bad," he lied.

"It is, and you know it."

He rubbed a hand over his jaw self-consciously. "Sorry. I didn't realize I was such a brute."

"Well, of course it wasn't deliberate." She thought for a moment. "I also can't go down there in that outfit and no underwear. It's one thing to wear it in the evening—quite another to sashay around in the daytime, looking like I'm open for business."

He grinned. "Okay. How about I go check us out and then bring you back some coffee and a sweet roll for the drive?"

"Perfect. Let's just meet in the parking lot, at the truck."

She got herself together as best she could while he was gone, wrinkling her nose at having to put on Kiki's boots again. She'd completely forgotten to inspect his back for tiny little claw marks.

Again, she told herself sternly that it didn't matter. He could have the claws of a thousand vixens embedded in his torso—he wasn't hers. She'd only borrowed him for one night.

She opened the door and slunk out, feeling like the Whore of Babylon. The coast was clear. She closed the door behind her, took a few steps, rounded the side of the cottage and almost walked smack into the hostess of the B and B. "Oh, excuse me!"

"No, excuse *me*. I wasn't looking where I was going, behind this stack of towels. Did you enjoy your stay, hon?" She inspected Sydney's face covertly.

"Um, yes. Very much."

"I can see that. Would you like me to get you something for your face?"

Her ears buzzed pink with mortification. "Thank you, but no. It'll be fine."

"Whisker burn on a redhead's skin." The lady shook her head. "That won't fade for ages unless you put cream on it." She took Sydney's arm. "Come with me, now. I don't want to hear another word. I was young once, too."

Syd closed her eyes and stumbled after her, hoping Alex had checked in under a false name. His family was as prominent around here as the blasted Sonntags.

The lady brought her into the kitchen from an exterior back door, and rummaged through a cabinet while Syd wished for a speedy, painless death.

"Aha! Here it is. My niece just gave this to me a couple of days ago. Supposed to help soothe any skin condition. Now, don't mind the funny color or the baby-food jar: It healed a burn on my hand overnight! Great stuff." Sydney looked down in disbelief at a jar of Emulsion.

She eventually disentangled herself from the hostess, her face covered with a coating of the cream. She walked the short distance to the truck to find that Alex already had the engine on and was waiting for her impatiently. Not a trace of dream lover remained.

"Alex, what's wrong?"

"Get in." She did as she was told, and he sped out of the parking lot almost before she had the passenger door closed. "I just got a call from my father. Mama—" He broke off, swallowed and took a deep breath. "Mama is out weeding the front garden in a black silk slip, rubber flip-flops and a Texas Rangers baseball cap. He can't get near her—she has a hoe and she doesn't recognize him."

# Chapter Nineteen

Alex drove the pickup like a bullet out of a Colt .45. Jersey hung onto the door handle and kept her eyes—and her mouth—shut. They burned up the tarmac, racing the double yellow lines of the highway, and squealed through intersections. He briefly admired her forbearance.

Gravel flew from the tires as they sped down the road that led to the Kimball homestead. Mama's bent figure was clearly visible from the highway, baseball cap askew, with the brim turned sideways and mostly backward. The skimpy black satin nightie gleamed in the late morning sunlight and one spaghetti strap trailed off her shoulder. The flip-flops were his own, the ones he occasionally used when boating. Gigantic on her small feet, they provided absolutely no protection from insects, or worse, snakes.

The sight of her punched him in the gut. For the first time in his life he was tempted to run.

He hit the brakes. Nausea climbed into his throat as he eased his foot down on the gas pedal and brought them crawling closer. Mama had on a strand of pearls, one matching earring and a pair of garden gloves. Her salon-rinsed hair quivered violently each time she hit the dry ground with the hoe. Dad squatted miserably about fifty yards from her.

Sydney made the distressed noise that Alex couldn't allow himself—wasn't sure he was capable of. Somehow his internal organs had been replaced with a heavy, padlocked steel box.

He didn't have a shred of a concept of what to do.

Mama saw the truck and waved cheerfully at him. After a glance at his father, he waved back. He inched forward, parked the truck in the middle of the road, and got out. Sydney did, too.

Mama's face brightened as she saw her. "Well, hello, Nell! Come here and give me a kiss. How are the girls?"

Sydney walked to her and bussed her cheek while Alex stood rooted to the ground like an idiot. Jersey gracefully entered an imaginary conversation about a fictional world, telling Mama how well "the girls" were doing in school, how Kelsey was in an elementary theater production and Bonnie had developed quite a talent for hoops.

Alex watched her, standing there in last night's

outfit, whisker burn and all, unflinching. She was utterly unself-conscious, focused on his mother and the situation. He felt some kind of emotion hammering to get out of the steel box inside him, but he wasn't sure what it was. Gratitude? Admiration? Sheer relief that Sydney was present? He hadn't even thought to drop her off at the Motor Inn first. She'd been at his side, and it seemed natural that she remain there.

"How do you keep your figure, Nell?" Mama asked her. "I never can get over how that little ole tummy of yours snapped back after twins." She playfully poked at the two inches of flesh displayed under Syd's halter top. And then a few minutes later she said, "I've never seen jeans quite like that, honey. Where did you get them?"

As the two women talked, Sydney bent, helped Mama pull weeds from the area she was clearing, and eventually took over the hoe.

Alex put one leaden foot after the other and went to his father. Dad had moved to sit on a large rock near some shrubs. Sweat soaked his shirt, his shoulders were shaking and he'd thrown up. "Thirty-six years," he repeated, over and over again. "Thirty-six years." He put his head between his knees.

Alex exhaled and squatted down next to him, placing his hand on his father's shoulder.

Drops of moisture fell in the vicinity of Dad's work boots. One of them hit the tip of a blade of grass, rolled down it and plopped onto an unsuspecting ant. The ant reeled and headed the other way, but tears were falling like artillery all around it and the little creature didn't know what to do.

"Thirty-six years." Dad's voice broke. "How can . . . she . . . not recognize me?"

Alex closed his eyes and tried to block out memories of the time he'd come home and walked into the kitchen: The look of fear on Mama's face; the squeak of terror she'd made as she put the butcher block between them. He couldn't even feel his heartbeat because of the locked box between his ribs.

"I love her more than I love myself." Dad's voice was low and fierce.

Alex knew he spoke the truth. He reached for his father's hand, rougher and more weathered but almost a carbon copy of his own. "I know you do."

"I've been in love with that woman for thirty-seven years, four months, twenty-three days and ten hours. I remember the first time I saw her, and the blue sweater set she wore and the way she smiled at me."

Alex bent his head and squeezed the old man's hand: the man he'd once looked to for comfort and wisdom and discipline; the father who'd given him the compass with which to navigate his life—the same man who looked so lost now, and in need of comfort and wisdom himself.

"I love her more than I love myself," Dad repeated.

"Then," Alex told him, "you have to forgive her. She doesn't mean to hurt you—just like she didn't mean to hurt me."

"I know that, God damn it!" His father raised his head and glared at him. "Don't you think I've forgiven her already? It's done." He yanked his hand back and gestured angrily.

"What I *don't* know is what to expect, how to brace myself. Who will she be tomorrow? And the next day? Where is my wife?"

He looked at the sky and gulped for air, a harsh, rasping sound. *"Where is my Emily?"* He screamed it to the clouds, to the sun, to God. They didn't answer him.

Alex ignored the almost physical pain that swept over him at witnessing his father. His eyes and throat burned with it. He shoved it aside, stuffed it into the box. "Dad, your heart. You're not well."

"Screw my damn heart." He dropped his head back between his knees.

"No. You've got to keep it going, if not for yourself, then for her. You have to calm down. Where are those pills?"

His father sighed. "I'm fine. I'd'a keeled over when she came at me with the hoe, if I was going to. Medication's all on the kitchen windowsill, where it always is. With that stupid soap that looks like a potato, and the nail file and the little china box of dirty rubber bands that come on the newspaper. The ones your mother won't let me throw away."

Alex hitched up a corner of his mouth and touched his father's shoulder again. "Maybe you can do it when she's not looking and blame it on 'Nell.' "

Dad produced a weak chuckle. "She sure has taken a shine to that girl."

*She's not the only one.* Alex looked over at the two women, who were now walking toward them.

Just a few yards away, Sydney's voice carried to them on the wind. "So why don't we finish the weeding in the evening, when it's cooler?"

And his mother's: "I always said you were a smart young lady. Can I interest you in some chicken salad for lunch?"

"Only if you'll give me the recipe without leaving anything out this time." Sydney winked at her.

"The secret is to make your own mayonnaise, Nell—I *told* you that."

"You know I'm too lazy. Kraft has always been good enough for me."

"Well, then, you'll be asking me for the correct recipe until the day I die. Won't you?"

They shared in companionable laughter as they approached, and Alex held his breath. His father closed his eyes.

Mama walked right up, frowned at Dad and slapped him lightly on the shoulder with her gardening gloves. "Jonathan, don't you have anything better to do than sit like a bump on a log all day? What's wrong with you, silly?"

Just a few simple words, and they lit up the old man's face. He grinned so wide that Alex was afraid his head might fall right off.

A moment ago, he would have paid a billion dollars to see that smile. He felt weak with relief and couldn't stand up. He simply sat on the rock and blinked moisture from his eyes as Dad surged forward and swept Mama into his arms for a bear hug and then a kiss.

"What has come over you, Jonathan?" she asked.

He picked her up and started toward the house with her, giant flip-flops and all. The Texas Rangers hat fell off as she shrieked, "Put me down, you crazy man!"

"Hell," Alex said, finally finding the strength to get up. "That *cannot* be good for his heart."

One flip-flop flew through the air, then another. Mama didn't look like a strange hybrid of Madonna and some rapper. She looked like a woman on a second honeymoon.

Sydney linked her arm through his and gazed up at him with tears in her cinnamon eyes. "Oh, I'd say that it's *very* good for his heart."

\* \* \*

Sydney glanced at Alex's profile as he drove her the couple of miles back to Orange Street and Marv's Motor Inn. He looked exhausted. Since neither of them had slept much the night before and he'd just been through emotional turmoil, that wasn't surprising.

She knew it was a bad time to bring up the subject, and she wondered how she'd gotten so involved in *his* family issues instead of her own. She should be concentrating on how to stop Julia's ridiculous wedding. But frankly, she wasn't sure how to do that.

And somebody around here needed to get through to him. "Alex," she began, "I know you don't want to hear this, but you have got to get some help with your mother. You can't go on like this, and neither can your father."

His jaw tightened and his hands gripped the steering wheel more tightly. A tiny vein pulsed at his temple.

"She may very well be normal for the rest of the afternoon. She may be completely lucid next Tuesday and have total command of her memories. But Wednesday she could get in the car, drive to Dallas and get lost in a shopping mall, unable to remember where she lives. Friday she could forget a cake in the oven or a pot on the stove, and burn the house down. Saturday she could go violent and hit somebody on the street. You *just don't know.*"

Alex stared straight ahead, giving no indication that he'd heard her.

"Listen," she said. "There are trained staff you can bring into the home. Or there are adult day-care centers—she could go from nine to five, and then come home for the night. And then there are assisted living centers . . . until it gets really bad."

Alex turned into the Motor Inn's parking lot. "Thank you for the information," he said in clipped, polite tones. "But I think we'll pass."

"But—"

"My father does not want a stranger in his house taking care of the woman he loves. And there is no way in hell, *not over our dead bodies,* that we will ever put her away."

"Alex, it doesn't have to be a stranger, and I never said anything about putting her 'away.' That's an awful term. For now, you could have friends come in to be with her, and that buys you time to find someone really good, someone from around here that you can trust."

"No, Sydney. You think Dad will let her friends see her when she's acting crazy? When she might go after them with a barbecue fork or the electric beaters, for God's sake? Yeah, that's a great idea! Let's have the garden club over to watch her whip off her bra. Let's turn her into a freak show for all the local gossips! Thelma Lynn Grafton'll have a ball."

"You know what? Her true friends won't care. They'll just love her anyway. And I'm telling you, there are times coming—and not far in the future—

that you will not know how to handle. You froze back there even today. You are going to need help."

"I didn't freeze. I'm not going to lie to you, Sydney: I'm glad you were there. I do thank you, and my father thanks you, for your help. But it doesn't make you the expert around here. And it certainly doesn't qualify you to make decisions regarding my family. Is that clear?"

Every bone in his face jutted toward her aggressively and his brown eyes snapped, hot and angry.

She could have shrunk from him and run inside. Or she could have gotten offended and snapped back. She could have told him that his rage wasn't directed at her, but at the situation and the helplessness he felt and the decisions he did not want to have to make.

But she shut her mouth and swallowed her hurt. "Crystal." She looked at him for a few moments. He turned away and stared out the window. She reached out a hand and gently touched his cheek. Then she kissed it. "I had a wonderful time last night, Alex. Thank you."

She slid over to the door, opened it and swung down. "Goodbye," she said. She walked in Kiki's boots and Julia's clothes to the smoked brown glass of the door. But she held her head high: It was her own grace underneath it all.

# Chapter Twenty

Alex stared after Sydney, her kiss still lingering on his cheek. He felt like a complete dickhead. Yet he'd had every right to say what he'd said. Her experience with her grandmother did not qualify her to step in and take the reins of his runaway life. She had gall, she really did, to give him advice after knowing him for what, a week?

*Christ Almighty.* He put the truck into reverse and got the hell off Marv Spinelli's ugly-ass property and away from his maddening, mouthy, sexy daughter—walking contradiction that she was.

A prim redhead. A bossy little numbers geek who was confident enough to order people around and interfere in their lives, but vulnerable and full of self-doubt. A girl who'd run from a kiss and then show up for a date without a stitch of underwear.

What in the hell did you do with a woman like that?

*Marry her.*

Alex almost drove through the red light at Milam and Main. Only a honk from another car crossing Main stopped him. Where in the Sam Hill had such an idea come from?

Mama. It was just Mama's little fantasy that he and "Nell" were joined at the hip and busy procreating. Poor crazy Mama . . . and he was her son. There wasn't a whole lot of conclusive information out there about Alzheimer's yet, but besides the curious fact that traces of aluminum were found in most patients, medicine's best guess had to do with genetics.

As he headed out North Milam to 965, Alex couldn't help wondering if he'd go barking mad in his fifties, too. Would they find him on the Riverwalk one day, puffing a cigar in his skivvies? Lost on South Lincoln in plaid and stripes? Urinating in somebody's garden?

If so, he didn't want a humiliated, heartbroken wife running after him, trying desperately to keep him corralled and out of mischief. He didn't want a pack of mortified children watching as he slowly lost all the qualities that made him human. He didn't want them all hovering over him as he lapsed into a vegetative state and did nothing but blink and drool.

*I'm not subjecting anyone to that. No way in hell.* Jake could get married to every stripper in Dallas before Alex would walk down the aisle.

He hadn't been paying any attention to his speed.

The flashing red lights behind him told him that had been a mistake. He pulled over and waited for the state trooper to get out of his squad car and write him a ticket for going ninety-five in a sixty-five mph zone.

*Crunch, crunch.* The state issue black boots approached and Alex grimaced, wondering how much his auto insurance was going to shoot up.

"Sir, do you know what rate of speed you were traveling at?" asked a familiar voice. Then, "Aw, shit. It's you, you dumb bastard." Wesley Taunton, a high school buddy, grinned down at him.

"Hey, Wes. Just give me the damn ticket."

"Could you at least whine a little? Tell me how you're racing to the hospital because your sister's havin' a baby?"

"You know I don't have a sister. And I don't whine."

"You are no fun at all. I want to flex some muscle here, feel my power. C'mon, beg a little, and I might let you off."

Alex smirked and shot him the finger. "Flex this."

"Oh, fine. Be that way. Tell you what, some woman just called in with emu splattered all over her windshield. There's been another jailbreak."

*Great.* "Is she okay?"

"She's fine. Pissed off and shaken up, but fine." Wesley snapped his gum and squinted at Alex.

"You get the hell over to your Uncle Ted's, help

clear the hundred Big Birds off Highway 290 and we'll call it even. I ain't goin'. Those birds stink."

"Goddamn giant chickens," Alex said. He sighed. "It's a deal. You want a few steaks from the one we scrape off the windshield?"

"Hell, no. I'm not eatin' no mutant ostrich." Wes stumped back to his squad car. Alex laughed. Then he banged his head on the steering wheel.

Sydney stood with her back to the wall in the Motor Inn foyer and craned her neck for any sign of Julia. So far, so good. The last thing she needed right now was for her sister to see her creeping in at eleven a.m. in last night's clothes with all her makeup eaten and/or showered off. She put a hand up to her face, slick with Emulsion, and prayed the stuff would work fast to fade Alex's whisker burn.

She slunk down the hallway to the stairwell. Two flights, fifty feet down another hallway to room 239, and she was safe. Syd stuck her head around the corner. The coast was clear. She made a run for it, taking the brown-carpeted stairs two at a time and rounding the landing like a jackrabbit.

"Good morning!" Julia sang, her eyes bright with cheerful malice. She sat cross-legged at the top of the stairs, doing paperwork on a clipboard.

*Ugh.* "Good morning."

"I waited up for you last night, so that I could

hear all about your hot date, but around three a.m. I finally had to turn in.''

"Oh, sorry.'' Syd tucked her hair behind her ears. "Alex got a flat tire. Must have run over a broken bottle or something in the parking lot.''

"What bad luck. But he's got a spare in the bed of the truck, doesn't he?'' Julia's gaze raked her from top to toes and honed in like a laser on her face.

"Uhhhhh. Yes. Yes, he does, but he didn't happen to have a jack with him. So we just ended up staying the night in Gruene.''

"Did you. Gosh, Syd, that rash of yours is back. You've really got to stop using that cleanser you told me about. Funny how you had some in your evening bag last night.''

*Shit.* "Yeah. Can you recommend a dermatologist around here?'' She yawned and sidled past her younger sister. "I am so tired. I'll see you later, okay?''

"Nice try, Sydney. I'll just bet you're tired. Because you've been up all night doing dirty deeds with Alex Kimball! That is the *worst* case of whisker burn I've ever seen in my life, and you are a very, *very* bad liar.''

Sydney hunched her shoulders, honed in on door 239 and tried to make a run for it, but Julia hopped right out of her Manolo slides and raced after her.

Syd tried to shut the door in her face, but Jules got

the clipboard between it and the jamb and muscled her way inside—in spite of the fact that her sister had a good twenty pounds on her.

"You're shameless. Leave me alone," moaned Sydney.

Julia put her hands on her hips. *"I'm* shameless? *I'm* shameless? I didn't just slither inside after a one-night stand, Miss Morality!"

"I never said I was Miss Morality. Go away." Syd collapsed facedown onto the bed, smearing Emulsion onto the brown and mustard bedspread.

Julia plopped down right beside her. "No, you just acted like I was a loose dimwit for sleeping with Roman. My *fiancé.*"

"The issue was not sleeping with him. The issue was unplanned pregnancy; the reliability of the pill, maybe using a—" Sydney shut her mouth. *Yeah, one of those. One of those things you forgot to use in the heat of the moment, until he reminded you. Wanna start a South River chapter of Hypocrites R Us?*

"And are you on the pill, Sydney?"

*Oh, boy.* "N-no."

"Oh, really? Then you must have used a condom."

"Y-yes."

"Gosh, I think I detected a little pause there. A little hesitation. Where's the phone book? Those drugstore test kits aren't always accurate, so we need to make an appointment for you at the women's clinic, right away! You should get a pregnancy test.

And if Thelma Lynn Grafton should happen to be driving by as you leave, you can just tell her it was immaculate conception."

Sydney heard the nightstand drawer open and close, and then the riffle of pages, the rattle of the telephone receiver being picked up. "What are you doing?" She bolted upright.

"I'm calling the women's clinic, Syd. I wouldn't be a good sister if I didn't make you an appointment so we're sure you aren't pregnant. What if you had to turn around and marry Alex without thinking things through? My God, you don't even know the guy—"

Syd bounced across the mattress and ripped the phone out of Julia's hand. "Okay, okay. Point taken." She dropped the receiver back into the cradle.

"Point taken? That's all you're going to say? How about an apology? An admission that you were wrong? That Roman is a wonderful guy, and I'm marrying him because I love him, and for no other reason?"

*So wonderful that he gave you a fake engagement ring.* Sydney glanced at it and felt her anger kick up all over again. He would be back from his little business jaunt today, and she was going to give him a piece of her mind.

"Julia, I don't know what to say. I still think you're making a mistake to rush into this whole thing. Roman might not be who you think he is. You just don't know a lot about him."

Julia's perfect chin jutted and trembled at the same time. Her lovely eyes went stormy and her no-need-for-Botox lips flattened. "You just can't be happy for me, can you? And it's because you're *jealous*."

Syd's mouth dropped open. "What? That is so untrue!"

"Oh, it's true, all right."

It took a sickening lurch in her stomach for Sydney to realize her sister was right. What wouldn't she give for Julia's looks? To have Julia's choices in men? To inspire the kind of devotion in them that she did? To have them running after her, begging for her heart? How many of Julia's boyfriends had proposed to her? Five? Six?

"You and Marv and everyone else—you all think I'm just a dizzy blonde. That I have a dim perception of the world and no depth of feeling."

"No! I always defend you to Marv—" *Oh, shut up, Syd. You just admitted that Marv insults her intelligence, even though he adores her.*

"You're jealous, and you had to fly down here and treat me like a child and question my decisions and make me take a pregnancy test. And I put up with it! That's the part I can't believe."

"So why *did* you put up with it, Julia?" *Because the more I think about it, I have to admit that I wouldn't have.* Her nausea grew with her awareness.

"Because you're intimidating. You've always been

the older sister, the one who knew there was no Santa and despised me for crying when you told me.

"You've always known better than me, and I just fell into the same old pattern—'Sydney must be right.' Even when you're wrong, like in this case, you're still somebody I have to *prove* things to. Miss Good Grades, Miss Together, Miss Know-It-All, the one Marv trusts with his precious business books!"

Sydney would have laughed at this last statement if she hadn't felt so sick to her stomach, and hadn't been so horrified that Julia was right. She *had* been unable to be happy for her. What kind of person couldn't be happy for her own sister?

"Just once," Julia continued. "Just once! I would love for Marv to look at me the way he looks at you: with *respect*."

Syd swallowed. Happy-go-lucky Julia envied *her*? She tried to absorb the information, tried to bend her mind around it.

"But that'll never happen. So forget it. Roman, however, respects me. He loves me, and I love him, heart and soul. Our engagement has nothing to do with impulsiveness or flakiness, got that? I'd marry him no matter what. I'd marry him if he was a crook. I'd marry him with a ring made out of tinfoil. Who cares about this rock that you seem so fixated on— that you just had to have cleaned!"

Sydney closed her eyes. *Oh, God. I should tell her.*

*Her, not Roman. But how in the hell can I possibly bring up the issue now?*

"Julia," she said slowly. "I'm so sorry. I never meant to hurt you. I—I guess, deep down inside, I *was* jealous. Everybody loves you. You're beautiful and friendly and bubbly . . . you look like you just stepped out of *In Style* magazine. You've always had guys after you. They always want to marry you. And I've always had to work . . . work so hard to get attention. Hey, check out my straight A's. See my Phi Beta Kappa membership? Be impressed by how competent I am. Just don't, for God's sake, notice my nose or tell me how I look nothing like my adorable sister."

"Oh, Sydney. That's ridicu—"

"No, let me finish. Last night I pretended that I was more like you. I had a chance to go out with this incredible-looking, funny, sweet guy. And he made me feel beautiful and sexy." She smiled. "He made me feel like I was some amazing gift that he got to unwrap . . ." Her smile faded. "But you're right, it was a one-night stand. Because I'm not you. And the Alex Kimballs of the world don't fall in love with the Sydney Spinellis. It just doesn't work that way." She lapsed into silence.

*No, we fall in love with them. And they don't even notice.*

Julia scooted over and put her arms around Sydney. She started to speak, but Syd interrupted her, and surprised herself, with a loud, anguished honk and a minirainstorm. "He told me he loved my nose," she bawled.

"Oh, Sydney." Julia tightened her hug. "He's right. It's a great nose . . . you're beautiful . . . you just won't see it."

"And he said I have a ch-ch-charming ch-chin. And he's so sweet with his parents, and he was impressed that I could calculate a 19.3 percent tip in eight seconds . . ." She gasped for air.

"But he won't ask me out again, and anyway, I live in Princeton even if he did . . . and I, oh God, I think I love him." Horrified that she'd thought it, much less said it out loud, she lifted her head from Julia's shoulder, wiped her nose with the back of her hand and stared at her. "I take that back."

"Oh, sweetie, I don't think you can."

"I can." Syd nodded vigorously.

"Okay." But Julia drew her brows together and sighed.

"I'm not going to see him again. I've got to go back to New Jersey in the next couple of days." Syd got up and searched for a Kleenex box, but there was none.

"Marv's too cheap to put tissue in the rooms," said Julia matter-of-factly.

Syd shook her head in disgust and went for the toilet paper roll. She blew her nose and then eyed her sister. "By the way, don't *ever* envy the fact that

Marv turns to me for accounting help. He cooks his damn books."

Julia's jaw dropped.

"Yeah, and he wants me to be head chef. I won't do it. I've combed through and found all the traces of Betty Lou's sticky fingers, but I'm retiring as soon as I confess that I know she took his thirty thousand to Vegas and lost every dime."

Julia winced.

"Yeah, you want me to have that conversation on speakerphone, so you can share in the joy?"

"I think I'll pass."

"Julia," Syd said. "I love you. So much. Always have."

"I love you, too, Sydney."

"I'm really sorry about Santa."

Julia's lips twitched. "That was so mean, but I guess I'm over it now. After lots of therapy." She winked.

Sydney wanted to tell her that she was happy for her. But, knowing what she did, the words stuck in her throat. So she said instead, "I love you in spite of the fact that I sometimes want to shove fried food down your throat while you're sleeping. And maybe draw a black mustache on you with a permanent marker."

"Sydney!" But Julia convulsed into giggles.

Syd grinned at her and shrugged. "Hey, at least I'm honest, right?" Yet she wasn't being entirely honest—at least, not about that damn ring. What was she going to do?

# Chapter Twenty-one

Sydney kicked off Kiki's boots, peeled off the Cavalli jeans and ditched the Pucci halter. As she showered she looked forward to the comfort of her own baggy clothes: an actual pair of panties, Levi's that were a size too big and a nice cotton T-shirt.

Every part of her ached from her night with Alex, but she refused to think about him further. He'd made it quite clear that she should butt out of his life. It still hurt, even though he'd had every right to say it.

She'd been busy lately, meddling in other people's lives. Perhaps it was time to get back to her own. To tell Marv once and for all that he could do his home book-cooking on his own. He could rave and holler about ingratitude to his heart's content: She did not owe him a guilty conscience, a criminal record or jail time for her stint at boarding school or her college education.

Speaking of a guilty conscience, though . . . she had to do *something* about the damn engagement ring. After the talk they'd had, she couldn't just drop the bomb on Julia. And hadn't she said she didn't care about the ring? That she'd marry Roman even if he was a crook?

She had. So why tell her? What was the point?

*Because she should know what a creep he is.*

What if it doesn't bother her that he's a creep?

*It bothers ME.*

Aha. But you are embracing a new philosophy of Butting Out. Isn't that right?

*Yes . . . but I still can't let him get away with it. I have to confront him. I just have to.*

The telephone rang beside her, making her jump. "Hello?"

"Miss Sydney, you have a delivery here," said Hector's voice. "You want me to bring it up to you?"

*A delivery?* "No, that's okay, Hector. I'll come down. Thank you."

She padded downstairs in her bare feet, not wishing to put on her emu crap–encrusted sling-backs, her hiking boots, or Kiki's again.

Her bare feet were apropos for the occasion: On the registration counter sat a pair of beautiful, hand-tooled Western boots full of Indian paintbrush and bluebonnets.

"It's illegal to pick those," Hector informed her as she gaped.

"What?"

"Bluebonnets are the Texas state flower. You ain't allowed to pick 'em."

"These are for me?"

"Yep. There's a card, too. I tried real hard, but I couldn't see the signature through the envelope."

They had to be from Alex. She opened the card, being careful to step away from Hector's prying eyes.

*Dear Jersey,*

*I thought you might want a pair of your own cowboy boots, since you're now an expert two-stepper. I had a great time last night, Gorgeous. Sorry I was so gruff this morning.*

*Love, Alex.*

She felt tears well up in her eyes for the second time that day. The boots were polished, chestnut brown hide with a deep burgundy inlay over the shank. They had a medium heel and a sexy, pointed Texas toe. She would love them forever.

He'd remembered her mortification over wearing his ex's boots. He'd called her Gorgeous. He'd sent her flowers and apologized.

She'd fallen into deep, deep trouble when she'd met Alex Kimball. She'd fallen in love.

A half hour later, she'd put the flowers in her room, the narrow twin vases side by side on Marv's cheap, mass-manufactured idea of a dresser. She'd slid her feet into the boots, spun around in them a couple of times, and had to stop herself from calling Alex to say thank you.

*Focus, Sydney. Focus on what you're going to say to that rat bastard Roman out at the vineyard.* She needed to get it over with, and before he and Julia met for dinner and other indoor sports.

She made her way out to her rental car, and had the sense to open both the driver's side door and the passenger side door, turn on the ignition and let it cool down a bit before she got inside. She was not going to show up at the vineyard in a pool of perspiration this time. No—it was her turn to make *Roman* sweat.

*You're a fake, just like your ring,* she'd say. *You are as twisted as one of your damn vines. I'm going to yank off your little twin grapes, you jerk.*

Yup. That pretty much summed up her message.

*You either tell her that ring is fake, or I will.* She needed to add that, too.

Sydney finally got the car cooled down enough to get inside without singeing her butt on the black vinyl seat and then melting. She took the roads she remembered Alex taking, and within about fifteen minutes she was pulling in to the Sonntag Winery. She parked the car, wiggled her toes in her new boots for courage, took a deep breath and headed inside.

There was nobody there. The lights were on, the

shelves were stocked, the stemware gleamed from the hanging rack behind the counter, but she saw no human being.

Then she discerned the puff of cigar smoke coming from just beyond the little verandah, the one looking out over the vineyard. The door was ajar. Sydney stepped to it and pulled it open, her pulse kicking up as she mentally prepared for her standoff with her sister's fiancé.

Roman's laughter carried to the door. "Yeah. Oh, absolutely. Uh-huh. Listen, Alex, I can't thank you enough for distracting her and keeping her out of the way. She was sending Julia right over the edge, especially with that pregnancy thing . . ."

Sydney stood rooted to the spot, her heartbeat arrested. *Please, God. I didn't just hear that, did I?*

But she had.

*Listen, Alex, I can't thank you enough for distracting her . . .* He'd taken her out because Roman had asked him to! He'd been *assigned* to keep her out of the way. To insulate Julia.

The breath she didn't know she'd been holding whooshed out of her, and she never wanted to take another. But her lungs disagreed and forced her to gasp for air.

She turned on her heel and ran from the place, because if she didn't she would either throw up on Roman or break down in front of him, neither of which was acceptable.

She reached the car and fumbled in her pocket for the keys, her whole body shaking. Then she had to fit the damn thing into the cheap compact's door and then into the ignition.

The makeover. The skintight bondage jeans. The tiny top. The lack of underwear. All of that she had done for Alex. He must have found her oh, so amusing! All the smarmy, ingratiating compliments that she'd fallen for, hook, line and sinker. The way she'd kissed him back and let him touch her—oh, God, the way she'd yanked on him to get him inside her. He must have been laughing his ass off.

And he was probably sharing it all now with his best buddy, Roman Sonntag! How he'd sent the desperate, homely sister into orbit, calling his name.

Sydney sat in the rental car, hyperventilating with rage at Alex and humiliation. Her palms sweated, but the rest of her body was ice cold in the sweltering heat, and she hadn't even turned on the ignition and AC.

Little by little she got control over herself and evened out her breathing. Then she put the compact into drive and sped out of the winery's gates.

The little piece of junk didn't want to go over seventy. Sydney didn't care. Pedal to the metal, she got it to ninety-two miles per hour, though the mechanical whine set her teeth on edge and the vibrations almost knocked her hands off the wheel.

She was about two miles away from the Kimball house when the siren went off behind her and she saw red flashing lights. Too bad. She was not pulling over, not when she was this close to ripping Alex a new one.

She ignored the trooper, even though she knew it was a crazy thing to do. The compact wouldn't go any faster, so she couldn't outrun him. He'd already clocked her at ninety-two, so she saw no reason to slow down. The ticket would be for the speed, not the duration of the speed.

She clenched her teeth and continued to drive like a madwoman.

Obviously frustrated, the trooper rolled down his window and stuck out a bullhorn. "Ma'am, please pull over to the shoulder and stop your vehicle."

She kept driving. Her gaze honed in on the two square stone posts that marked the entrance to the Kimballs' drive, and she slowed down only enough to squeal through them.

Gravel sprayed from the car's wheels and her teeth rattled in her head as she bumped down the road with the cop following her.

"Pull over immediately, ma'am. That is an order!" he squawked through the bullhorn.

Alex's tall figure appeared on the front steps, no doubt because of the noise, and she was only too happy to obey. She slammed on the brakes, almost causing the hapless lawman to rear-end her, and ripped the key from the ignition. Then she was out of the car and running at a startled Alex.

"You bastard!" she spat. "You son of a—" She stopped as she saw Mrs. Kimball's head pop into the kitchen window. "You took me out as a *favor* to *Roman Sonntag*? He asked you to distract me and keep me away from my own sister?"

"Whoa!" Alex threw up his hands. "No, you have got this all wrong."

The trooper came panting up behind her and grabbed at her arm. "Ma'am—"

She whirled on him. "I *know* I was speeding! You can give me five tickets, but you'll just have to wait until I am done with this man!"

"Hello, Wesley," said Alex. "Nice to see you again."

The trooper opened and closed his mouth. He looked from one to the other.

"Wes-Man, why don't you go on into the house and get a glass of iced tea from Mama. Doesn't that sound good?"

The uniform frowned. He cleared his throat, about to turn down the invitation in the name of duty.

"She just made a *nice* peach pie, too. I bet she'll set you up with a slice," Alex said.

The man's head came up like a gopher's, his expression yearning.

"Go on. Let me talk to the lady."

Wes pursed his lips and gave Sydney a severe look. But he was a pushover. He nodded sheepishly and headed for the front stoop.

Alex turned back to Sydney as the door shut behind the cop. "Now, where were we? I'm a bastard?"

"Yes!" But she sent an apologetic glance toward the kitchen window. Not double-paned. Not insulated. And she adored Mrs. K.

She grabbed Alex unceremoniously by the collar and hauled him over a few feet and down to her level. Then she was able to tell him exactly what she thought of him—pipe it right into his ear. His eyes widened and then he nodded.

"Okay. I think I get the gist of that, thank you very much. But I did not take you out last night because Roman asked me to."

"You lying sack of—you did, too! I heard it out of his own mouth just minutes ago, and he was talking to *you*."

"Roman was concerned about Julia, so—"

"Oh, spare me! Roman's so devoted to my sister that he gave her a fake diamond! Three carats of glass, that's what's on her hand. Proof of his undying love."

Alex's face reflected shock. "What? That can't be true. That ring was his grandmother's."

"And you—talk about birds of a feather. You are just as low-down as he is. Did you *screw* me because

263

Roman asked you to? Were you laughing inside the entire time? At my gullibility? Did you figure you were doing me a favor because with this nose—oh, your *favorite* part of me—I couldn't be getting much, anyway?"

"No! Aw, Christ—"

She disregarded his horrified expression and poked him in the chest with her index finger. "And then, today, when you thought it over, you felt a little guilty. Maybe you took your favor to Roman too far. So you sent me a gift to salve your conscience!"

She backed away from him, bent over, and tugged at one of the boots. The damn thing wouldn't come off. She stepped on the heel of it with the toe of the other and tugged, dislodging her foot by a centimeter or two.

"Sydney. Sydney, listen to me. None of that is true. Roman did ask me to keep you away from Julia, because you were upsetting her, and he's protective. I don't know where this business about the ring comes from—"

"I tricked her! I said the damn thing was filthy and we had to have it cleaned. While we were at the jeweler's I asked them to look at it. So don't bother trying to cover for that jerk. And you've just admitted all I need to hear." She got her foot free of the boot and threw it at him.

He dodged it. "No. That's *not* all you need to hear.

I said Roman asked me initially to keep you a little busy. But I don't take my orders from Roman. I drove you out around the hill country that day as a favor to him. I took you to Gruene Hall because I wanted to."

Sydney hopped around on the remaining boot, her sock-clad foot perched on the heel. It refused to budge.

"And I damn sure didn't sleep with you as a favor to Roman," Alex said emphatically. "I slept with you because I was dying to. You don't have a clue how hot you looked last night, and you don't have any concept of how beautiful you are right now, even doing a credible imitation of an amphetamine-crazed flamingo."

"Save—your—breath, Kimball." Hop, hop. *Fucking boot.* "You think I'm going to believe anything that comes out of your mouth?"

"You know what, Sydney?" He was starting to look steamed, not just shocked. "I don't care if you believe it. I'm no liar, and it's the truth."

"Bullshit."

"So quick to condemn."

"Yeah, sue me."

"Okay," Alex said. "Then let's look at this another way. If you hadn't flown down here like a bat out of South River and stuck your very pretty nose in where it didn't belong, then nobody would have seen it necessary to distract you!"

"Ooohh!" Syd leaned on the boot heel and pulled at her foot with all her might. No dice. "I can't even respond to that, it's so pathetic."

"Is it, Sydney? Think about it. You are a meddler. You came down here to stop your sister's marriage. Along the way, you tell me and Uncle Ted how to run our business. Then you start trying to make my family decisions. What gives you the right?"

She wouldn't look at him.

"I don't care what you think you've discovered about Julia's engagement ring. Roman loves her one hundred percent. With every fiber of his being. He loves her more than he loves himself." Alex stopped. He swallowed.

"I've only ever seen that kind of love one other time in my life," he said quietly. "It's very rare." He jerked his thumb toward the house behind him. "My parents have that. I doubt I ever will. But Roman and Julia—" He stopped. "Open your eyes, Sydney. Open your eyes and you'll see. You might even forgive Roman for the favor he asked of me. He won't let anybody hurt or upset the woman he loves."

Sydney gave up on the boot and clapped once, twice, three times. "A beautiful speech."

His jaw jerked in irritation.

"You've got quite a way with words, Kimball. That should come in handy for you later. Because I'm retiring from the meddling business. I'm not going to tell my sister about the ring—she wouldn't believe me at first, and then it would devastate her. And I'm not going back out to the vineyard to tell Roman, either. Because if I see that rat bastard, I am all too likely to wrap my hands around his lying throat and cling there like a koala bear until he keels over dead.

"Since you are the one trying to reform my evil, meddling ways, Kimball, you can tell Roman yourself. Tell him I know that ring is fake, that it's been examined by a gemologist, and that he'd better come clean with my sister or I will take the information straight to Thelma Lynn Grafton and we can see what's left of his name once it's been dragged through the mud."

Alex just stared at her.

"Do you think you can take care of that, Kimball? If you have a shred of fairness in you, then I bet you'll see you owe me that."

Sydney turned on her single boot heel and awkwardly stumped back to her rental car. She got in and started the ignition, only to see the trooper come flying out of the house brandishing a fork at her.

She rolled down the window. "Keep your shorts on, Deputy. Just send me the damn ticket, okay?"

He began to bluster.

"To Marv's Motor Inn on Orange Street."

"I'll vouch for her," Alex ground out. "Go finish your pie, Wes. If she skips it, I'll pay."

Sydney looked at him for a long moment, unsure of how she felt about that. She didn't want to owe him a shred of gratitude, much less money. She hated him.

He folded his arms and stared right back at her.

She rolled up the window and took off, a red-haired, one-booted rebel. Everything else in her life might suck at the moment, but she had to admit she relished her only experience of being an outlaw.

# Chapter Twenty-two

Sydney kicked the pizza box out of her path and listened to Marv, foaming at the mouth from South River. She'd stuck her cell phone on the nightstand and put it on speaker, so his nasal, profanity-spattered squawking filled room 239.

It was the crack of dawn, but Marv got up at five a.m. every day, and she'd wanted to get this conversation over with.

Normally his rages gave her tension headaches and curdled her insides. But at the moment she was curiously detached and only caught every other word.

". . . victim of a blue-haired bandit!" Marv screamed, followed by a couple of obscenities.

Sydney sighed and opened the pizza box with her toe, grimacing at the congealed mess of dough, cheese and pepperoni inside. She'd eaten one bite of one piece in twenty-four hours. What a waste. She closed the box and focused instead on the dent in the mustard-colored wall she'd made with her lone cowboy boot, before she'd ordered the pizza.

". . . poker chips up that broad's hemorrhoidal, saggy ass!" shrieked the cell phone.

*Ugh. Really, Marv. That's disgusting.*

Sydney had been forced to lie on the floor and hook the toe of the blasted boot under the bed frame in order to pull off Satan's Shit-Kicker.

Then she'd scarred the wall with it, stomped on it and tossed it into the bathtub.

She entertained herself with thoughts of schlepping the boot out to Uncle Ted's place and holding it under the backside of the biggest emu she could find. Then she'd break the window of Alex's truck, put it on the driver's seat and set it on fire.

Mature? No. Satisfying? Yes. And so much more original than slashing his tires.

". . . hunt her down and nail her fat carcass to the living room wall!" howled Marv.

Sydney sighed. "Ma would not appreciate the addition to her décor . . . and it really would clash with her scale-model Versailles dollhouse." Sydney imagined Betty Lou Fitch's stuffed head and shoulders presiding over the mantel, much as Lupe did at the Gristmill in Gruene, or the twelve-point buck at the Biergarten.

How would Marv describe his big-game trophy? As a ten-point bitch?

". . . another smart-ass word outta you, because this is all your fault!"

"*What?*"

"If you'd'a kept closer tabs on the books, this would'na happened . . ."

Her ears tingled and then began to burn. Sydney stalked to the phone, scooped it up and yelled, "Hold it right there, old man!"

An unintelligible but furious nasal New Jersey roar blared from the phone.

Through clenched teeth Sydney bit out her next words. "Meaning no disrespect, Marv, but *shut up*. I'm going to say this one time. I have my own business. I am not responsible for yours. And I will not help you falsify records.

"None, *none* of this is my fault! You hired Betty Lou. You supervised her—or didn't, as the case may be. And you would have been able to call the police and apprehend her with at least some of your money if your books were legit! So don't you dare blame me for this situation. I want an apology. And I quit." Sydney clicked the END CALL button on her phone and then turned it off for good measure.

She pumped her fist in the air, but without enthusiasm, and slumped back onto the bed among the brown and mustard flowers.

A knock sounded at the door. Julia's voice called, "Sydney? Sydney, it's me. Open up."

What was her sister doing up this early? She didn't move a muscle or say a word.

"Sydney, I know you're in there. And I've got a master key, so if you don't open the door I'll come in anyway."

Syd sighed. It seemed an almost overwhelming effort to heave herself up and off the bed. She kicked at the pizza box again as she passed it. "You forgot about the dead bolt," she grumbled through the door. "I can stay in here 'til next month if I want."

"Without food or clean underwear or fresh sheets?"

*Ugh.* Julia had a point. "What do you want?"

"Alex has called here about ten times."

"Alex who?"

"He was worried. He wanted to know if you got back here safely."

Syd snorted.

"He said the statistics on madwomen in one boot maneuvering sardine cans are not good."

Syd didn't even crack a smile.

"He wants to apologize," Julia told her. "He feels really bad."

"Next topic."

"Sydney, let me in. Please."

"Which part of 'go away' do you not understand?"

"Don't be nasty. I'm not the one you're mad at."

*She's right. None of this is her fault.* Sydney opened

the door, turned around and flopped back on the bed.

Julia surged in, bright and sunny in a little floral dress and mules. Syd felt like the Swamp Creature next to her. She grabbed a pillow and hugged it to her chest, glowering at her.

"Alex wants—"

"Four-letter word," snarled Syd. "Do not mention that name again."

Julia blinked. "Oh-kaaay. Let me start that sentence over. Roman—"

"*Five*-letter word," hissed Sydney.

"You cannot forbid me to mention my own fiancé's name." Julia glared at her.

Syd hunched over the pillow.

"Roman apologizes to you. He would have come to say it himself, but I told him that you would close his head in your laptop and then pitch him out the window."

"Correct."

"Anyway, he apologizes. He knows he stepped over the line. And he also told me that Al—"

Sydney growled in warning.

"—sorry, *Jackass* doesn't do anything that he doesn't want to do.

"And"—Julia took a deep breath—"I know about the ring. Roman told me. And he was mortified, absolutely beside himself."

*I'll just bet he was.*

"It's been in a bank vault, Sydney, ever since his grandmother died. The first time it came out of there was when Roman signed it out, the night before he proposed to me."

Julia nodded. "I can tell by your face that you don't believe it, but Roman is not responsible for switching the stones. He racked his brains and finally went to talk to his father. His dad remembers a period of about two weeks when his mother wasn't wearing the ring. She claimed the setting was loose, and it was at a jeweler."

She leaned forward. "Here's the proof, though: Roman's dad called the San Antonio dealer that *his* dad always used whenever he bought Olga jewelry. The one place that she would have trusted to reset the ring, which came originally from Belgium."

Julia's eyes sparkled. "That dealer kept meticulous records, and there's no record at all of him ever resetting the diamond for Olga."

"So?"

"So she took it somewhere else! To Houston, maybe. She sold the stone and had it replaced with a copy. Here's the kicker: It's not a cubic zirconia. It's a very old, very well-cut crystal."

"I'm not following you."

"Syd, if Roman had replaced the stone with a fake, it would have been a CZ—almost impossible to tell from a diamond with the naked eye. And it's a modern development. CZs weren't around when Olga did her switcheroo."

"Why would she have done it to begin with?"

"Roman's dad remembers his parents always fighting about money, and Olga liked to shop. She also ran with a social crowd that gave a lot to charity. He thinks she probably switched the ring to save face around her friends and have some pocket money to boot."

Sydney looked at Julia incredulously. She supposed that maybe, just maybe, the story made some sense. But she wasn't sure she believed it. She looked at her sister's fourth finger. The disputed engagement ring still flashed there. "Why are you still wearing it?"

Julia looked down at the stone and smiled softly. "Because Roman gave it to me. He swears that he's going to get me a real one, but you know what? I don't care. This is the ring he put on my finger when he proposed. And that's good enough for me."

When Julia left, Sydney flipped open her laptop and made an airline reservation for the next day. Her little Roman Holiday had come to an end. It was back to Princeton and her condo and her own business, which wouldn't stand any more neglect.

She'd wing through South River and visit Ma when she knew Marv was out, and she'd bring Humphrey home with her. Speaking of the poor dog, she

275

should round up some rawhide scraps for him before she left Texas. She supposed that she could get up the energy to do that: hit Main Street later and go to Dogologie, the chic little Fredericksburg shop catering to canines.

Syd checked e-mail quickly before logging off the Internet. Predictably, there was a reply from Vivien.

Subject: FAKE ring???
Date: XXXXXXX
From: vshelton
To: numbersgeek
What do you mean, the ring he gave her is fake?! HOW COULD HE??? Gotta fly, due in court. xoxoxo, Viv

*This electronic message transmission contains information from the law firm of Klein, Schmidt and Belker that may be confidential or privileged. The information is intended solely for the recipient and use by any other party is not authorized. If you are not the intended recipient, be aware that any copying, disclosure, distribution or use of the contents of this transmission is prohibited. If you have received this electronic transmission in error, please notify us immediately. Thank you.*

Sydney wearily composed a response.

Subject: Re: FAKE ring???
Date: XXXXXXX

From: numbersgeek
To: vshelton@kleinschmidtbelker

Viv, supposedly it's not his fault. The grand-mother sold it way back when and he didn't know. (Do you believe this? Not sure, myself.) But it doesn't matter! Our Julia has got it bad: she's STILL WEARING the ring, and says she doesn't care that it's fake. Why? Because HE gave it to her. I give up . . . I'm going home. Can you at least get her to sign a prenup? I'm serious!!!!!!!

Syd

She logged off and closed her laptop. It was about time she pulled herself together and left room 239. She'd holed up to lick her wounds and have a good sobfest, but the tears had never come. She'd entered a weird, robotic state where she couldn't experience any emotion. She knew she hurt. She knew she felt betrayed. She knew she hated the man whose name was a four-letter, unmentionable word.

But she'd turned off the tap to her feelings, other than briefly confronting Marv. Where Al—where *Jack-ass* was concerned, she was numb. She'd let him inside her once. He didn't get to return, not even mentally.

She decided that as long as she was here for another day, she would go and climb Enchanted Rock, a mas-sive outcropping of stone in a public park close by. Then she'd stop by the dog place on the way back.

Syd pulled her mess of hair into a ponytail and figured she should add pants to her lovely ensemble before leaving the room. A T-shirt and underwear did fine for number 239, but she didn't need her own tail hanging out in Dogologie.

She shoved her feet into her hiking boots, laced them up and jammed shades onto her nose. Then she grabbed her bag and left.

Blue skies and a rising sun greeted her outside, and if the air wasn't exactly cool, at least it didn't scald her skin. Sydney drove on Orange Street north to Travis, and then from Travis to North Milam and 965. Enchanted Rock was about eighteen miles northwest of Fredericksburg.

She'd gone about three of those miles and had steeled herself to pass the turnoff to Jackass's parents' house, when she saw a lone figure traipsing along the road. The figure looked female, and was clad in a blue nightgown and matching robe with terry-cloth slippers.

Something about her gait and the way she held her head struck a familiar chord in Sydney, and as she got closer she saw the familiar shade of salon-rinsed blond hair.

Sydney's heart dropped into her boots. Mrs. Kimball was nowhere near her home. She had shuffled two and a half miles in those terry-cloth slippers.

Syd turned the wheel of the rental car and pulled over onto the shoulder of the road, pasting a bright smile onto her face. She got out and waved to Emily, whose expression transformed from puzzled and lost to pleased. "Nell!" she exclaimed. "How are you?"

Her poor toes were blackened and grimy, the pink polish on them barely visible. The slippers, coated with dust and mud, had just barely protected her feet from the gravel and tarmac. One of them had almost disintegrated on her two-mile journey, the open terry-cloth toepiece flapping and secured by perhaps six threads.

The tears that had eluded Sydney for the last twenty-four hours sprang to her eyes, but she blinked them fiercely away so she wouldn't confuse Mrs. K. "I'm fine," she said. "Heading out to Enchanted Rock for a hike. Where are you off to?"

"Oh," said Alex's mother vaguely, "I just came out for the morning paper." The warm breeze lifted the hair at her forehead, and she looked like a lovely, late middle-aged child.

Sydney swallowed. "I don't see the paper anywhere. Maybe they're late with it today."

"You could be right. Or maybe I'm not looking in the correct place . . ."

"Would you like me to help you find it?" Sydney asked. She needed to get her into the car somehow so she could take her home—home to her husband and home to her son, the last person on the planet Syd wanted to see.

But under the circumstances, that just didn't matter. Mrs. Kimball could have gotten picked up by a friendly trucker, and not been able to tell him where she lived. She could have gotten a ride with someone not so friendly, which didn't bear thinking about. Or she could have been killed if she'd wandered into the middle of the highway.

"That is so nice of you, Nell. I'd greatly appreciate it."

Sydney put her arm around Emily Kimball's shoulders and walked calmly with her to the compact. "My car's not very luxurious," she said, "but it'll get us where we're going."

She helped her into the passenger seat, got her belt fastened and then slid in herself on the other side. "Let's head north," she suggested.

"Okay, dear." Mrs. K folded her hands in her lap and smiled trustingly at her.

Syd turned the key in the ignition and headed for the familiar square stone posts. Had she really been here just yesterday, poking Alex in the chest and defying the law?

She turned between the pillars, disturbing a dove perched on the right one. It fluttered into the air, then settled back into position as the car moved on.

Alex almost ran into them. He was squealing down the drive in the Mercedes, his father strapped in next to him.

Sydney braked hard, flinging her arm across Mrs. Kimball—a reflex to protect her from harm.

Alex braked viciously, too, when he saw them. He wrenched the wheel of the car hard to the right so that when both vehicles slid in the gravel, only the left headlight of the Mercedes grazed the compact's front bumper.

Accident avoided, they stared at each other for a long moment through their respective windshields. Alex saw his mother. He slumped, boneless, over the steering wheel. Mr. Kimball got out of the passenger side, visibly shaken, and approached his wife.

"Lord have mercy, Jonathan!" she said, opening the door. "What on earth do you two think you're doing?"

He bent down, took her in his arms, and looked an anguished thank-you at Sydney. "I don't know," he said heavily. "Emily, I just don't know."

# Chapter Twenty-three

"We didn't even know she was gone," Alex said to Sydney. He looked at his watch. "Good Christ, it's only seven fifteen a.m.!" He scrubbed a hand over his shadowed jaw. "Dad woke up just now and there she wasn't. He went to the kitchen, thinking she'd be there, making coffee. He looked everywhere. He panicked and woke me."

Sydney avoided looking at him. She said not one word of I-told-you-so, not one word of you-need-to-get-help. She seemed a cardboard cutout version of herself, pale and calm. The virago of yesterday had vanished. "I found her about two and a half miles down the road."

"Miles?"

"Yes. She said—" Her voice hitched, but her face remained expressionless. "She said she'd just stepped out to get the morning paper."

Alex closed his eyes. "She could have been . . ."

"Yeah."

He opened his eyes and looked at her: scraped-back hair, no makeup, baggy shorts and hiking boots. She wasn't herself. Even her freckles looked faded, tired and disillusioned.

*I did this to her. Without even meaning to.* He hated himself for it. "Sydney . . ."

What? What in the hell did he think he could say to her now, when in her eyes, he'd betrayed her in the worst way possible? She'd called it a mercy date, and he'd convinced her otherwise. She'd trusted him enough to sleep with him. And now she thought he'd manipulated her—done it all as a favor to Roman.

To her, it was particularly cruel, because she'd allowed herself to internalize his compliments. She had begun to absorb them. He'd watched her stand up taller, swing her hips, flash a wider smile full of confidence. He'd loved giving her that knowledge: that she was a sexy, desirable woman. That he'd wanted her. He still did—but she'd never, ever believe it again.

So he said what he could. "Sydney, I can't thank you enough for what you did today. For what you did yesterday. And the time we met at the salon."

She shrugged, not absorbing the words. "What is it you say around here? *De nada*?"

"It's not nothing. I know I'm the last person in the universe you wanted to see, but you brought Mama home anyway. And . . ." He took a deep breath.

"And you're right, Sydney. If nothing else, this incident has shown me that we're going to have to get some help."

She turned to get back into the compact. "I'm just glad she's okay. That I found her before anything bad could happen."

She tugged open the door, but he strode to her and pushed it closed again. She expelled a breath but didn't look at him. "You'll need to check her feet. They may be pretty bruised on the bottom."

"Yeah. I'll sit her on a bucket and hose them off."

She flinched almost imperceptibly.

"Jersey—"

"*Don't.* Don't call me that. I can handle anything but that."

"I'm so sorry. And I swear to you that our date was a real date. And I swear that you are one gorgeous woman."

"Alex. Get over it. I have. Tomorrow I'm on a plane and out of here. You won't have to feel guilty any longer. And you were actually right about one thing: If I hadn't interfered, nobody would have asked you to distract me. So I can take some responsibility for what happened, too."

"No. That was a low blow on my part. I'm sorry for saying that."

She tossed her keys in the air and caught them again. She moved his hand off the car doorframe. Her touch was beyond impersonal. "A low blow that happened to hit home. Okay, I'm gone. Nice knowing you. I guess we'll have to see each other at the wedding."

Sydney got into the car while he stood there, the steel box back within his ribs. She started the ignition, backed and turned. Then she bumped away, down the gravel road.

He wanted to run after her. He wanted to tuck the errant, flapping label of her T-shirt inside the collar. He wanted to pull the elastic band from her hair and smooth down the escaped lock that formed a fuzzy loop at the back of her head. He wanted to kiss away her competence and see her trusting smile again, the joy she'd taken in feeling sexually attractive to him.

And he wouldn't, couldn't do it.

He had the genes of the woman who'd just walked two and a half miles in search of the morning paper; the woman who'd tried to expose her violet bra on Main Street; the woman who'd given birth to him and raised him to be strong and fearless in the face of anything—anything but a slow spiral into madness and dependency and finally, a vegetative state.

The horror he felt at watching the process rivaled and surpassed anything that Stephen King or Hollywood could possibly dream up. The terror that it might happen also to him was selfish, but visceral and primal.

He could shrug off the fear for an evening of dancing, a day of running numbers, even a week or two

of normalcy. But it crowded out most urges to inti-
macy or emotional honesty.

And the fear turned into downright cowardice
when he contemplated a relationship with a woman,
much less a relationship that might lead to something
lasting, like marriage.

Alex watched the dust settle as Sydney's little
rental car buzzed away. "Goodbye, Jersey," he
murmured.

Desolation beat down on him like the Texas sun.


"Get up," said an implacable voice. It echoed in
Alex's head, getting louder and more dramatic like
the soundtrack to a bad B movie.

"Whah?" His tongue had obviously been stung by
a swarm of insects, because it had swollen to eight
times its normal size and soaked up any saliva in
his mouth.

"Drop your cock, pull up your socks, and let's go."
Roman. It was Roman who was hassling him. It must
also have been Roman who put the heavy artillery
in his head and ordered whoever manned it to fire
repeatedly, mercilessly.

"Blow me," Alex muttered. He attempted to roll
over, but it took too much effort and was too painful.

"Kimball, do not make me put this boot up your
ass." Roman picked up the boot Sydney had thrown
at Alex from its place of honor on the nightstand.
"Get the hell out of that bed."

Alex moaned. With distaste, he felt warm breath at his ear.

"*Now!!!*" Roman roared.

Alex shot off the mattress and stood on barely functional legs. "Christ Almighty! What the hell do you want!"

"Put these on," Roman ordered, tossing a pair of jeans at him. "And this." The collar of a clean shirt hit him in the jaw. Alex fumbled with the clothing, disgusted to find that something had died and rotted in his mouth overnight.

"What rock did you crawl out from under, and why are you in my face?"

"Your father called me this morning around two o'clock. He said you'd fallen into a bucket of Johnnie Walker and you were two-stepping around the front yard with a rake as a partner, howling that Two Tons of Steel song about it taking a redheaded woman to get a dirty job done."

"Bullshit," said Alex, confident in his disbelief.

"I said to Mr. K, 'No, I've known Alex for thirty years, and I've never seen him do anything *that* stupid.'"

"Nope, no way."

"And your dad said, 'Well, I've known him for thirty-five years, and the only thing I've seen him do stupider than this was let that little auburn-haired gal drive away. You might know her? She's related to your fiancée.'"

Alex had stopped with one leg into the jeans.

"Get your damn pants on, you dumb yokel. Your dad and I had a little chat when I came over to pull you out of the Johnnie Walker."

"That so," mumbled Alex. He buttoned his fly.

"She's leaving today."

"She who?"

"Listen to me, Alex. From what Julia's told me, Sydney spent hours with her grandmother when the old lady had Alzheimer's. Grandma told tall tales, threw food, wore bizarre combinations of clothing, and cussed and bitched. Sydney loved her through it all. She never walked away. Her feelings for her never changed."

"Is there a point to all this?"

"Do you love your mother any less now that she's changing?"

"What is this? Fuck off, Dr. Phil!"

"Does your father love her any less? Does Mrs. K love *you* any less?"

"Go away."

"Alex, the point is this: You probably won't even get the damn disease. It skips generations. But if you did, you'd have lived a full and happy life. And you should live that life with a wife and kids if you want them."

"Yeah, great, I should pass it on! Pull your head out, Roman. Look at what's going on in this house. I can't do that to someone."

"You're not doing anything to anyone. You don't control the odds. The Guy Upstairs does. And he generally laughs the hardest at the people who try to dodge what's in store for them."

"Roman. You're way too profound for eight o'clock in the morning. Now for pity's sake, at least bring me some aspirin."

After supplying him with painkillers and water, Roman kept at him. "I don't know what's gone on between you and Sydney Spinelli, man. It's not really my business, except that I feel awful for any role I've had in hurting her. But if you're dancing a rake around in the small hours, and yodeling about red-headed women, I'm going to extrapolate from that an interest in Sydney on your part."

Alex opened his mouth.

"While I realize that she wants to rip my balls off and feed them to me, I think she feels differently about you. So ask her to stay for a few more days. Figure out what this is between the two of you."

Alex closed his mouth.

"I'm going to drive you over there. You're in no condition to get behind the wheel."

"She hates me, Roman. She outran Wesley Taunton in his squad car to rip me a new one."

"Would all that hate be there, buddy, if some kind of feeling weren't on the flip side?"

Alex sighed. "I'm not sure."

# Chapter Twenty-four

Sydney hugged her sister goodbye and walked outside to the Marv's Motor Inn parking lot. She would no longer be counting sheep for cheap.

A little hurt that Julia hadn't accompanied her outside, she unlocked the trunk of the junky little rental car, opened it and tossed her laptop and small suitcase inside. She closed the trunk and emitted a small shriek when she turned and saw Alex Kimball.

He looked worse than hell and twice as sexy: bad boy, movie star, messed up hair; circles under his eyes that hung to his belt buckle; and his trademark five o'clock shadow.

"Hey, Jersey," he said softly. His voice held something she couldn't quite put her finger on—something alien to his personality. With surprise, she realized it was uncertainty.

He reeked of whiskey and cover-up mouthwash. The liquor sprang from his pores, and no amount of minty-fresh anything would hide it. She hoped he hadn't been driving.

"I'm looking for the woman whose foot fits this boot." He held up the one she'd thrown at him.

Sydney's mouth dried on the spot. *I am not this easy*, she told herself. When she could breathe, she said, "I believe she may have left the, um, kingdom."

"Nope," said Alex. "I don't think so."

She noticed that, for the second time, the man who never sweated had drops of perspiration rolling down his temples and dotting his forehead.

"Listen, if you happen to see her . . ." He cleared his throat. "Could you tell her there's a . . . big toad . . . who'd really like her to stay a few more days. At a decent hotel, on his tab."

Sydney's brows rose, and he winced. "I mean. Uh. I only meant a hotel other than the one her sister's running."

"I know what you mean."

"A hotel where she and the, uh, toad could have some privacy and talk. About whatever this feeling is that the toad has . . . and hopes she has for, uh, him . . ." He trailed off and winced at her expression.

Sydney folded her arms. "How many brain cells did you kill off last night?"

"One or two." He caught his upper lip under his teeth and squinted at her hopefully.

"Toad, I'm going to say something to you that you once said to me. You stink!"

His face fell. "Yeah. I hear tell that I fell into a vat of Johnnie Walker last night and two-stepped with a garden rake. Worse, I howled at the moon about a redheaded woman."

"Talented toad." But her lips twitched in spite of herself.

"He aspires to a higher station in life."

"And what might that be?"

"Well . . ." He sidled closer to her. "I've heard this theory that if you kiss a toad, he immediately turns into a—"

"Forget it," she said. "Your crown is most definitely in the shop for repairs."

"I was afraid of that."

"And it'll probably come back as ten-carat plate over surgical steel."

"Ouch."

"You remain a lowly amphibian for the next few days."

Alex dared to step closer and slip his arms around her waist. "And then?"

*Damn, I am this easy.* "Then it's either formaldehyde for you, or a kiss."

"Are you sure I can't get a preview of coming attractions?" he whispered, closing his mouth over her earlobe.

"Oh," she said, "I'm sure that somewhere we can

find a ruler, a spiral notebook and a sadistic kid with braces for you." She grinned evilly.

"Jersey," Alex said, "I think I'm in love with you. And you have a mouth that just won't quit." Then he closed his own over it, for quite some time.

If you enjoyed watching Sydney Spinelli race to Texas to save her baby sister from marrying a pretty boy Texan in *First Date*, you'll definitely want to see how the Sonntag family feels about their future sister-in-law. . . .

Meet Kiki Sonntag. She's the perfect bridesmaid—sexy, stylish, and a former Miss Texas beauty pageant queen with the talent and determination to become a big actress in New York City. When she gets word of her brother Roman's upcoming nuptials to a Jersey girl she's never met, she's sure she needs be her wedding consultant and plan the grant event, no matter who her in-laws will be. But a nasty tabloid scandal forces her into hiding in Manhattan's swankiest new hotel—and the playboy owner has some plans of his own for Kiki that begins with their . . .

## *First Kiss*

### BOOK TWO IN

## THE BRIDESMAID CHRONICLES

(Read ahead for a sneak peek of Kiki's story.)

From: kikid@misstexas95.com

To: suzix2@hotmail.com
80sdancer@aol.com

Subject: Venting

Suzi-Suzi and Danni!

It's after midnight and too late to call, so here I sit banging away on my laptop. May I please share two things that are currently driving me insane?

1) Polygamy! Why is this a crime? The multiple wives/husbands are at least sharing responsibilities. Meanwhile, there are no laws to protect bridesmaids. I'm already booked for four weddings this summer, and now my brother is getting married. That's five new dresses to buy that I will only wear once! Five trips to spots on the map that require me to get on a plane and fly coach! Five bridal shower gifts! Five wedding gifts! And you know my luck. If there was one straight, single, smoking-hot groomsman to look forward to, then it might be worth it. But that's never the case. I get stuck trudging down the aisle with the teenage boys fighting acne, boring salesmen who are already married, and gay cousins. Never the straight hot guy. Ugh! It's so unfair. I should write my congressman. Hmm. Who is my congressman? Wait! I'll e-mail Hillary. She's a senator. That's higher up

the political food chain. I'm sure that she'll want to help. I mean, Chelsea's probably just starting to go through this sort of thing. I imagine that she'd be a very popular bridesmaid. Don't you think?

2) Botox! I can't afford it this month. Why? Because of all these wedding expenses! And there's also the fact that I'm not working right now. That doesn't help. Anyway, I don't know what's worse for my frown lines—not getting Botox, or stressing out about not getting Botox. All I can do is double up on my new Principal Secret products. Victoria's new Reclaim line has an ingredient called Argireline that's supposed to smooth out lines. I've been applying it every two or three hours. You know, I think it's starting to work.

P.S. This is way off point, but I would totally get behind the controversial cloning issue if a brilliant scientist agreed to duplicate Jude Law.

Air Kisses,
K

Kiki plunked down with a dramatic sigh and immediately flagged a waiter for a Diet Coke with lime. "You don't know what I went through to get here." She glanced around quickly for famous faces. Celebrities frequented the eatery all the time. Ooh. Wasn't that the hot guy from *Survivor*? Yummy. Civilization definitely agreed with him. "I have two dollars to my name," she announced without preamble. "And a credit card that the manager will probably cut up in front of my face."

Danni opened up her clutch to flash a thick wad of cash. "No worries, sweetheart. I did a new routine to 'Pour Some Sugar on Me' by Def Leppard last night. After I nailed my new move on the pole, it rained money."

Danni Summer worked as an exotic dancer at Camisole, the hottest gentleman's nightspot in Manhattan. The hysterical part was this: She never took off her clothes. For Danni, a nice Christian girl from Mississippi, it got no skimpier than a modest bra and panties set. She merely loved choreographing and performing dance routines to songs by her favorite bands from the eighties—Def Leppard, Poison, Bon Jovi—the list went on. Where else could a girl do that but a strip club? And who else could get away it but Danni Summer? She was drop-dead beautiful. A near dead ringer for Nicole Kidman with her auburn hair, lissome body, and porcelain skin. Management at Camisole kept her on because she packed the club even without flashing the goods.

Suzi-Suzi glanced at Danni with imploring eyes.

"Everything's on me today," Danni offered. As if anyone had to hold their breath. She was one of the most generous people Kiki had ever known.

"Did you get my e-mail?" Kiki demanded.

The girls nodded.

"It was hilarious," Suzi-Suzi put in. "I want to know who this girl is that your brother's marrying all of a sudden. But I guess the more pressing question is . . . when's the baby due?"

A chorus of girlish giggles.

"She's from *New Jersey*," Kiki said, putting enough topspin on the words to equate New York's neighbor state to the hills of Appalachia.

Danni pointed to Kiki's Diet Coke, which sat there untouched and sweating, as if angry about its no-line status. "*New Jersey?* You're going to need a stronger drink than that."

"Ugh—that's only the beginning," Kiki said. "Her family owns a chain of motels. *Mary's Motor Inns.* Can you imagine?"

"Is that the kind of place where kids with no money go on prom night?" Suzi-Suzi asked.

"They're actually not that bad," Danni put in. "I have an aunt and uncle who love road trips. I've heard them rave about the chain."

Kiki remained skeptical. "Oh, and here's another fun fact. Guess who's best friends with the bride?"

Suzi-Suzi's eyes sparkled. "Is she famous?"

"Yes," Kiki answered. "Famously awful. It's *Vivien*. That horrible woman who represented Walter in our divorce."

A look of alarm flashed across Danni's face. "Is she a bridesmaid?"

Kiki nodded. "Why can't my brother elope? Or just get drunk in Vegas and be done with it like Britney and Nicky Hilton managed to do."

"Um, I think both of those marriages were annulled," Suzi-Suzi pointed out.

"Whatever," Kiki grumbled. "It's just so unfair. I don't expect this Julia girl to know any better. I mean, she's from New Jersey. But Roman's my brother! And did he consider *me* in any of this? How self-involved can one person be?"

The waiter returned with the lime and stood poised for their orders. It was salads all around plus an entrée to share of steak *frites* with the thinnest, most perfectly salted fries in the world.

"Why couldn't Roman have been gay?" Kiki went on. "It would've been like having a sister all these years, and I wouldn't be dealing with any of this."

"Look at the bright side," Suzi-Suzi offered. "In a few months, you'll have a niece or nephew to spoil rotten."

Kiki blanched. "NO more baby jokes. *Please.* One day, yes, but not so soon after the wedding. I think a couple should be married for at least five years before having kids. I mean, you have to build in time for the possibility of divorce." She shook her head and sipped on her drink before erupting with, "All these weddings! And none of them are mine?"

Suzi-Suzi piped up again. "That's okay. We

shouldn't be made to feel less than just because we don't have husbands." She halted. "Well, I sort of have one, but he's not mine legally, and I never get him on holidays. And when he's around, he never wants to do manly things like fix the running toilet or move furniture. He saves that part of himself for his real wife. Chad just wants to have sex. Come to think of it, he's really just some asshole guy who calls me up when he happens to be free and horny. Remind me to break up with him. But back to my point. Most of the married women I know are not the happiest bunch. They pop Xanax and Paxil like Tic Tacs and constantly complain about their husbands not being interested in anything they have to say. If that's the case, aren't we better off single?"

"Most days," Kiki said. "But right now I wouldn't mind having a husband with a nice income to rely on." Thoughts of Kiki's short-lived first marriage smoked her brain. Walter Sharpe. What had she ever seen in that rich old bastard? Besides all the exotic trips, new clothes, and jewelry. Hmm. That list seemed fairly complete.

"Don't worry. Everything will work out," Danni whispered soothingly. "You're just in a bit of a slump. I can help you out. In my bedroom closet, I've got shoe boxes stuffed with cash I've earned from dancing. Just take one. I'll never know the difference."

"Do you really think it's safe to keep all that cash

around?" Suzi-Suzi asked. "Why don't you put it in the bank?"

Danni shrugged. "I keep meaning to, but the banks are closed when I get off work." She reached for Kiki's hand and squeezed it for emphasis. "I'm serious. Come over and grab a box. Take the one my Gucci boots came in. That's a big box with lots of money."

Kiki was touched. "You're so sweet. But since I'm taking the box anyway, do you mind if I borrow the boots, too?"

"Not at all," Danni said. "And they will look so cute on you."

Kiki experienced a surge of relief. Financial crisis averted—for the moment. Suddenly, it dawned on her that there would be no funds emergency at all if Walter had not been so well represented by Vivien. Evil divorce lawyer. Sworn enemy. Now a fellow bridesmaid. "Whenever I think about that prenup, I just feel like screaming. So what if I didn't read it before I signed. I barely have time to read *Us* magazine, and the courts expect me to study a thick legal document? Besides, what sane person would agree to anything other than lifetime alimony? I should've been declared incompetent just for signing it in the first place. God, it's ridiculous. I gave that man ten months of my life, and all I got in return was three years of support and a gag order to never speak about him in public."

Excerpt from FIRST KISS

"It's all because of that Vivien," Suzi-Suzi spat. "How are you going to stand being in the same bridal party with her?"

"Keep in mind that what happened had no personal intent," Danni reasoned. "Think about it. Walter hired her to do a job. She would've fought just as hard no matter who was on the other side."

"You know, I've read that women are the real sharks in divorce law these days," Suzi-Suzi said. "Men are hiring them left and right because they work like hell upholding prenups and even get fathers full custody of their children. What, I ask you, has happened to sisterhood?"

Kiki sighed wearily. "I don't know. But I bet you anything these women were *not* popular in high school. I mean, take Vivien. She's *very* tall. You know how boys are about that. I can't see her having many dates back then."

"It's so classic," Suzi-Suzi remarked. "She makes *you* pay for her childhood wounds."

"I know," Kiki said. "It' so wrong. And they say beautiful people go through life with such ease. If you ask me, it's the pretty girls who suffer the most."

\*       \*       \*

If you fell in love with Sydney in *First Date* and laughed out loud at Kiki's misadventures in *First Kiss*, there's one more bridesmaid you'll have to meet before the big wedding in . . .

# *First Dance*

## BOOK THREE IN

## THE BRIDESMAID CHRONICLES

Vivien Shelton is Manhattan's top female divorce attorney . . . and Julia Spinelli's best friend and future bridesmaid. Except Vivien has seen the ugly side of love—and alights at the wedding in Texas with the perfect present: an ironclad prenup. But the groom's good ole boy lawyer is itching for a fight—especially with Vivien, a woman he has tangled with in the past. . . .

You won't want to miss the first three books in THE BRIDESMAID CHRONICLES *First Date* (6/05) *First Kiss* (7/05) *First Dance* (8/05), and you're invited to the big day, the bride's story in *First Love*, following in September.

(Read ahead for a sneak peek of Vivien's story.)

A *bridesmaid*. Vivien didn't want to be anybody's maid, not even for a day. The whole concept was foreign; it implied servitude and worse, it spanned all the possibilities of polyester.

She'd already had to leave a deposition one day to find a full-length, strapless foundation garment in her bra size. Julia had then commanded that she purchase a pair of satin Manolo evening mules and a flaring *petticoat*. Viv had never in her life worn something as fussy as a petticoat, and she dreaded seeing the hideous taffeta creation that went over it. Oh, God! Please let her not have to wear anything with a bow on the butt . . .

Under any other circumstance, she'd laugh her ass off at the idea of one of Manhattan's top divorce attorneys moonlighting as a bridesmaid in a wedding. But all the humor went out of it immediately when *she* was the top divorce attorney in question. Viv had represented some high-profile clients, and

## Excerpt from FIRST DANCE

she only hoped the papers didn't get hold of this. She could see the headlines now: RAPTOR IN ROSEBUDS! WILL SHELTON SERVE GROOM PAPERS AT RECEPTION?

Viv shook off what she knew were selfish thoughts under the circumstances. She should be a lot more concerned about Julia than she was about herself. She'd already questioned her delicately on the phone about this guy Roman. She'd also told Julia that coincidentally she knew his sister, Kiki Douglas. Unfortunately Viv had represented her ex-husband in their Manhattan divorce three years ago.

"Listen, hon," she'd said to Julia. "If Roman is anything like Kiki, you want to be careful."

"Roman is nothing like Kiki!" Julia had exclaimed, even though to Viv's knowledge she'd never met her.

Viv had closed her eyes to ward off a migraine—impossible—and sent an urgent e-mail to Sydney Spinelli, Julia's older sister.

Today there was a reply, and Vivien scanned it quickly.

Subject:    Re: Your little sister has gone crazy!

Date:       XXXXXX

From:       numbersgeek

To:         vshelton

Tell me about it! Yes, I've met him, and there's something fishy with the guy. What kind of Texan

306

speaks Italian, wears designer clothes, and has a vineyard??? And Viv, here's the really awful part: the ring he gave her is FAKE!!!!!!!!!!!!!! I think he's marrying her for the $$$. But I can't talk sense into her.

Syd

*"Fake?!"* Viv said it loud, with enough force that Maurice squinted at her in the rearview mirror. *"What?* She has *got* to be kidding!"
Viv typed a quick reply. She'd called Sydney as soon as she got to the office.

Subject:   FAKE ring???

Date:      XXXXXX

From:      vshelton@kleinschmidtbelker

To:        numbersgeek

What do you mean, the ring he gave her is fake?! HOW COULD HE??? I'm speechless. xoxoxo, Viv

*\* This electronic message transmission contains information from the law firm of Klein, Schmidt and Belker that may be confidential or privileged. The information is intended solely for the recipient and use by any other party is not authorized. If you are not the intended recipient, be aware that any copying, disclosure, distri-*

## Excerpt from FIRST DANCE

*bution or use of the contents of this transmission is prohibited. If you have received this electronic transmission in error, please notify us immediately. Thank you.*

Sydney was obviously online at the same time, because before Viv had finished reading one of the work e-mails her reply popped into the mailbox.

Subject:   Re: FAKE ring? ? ?

Date:      XXXXXXX

From:      numbersgeek

To:        vshelton@kleinschemidtbelker

Viv, supposedly it's not his fault. The grandmother sold it way back when and he didn't know. (Do you believe this? Not sure, myself.) But it doesn't matter! Our Julia has got it bad: she's STILL WEARING the ring, and says she doesn't care that it's fake. Why? Because HE gave it to her. I give up . . . I'm going home. Can you at least get her to sign a prenup? I'm serious! ! ! ! ! ! !

Syd

Viv stared in disbelief at the text. Julia was still wearing a fake ring! She logged off and shut her laptop with a snap. This was insane. This Roman guy must be damn good in bed to have her so deluded.

He sounded like one hundred percent bad news, and if he was related to Kiki Douglas, whose face had been *all* over the tabloids lately, then he was a prize schmuck.

Julia needed a prenup, all right. The question was how to convince her of that. People in love and planning a wedding did not want to think about the ugly death of that love and the dissolution of the wedding. You couldn't really blame them.

Viv shuddered at the idea of grabbing Julia and telling her that the fabric, cut and design of her gown didn't matter, because she'd be burning it in a backyard bonfire in less than a year.

"Julia, honey," she saw herself saying, "don't worry that the doves they delivered for the event are both male. You'll be roasting them on the barbecue with veggie kabobs by Christmas." Or . . .

"Sweetie, don't bother freezing the top of that cake—unless you want something heavy and icicle-encrusted with which to brain your husband after he absconds with your trust fund." Or . . .

"Lacy white bridal lingerie imported from France? Don't spend the money—unless you've got some red or purple dye on hand. You can transform them for your divorce trousseau."

Viv winced. Julia, the poor thing, wouldn't want to listen to any of this. But Vivien had seen the rough side of marriage. She dealt with it every day: the ugly accusations, the dirty little secrets, the infidelity, the asset hiding, the custody squabbles—even the occasional kidnapping of the miserable couple's children by one spouse.

Viv had seen some strange things. She'd attended Divorce Dirge for a client of hers and downed a dirty martini as a doll of the ex-husband was burned in effigy.

A caterer client had baked a large, penis-shaped chocolate cake for a luncheon, serving a stunned Viv a good chunk of the balls on a china plate. The client had then thanked her in front of everyone for her great work.

And during one case the cheating SOB of a husband had propositioned Viv right in front of her client, his wife!

But Viv's mistrust of marriage went far deeper than her job. Not only were her own parents divorced, but their parents before them. She simply did not believe in marital bliss . . . and she was going to make sure her friend Julia was protected. . . .

One wedding.
Three bridesmaids.
Four sexy tales of modern-day romance.

Don't miss any of the books in
## *The Bridesmaids Chronicles*

**Coming July 2005**
### *First Kiss*
by Kylie Adams

**Coming August 2005**
### *First Dance*
by Karen Kendall

**Coming September 2005**
### *First Love*
by Julie Kenner

A romantic debut that's
**"Sharp, witty, wonderful!"**
—Karen Kendall

# *My Hero*

## by Marianna Jameson

Miranda Lane is a Southern romance writer, famous
for her sensitive heroes. But when her editor wants
her to write about a brooding, sexy cop, Miranda will
have to turn to the arrestingly handsome
Detective Chas Casey for a little inspiration.

Now Miranda is writing her own personal
romance story with a hero like no other—and a
happy ending all her own.

**"Marianna Jameson has hit the
jackpot...This book has it all."**
—Julie Kenner

0-451-21565-6

**Available wherever books are sold or at
www.penguin.com**

S885